I0676322

"She stood there . . . her slim body swaying in a perfect
rapture of admiration for her own beauty"

TALES OF SECRET EGYPT

By SAX ROHMER

Fredonia Books
Amsterdam, The Netherlands

Tales of Secret Egypt

by
Sax Rohmer

ISBN: 1-4101-0105-3

Copyright © 2002 by Fredonia Books

Reprinted from the 1920 edition

Fredonia Books
Amsterdam, The Netherlands
http://www.fredoniabooks.com

All rights reserved, including the right to reproduce this book, or portions thereof, in any form.

In order to make original editions of historical works available to scholars at an economical price, this facsimile of the original edition of 1920 is reproduced from the best available copy and has been digitally enhanced to improve legibility, but the text remains unaltered to retain historical authenticity.

CONTENTS

PART I

TALES OF ABÛ TABÂH

PART II

OTHER TALES

TALES OF SECRET EGYPT

PART I

TALES OF ABÛ TABÂH

I

THE YASHMAK OF PEARLS

THE *duhr*, or noonday call to prayer, had just sounded from the minarets of the Mosques of Kalaûn and En-Nasîr, and I was idly noting the negligible effect of the *adan* upon the occupants of the neighboring shops—coppersmiths for the most part—when suddenly my errant attention became arrested.

A mendicant of unwholesome aspect crouched in the shadow of the narrow gateway at the entrance to the Sûk es-Saîgh, or gold and silver bazaar, having his one serviceable eye fixed in a malevolent stare upon something or someone immediately behind me.

It is part and parcel of my difficult profession to subdue all impulses and to think before acting. I sipped my coffee and selected a fresh cigarette from the silver box upon the rug beside me. In this interval I had decided that the one-eyed mendicant cherished in his bosom an implacable and murderous hatred for my genial friend, Ali Mohammed, the

1

dealer in antiques; that he was unaware of my having divined his bloody secret; and that if I would profit by my accidental discovery, I must continue to feign complete ignorance of it.

Turning casually to Ali Mohammed, I was startled to observe the expression upon his usually immobile face: he was positively gray, and I thought I detected a faint rattling sound, apparently produced by his teeth; his eyes were set as if by hypnosis upon the uncleanly figure huddled in the shadow of the low gate.

"You are unwell, my friend," I said.

Ali Mohammed shook his head feebly, removed his eyes by a palpable effort from the watcher in the gateway, but almost instantly reverted again to that fixed and terrified scrutiny.

"Not at all, Kernaby Pasha," he chattered; "not in the least."

He passed a hand rapidly over a brow wet with perspiration, and moistened his lips, which were correspondingly dry. I determined upon a diplomatic *tour de force;* I looked him squarely in the face.

"For some reason," I said distinctly, "you are in deadly fear of the wall-eyed mendicant who is sitting by the gate of the Sûk es-Saîgh, O Ali Mohammed, my friend."

I turned with assumed carelessness. The beggar of murderous appearance had vanished, and Ali Mohammed was slowly recovering his composure. I knew that I must act quickly, or he would deny with the urbane mendacity of the Egyptian all knowledge of the one-eyed one; therefore—

"Acquaint me with the reason of your apprehensions," I said, at the same time offering him one of his own cigarettes; "it may be that I can assist you."

A moment he hesitated, glancing doubtfully in the direction of the gate and back to my face; then—

"It is one of the people of Tîr," he whispered, bending close to my ear; "of the evil *ginn* who are the creatures of Abû Tabâh."

I was puzzled and expressed my doubt in words.

"Alas," replied Ali Mohammed, "the Imâm Abû Tabâh is neither a man nor an official; he is a magician."

"Indeed! then you speak of one bearing the curious name of Abû Tabâh, who is at once the holder of a holy office and also one who has dealings with the *ginn* and the *Efreets*. This is strange, Ali Mohammed, my friend."

"It is strange and terrible," he whispered, "and I fear that my path is beset with pitfalls and slopeth down to desolation." He pronounced the *Takbîr*, "*Allâhu akbar!*" and uttered the words "*Hadeed! yá mashûm*"! (Iron! thou unlucky!), a potent invocation, as the *ginn's* dread of that metal is well known. "There are things of which one may not speak," he declared; "and this is one of them."

Sorely puzzled as I was by this most mysterious happening, yet, because of the pious words of my friend, I knew that the incident was closed so far as confidences were concerned; and I presently took my departure, my mind filled with all sorts of odd conjectures by which I sought to explain the matter. I was used to the superstitions of that quarter where almost every gate and every second street has its guardian *ginnee,* but who and what was Abû Tabâh? An Imám, apparently, though to what mosque attached Ali Mohammed had not mentioned. And why did Ali Mohammed fear Abû Tabâh?

So my thoughts ran, more or less ungoverned, whilst I made my way through streets narrow and tortuous in the direction of the Rondpoint du Mûski. I saw no more of the wall-eyed mendicant; but in a court hard by the Mosque of el-Ashraf I found myself in the midst of a squabbling crowd of natives surrounding someone whom I gathered, from the direction of their downward glances, to be prone upon the ground. Since the byways of the Sûk el-Attârin are little frequented by Europeans, at midday, I thrust my way into the heart of the throng, thinking that some stray patron of Messrs. Cook and Son (Egypt, Ltd.) might possibly have got into trouble or have been overcome by the heat.

Who or what lay at the heart of that gathering I never learned. I was still some distance from the centre of the disturbance when an evil-smelling sack was whipped over my head and shoulders from behind, a hand clapped upon my mouth and jaws; and, lifted in muscular arms, I found myself being borne inarticulate down stone steps, as I gathered from the sound, into some cool cellar-like place.

II

In my capacity as Egyptian representative of Messrs. Moses, Murphy & Co., of Birmingham, I have sometimes found myself in awkward corners; but in Cairo, whether the native or European quarter, I had hitherto counted myself as safe as in London and safer than in Paris. The unexpectedness of the present outrage would have been sufficient to take my breath away without the agency of the filthy sack, which had apparently contained garlic at some time and now contained my head.

I was deposited upon a stone-paved floor and my wrists were neatly pinioned behind me by one of my captors, whilst another hung on to my ankles. The sack was raised from my body but not from my face; and whilst a hand was kept firmly pressed over the region of my mouth, nimble fingers turned my pockets inside out. I assumed at first that I had fallen into the clutches of some modern brethren of the famous Forty, but when my purse, note-case, pocket-book, and other belongings were returned to me, I realized that something more underlay this attempt than the mere activity of a gang of footpads.

At this conclusion I had just arrived when the stinking sack was pulled off entirely and I found myself sitting on the floor of a small and very dark cellar. Beside me, holding the sack in his huge hands, stood a pock-marked negro of most repulsive appearance, and before me, his slim, ivory-colored hands crossed and resting upon the head of an ebony cane, was a man, apparently an Egyptian, whose appearance had something so strange about it that the angry words which I had been prepared to utter died upon my tongue and I sat staring mutely into the face of my captor; for I could not doubt that the outrage had been dictated by this man's will.

He was, then, a young man, probably under thirty, with perfectly chiseled features and a slight black moustache. He wore a black *gibbeh*, and a white turban, and brown shoes upon his small feet. His face was that of an ascetic, nor had I ever seen more wonderful and liquid eyes; in them reposed a world of melancholy; yet his red lips were parted in a smile tender as that of a mother. Inclining his head in a gesture of gentle dignity, this man—whom I hated at sight—addressed me in Arabic.

"I am desolated," he said, "and there is no comfort in my heart because of that which has happened to you by my orders. If it is possible for me to recompense you by any means within my power, command and you shall find a slave."

He was poisonously suave. Beneath the placid exterior, beneath the sugar-lipped utterances, in the deeps of the gazelle-like eyes, was hid a cold and remorseless spirit for which the man's silken demeanor was but a cloak. I hated him more and more. But my trade—for I do not blush to own myself a tradesman—has taught me caution. My ankles were free, it is true, but my hands were still tied behind me and over me towered the hideous bulk of the negro. This might be modern Cairo, and no doubt there were

British troops quartered at the Citadel and at the Kasr en-Nîl; probably there was a native policeman, a representative of twentieth-century law and order, somewhere in the maze of streets surrounding me: but, in the first place, I was at a physical disadvantage, in the second place I had reasons for not desiring unduly to intrude my affairs upon official notice, and in the third place some hazy idea of what might be behind all this business had begun to creep into my mind.

"Have I the pleasure," I said, and electing to speak, not in Arabic but in English, "of addressing the *Imám Abû Tabâh?*"

I could have sworn that despite his amazing self-control the man started slightly; but the lapse, if lapse it were, was but momentary. He repeated the dignified obeisance of the head—and answered me in English as pure as my own.

"I am called Abû Tabâh," he said; "and if I assure you that my discourteous treatment was dictated by a mistaken idea of duty, and if I offer you this explanation as the only apology possible, will you permit me to untie your hands and call an *arabîyeh* to drive you to your hotel?"

"No apology is necessary," I assured him. "Had I returned direct to Shepheard's I should have arrived too early for luncheon; and the odor of garlic, which informed the sack that your zeal for duty caused to be clapped upon my head, is one for which I have a certain penchant if it does not amount to a passion."

Abû Tabâh smiled, inclined his head again, and slightly raising the ebony cane indicated my pinioned wrists, at the same time glancing at the negro. In a trice I was unbound and once more upon my feet. I looked at the dilapidated door which gave access to the cellar, and I made a rapid mental calculation of the approximate weight in pounds of the large negro; then I looked hard at Abû Tabâh—who smilingly met my glance.

"Any one of my servants," he said urbanely, "who wait in the adjoining room, will order you an *arabîyeh*."

III

When the card of Ali Mohammed was brought to me that evening, my thoughts instantly flew to the wall-eyed mendicant of the Sûk en-Nahhasîn, and to Abû Tabâh, the sugar-lipped. I left the pleasant company of the two charming American ladies with whom I had been chatting on the terrace and joined Ali Mohammed in the lounge.

Without undue preamble he poured his tale of woe into my sympathetic ears. He had been lured away from his shop later that afternoon, and, in his absence, someone had ransacked the place from floor to roof. That night on his way to his abode, somewhere out Shubra direction I understood, he had been attacked and searched, finally to reach his house and to find there a home in wild disorder.

"I fear for my life," he whispered and glanced about the lounge in blackest apprehension; "yet where in all Cairo may I find an intermediary whom I can trust? Suppose," he pursued, and dropped his voice yet lower, "that a commission of ten per cent—say, one hundred pounds, English—were to be earned, should you care, Kernaby Pasha, to earn it?"

I assured him that I should regard such a proposal with the utmost affection.

"It would be necessary," he continued, "for you to disguise yourself as an aged woman and to visit the *harêm* of a certain wealthy Bey. I have a ring which must be shown to the *bowwab* at the gate of the *harêm* gardens upon which you would knock three times slowly and then twice rapidly. You would collect the thousand *ginêh* agreed upon and would deliver to a certain lady a sandalwood box, the possession of which endangers my life and has brought about me the hosts of Abû Tabâh the magician."

So the head of the cat was out of the bag at last. But there was more to come and it was not a proposition to plunge at, as I immediately perceived; and I parted from Ali Mohammed upon the prudent understanding that I should acquaint him with my decision on the morrow.

The terrace of Shepheard's was deserted, when, having escorted my visitor to the door, he made his way down into the Shâria Kâmel Pasha. Two white-robed figures who looked like hotel servants, and a little nondescript group of natives, stood at the foot of the steps. At the instant that doubt entered my

mind and too late to warn the worthy Ali Mohammed, the group parted to give him passage; then
. . . a terrific scuffle was in progress and one of
the wealthiest merchants of the Mûski was being
badly hustled.

I ran down the steps, the carriage-despatcher and
some other officials, whom the disturbance had
aroused from their secret lairs, appearing almost
simultaneously. As I reached the street, out from
the feet of the wrestling throng, like a football from
a scrum, rolled a neat *tarbûsh*.

Automatically I stooped and picked it up. Its
weight surprised me. Then, glancing inside the *tarbûsh*, I perceived that a little oblong box, together
with a quaint signet ring, were ingeniously attached
to the crown by means of silk threads tied around
the knot of the tassel. I glanced rapidly about me.
I, alone, had seen the cap roll out upon the pave-
ment.

A hard jerk, and I had the box and the ring free
in my hand. The tall carriage-despatcher, his ferocious efforts now seconded by a native policeman
who freely employed his cane upon the thinly-clad
persons of the group, had terminated the scuffle.

Right and left active figures darted, pursued for
some little distance by the policeman and the two
men from the hotel. There were no captures.

A very dusty and bemused Ali Mohammed, his
shaven skull robbing him of much of the dignity
which belonged to his *tarbûsh*, confronted me, rue-
fully dusting his garments.

"Your *tarbûsh*, my friend," I said, restoring his property to him with a bow.

One piercing glance he cast into the interior, then—

"O Allah!" he wailed—"O Allah! I am robbed! Yet——"

A sort of martyred resignation, a beatific peace, crept over his features.

"To war against Abû Tabâh is the act of a fool," he declared. "To have obtained the Bey's money would have been good, but to have obtained peace is better!"

IV

I awoke that night from a troubled sleep and from a dream wherein magnetic fingers caressed my forehead hypnotically. For a moment I could not believe that I was truly awake; the long ivory hand of my dreams was still moving close before me with a sort of slow fanning movement—and other, nimble, fingers crept beneath my pillow!

Of my distaste for impulse I have already spoken, and even now, with my mind not wholly under control, I profited by those years of self-imposed discipline. Without fully opening my eyes, cautiously, inch by inch, I moved my hand to that side of the bed nearer to the wall, where there reposed a leather holster containing my pistol.

My fingers closed over the butt of the weapon;

and in a flash I became wide awake . . . and had the ring of the barrel within an inch of the smiling face of Abû Tabâh!

I sat up.

"Be good enough, my friend," I said, "to turn on the center lamp. The switch, as you have probably noted, is immediately to the left of the door."

Abû Tabâh, straightening his figure and withdrawing his hand from beneath my pillow, inclined his picturesque head in grave salute and moved stately in the direction indicated. The room was flooded with yellow light. Its disorder was appalling; apparently no item of my gear had escaped attention.

"Pray take a seat," I said; "this one close beside me."

Abû Tabâh gravely accepted the invitation.

"This is the second occasion," I continued, "upon which you have unwarrantably submitted me to a peculiar form of outrage——"

"Not unwarrantably," replied Abû Tabâh, his speech suave and gentle; "but I fear I am too late!"

His words came as a beam of enlightenment. At last I had the game in my hands did I but play my cards with moderate cunning.

"You must pursue your inquiries in the *harêm* of the Bey," I said.

Abû Tabâh shrugged his shoulders.

"The house of Yûssuf Bey has been watched," he replied; "therefore my agents have failed me and must be punished."

"They are guiltless. It was humanly impossible to perceive my entrance to the house," I declared truthfully.

Abû Tabâh smiled into my face.

"So it was *you* who carried the sacred *burko* of the Seyyîdeh Nefîseh," he said; "and to-night Ali Mohammed brought you the reward for your perilous journey."

"Your reasoning is sound," I replied, "and the accuracy of your information remarkable."

I had scored the first point in the game; for I had learned that the wonderful silken *yashmak,* pearl embroidered, which I had found in the sandalwood box, was no less a curiosity than the face-veil of the Seyyîdeh Nefîseh and must therefore be of truly astounding antiquity and unique of its kind.

"The woman Sháhmarâh," continued my midnight visitor, the eerie light of fanaticism dawning in his eyes, "who was once a dancing girl, and who will ruin Yûssuf Bey as she ruined Ghûri Pasha before him, must be for ever accursed and meet with the fate of courtesans if she dare to wear the *burko* of Nefîseh."

I had scored my second point; I had learned that the lady to whom Ali Mohammed would have had me deliver the *yashmak* was named Sháhmarâh and was evidently the favorite of the notorious Yûssuf Bey. The complacent self-satisfaction of Abû Tabâh amused me vastly, for he clearly entertained no doubts respecting his efficiency as a searcher.

He was watching me now with his strange

hypnotic eyes, which had softened again, and his fixed stare caused me a certain uneasiness. For a captured thief, sitting covered by the pistol of his captor, he was ridiculously composed.

"You have performed an immoral deed," he said sweetly, "and have pandered to the base desires of a woman of poor repute. I offer you an opportunity of performing a good deed—and of trebling your profit."

This was as I would have it, and I nodded encouragingly.

"Unfold to me the thing that is in your mind," I directed him.

"I am a Moslem," he said; "and although Yûssuf Bey is a dog of dogs, he is nevertheless a True Believer—and I may not force my way into his *harêm.*"

"He might return the veil if he knew that Shâhmarâh had it," I suggested ingenuously.

Abû Tabâh shook his head.

"There are difficulties," he replied, "and if the theft is not to be proclaimed to the world, there is no time to be lost. This is my proposal: Return to the woman Shâhmarâh, and acquaint her with the fact that the sacred veil has been traced to her abode and her death decided upon by the Grand Mufti if it be not given up. Force the merchant Ali Mohammed to return the money received by him, using the same threat—which will prove a talisman of power. Return to the infidel woman the full amount; I will make good your commission, to which, if you be successful, I will add two hundred pounds.''

I performed some rapid thinking.

"You must give me a little time to consider this matter,'' I said.

Abû Tabâh graciously inclined his head.

"On Tuesday next a company of holy men who have journeyed hither from Ispahân, go to view this relic; you have therefore five days to act.''

"And if I decline?''

Abû Tabâh shrugged his shoulders.

"The loss must be made known—it would be a great scandal; the merchant Ali Mohammed, and the woman, Sháhmarâh, must be arrested—very undesirable; *you* must be arrested—most undesirable; and your banking account will be poorer by three hundred pounds.''

"Frightfully undesirable,'' I declared. "But suppose I strike the first blow and give you in charge of the police here and now?''

"You may try the experiment,'' he said.

I waved my hand in the direction of the door (I had reasons for remaining in bed). *"Ma'salâma!* (Good-bye),'' I said. "Don't stay to restore the room to order. I shall expect you early in the morning. You will find the door of the hotel open any time after eight and I can highly recommend it as a mode of entrance.''

Having saluted me with both hands, Abû Tabâh made his stately departure, leaving me much exercised in mind as to how he proposed to account to the *bowwab* for his sudden appearance in the building. This, however, was no affair of mine, and, first reclosing the window, I unfastened from around my left ankle the sandalwood box and the ring which I had bound there by a piece of tape—a device to which I owed their preservation from the subtle fingers of Abû Tabâh. Furthermore, to their presence there I owed my having awakened when I did. I am persuaded that the mysterious Egyptian's passes would have continued to keep me in a profound sleep had it not been for the pain occasioned by the pressure of the tape.

Opening the sandalwood box, and then the silver one which it enclosed, I re-examined the really wonderful specimen of embroidery whereof they formed the reliquary. The *burko* was of Tussur silk, its texture so fine that the whole veil, which was some four feet long by two wide, might have been passsd through the finger ring and would readily be concealed in the palm of the hand.

It was of unusual form, having no forehead band, more nearly resembling a *yashmak* than a true *burko,* and was heavily embroidered with pearls of varying sizes and purity, although none of them were large. Its instrinsic value was considerable, but in view of its history such a valuation must have fallen far below the true one. When its loss became known, I estimated that Messrs. Moses, Murphy & Co. could readily dispose of three duplicates through various channels to wealthy collectors whose enthusiasms were greater than their morality. The sale to a museum, or to the lawful owners, of the original (known technically as "the model") would crown a sound commercial transaction.

Cock-crow that morning discovered me at the private residence, in the Boulevard Clot-Bey, of one Suleyman Levi, with whom I had had minor dealings in the past.

v

At nine o'clock on the following Monday night, an old Egyptian woman, enveloped from head to foot in a black *tôb* and wearing a black crêpe face-veil boasting a hideous brass nose-piece, halted before a doorway set in the wall guarding the great gardens of the palace of Yûssuf Bey. I was the impersonator of this decrepit female. Abû Tabâh, who thus far had accompanied me, stepped into the dense shadow of the opposite wall and was thereby swallowed up.

I rapped three times slowly upon the doorway, then twice rapidly. Almost at once a little wicket therein flew open, and a bloated negro face showed framed in the square aperture.

"The messenger from Ali Mohammed of the Sûk en-Nahhasîn," I said, in a croaky voice. "Conduct me to the Lady Sháhmarâh."

"Show her seal," answered the eunuch, extending through the opening a large, fat hand.

I gave him the ring so fortunately discovered in the *tarbûsh* of my friend the merchant and the hand was withdrawn. Within a colloquy took place in which a female voice took part. Then the door was partly opened for my admittance—and I found myself in the gardens of the Bey.

In the moonlight it was a place of wonder, an enchanted demesne; but more like an Edmond Dulac water-color than a real garden. The palace with its magnificent *mushrabîyeh* windows, so poetically symbolical of veiled women, guarded by several fine, straight-limbed palm trees, spoke of the Old Cairo which saw the birth of *The Arabian Nights* and which so many of us imagine to have vanished with the *khalîfate*.

A girl completely muffled up in many-hued shawls and scarves, so that her red-slippered feet and two bright eyes heavily darkened with *kohl* were the only two portions of her person visible, stood before me, her figure seeming childish beside that of the gross negro—whom I hated at sight because he reminded me of the one whom I had encountered in Abû Tabâh's cellar.

"Follow me, quickly, mother," said the girl. "You"—pointing imperiously at the black man—"remain here."

I followed her in silence, noting that she pursued a path which ran parallel with the wall and lay wholly in its shadow. The gardens were fragrant with the perfume of roses, and in the center was a huge marble fountain surrounded by kiosks projecting into the water, tall acacias overshadowing them. We skirted two sides of the palace, its *mushrabîyeh* windows mysteriously lighted by the moon but showing no illumination from within. There we came to the entrance to a kind of trellis-covered walk, mosaic paved and patched delightfully with mystic light. It terminated before a small but heavy and nail-studded door, of which my guide held the key.

Entering, whilst she held the door ajar, I found myself in utter darkness, to be almost immediately dispelled by the yellow gleam of a lamp which the girl took from some niche, wherein, already lighted, it had been concealed. Up a flight of bare wooden stairs she conducted me, and opened a second prison-like door at their head. Leaving the lamp upon the top step, she pushed me gently forward into a small, octagonal room, paneled in dark wood inlaid with mother-o'-pearl and reminding me of the interior of a magnified *kursee* or coffee table.

Rugs and carpets strewed the floor and the air was heavy with the smell of musk, a perfume which I detest, it having characterized the personality of a certain Arab lady who sold me so marvelous a Damascus scimitar that I was utterly deceived by it until too late.

Raising a heavy curtain draped in a door shaped like an old-fashioned keyhole, and embellished with an intricate mass of fretwork carving, my guide went out, leaving me alone with my reflections. This interval was very brief, however, and was terminated by the reappearance of the girl, who this time made her entrance through a second doorway masked by the paneling. A faint musical splashing sound greeted me through the opening; and when my guide beckoned me to enter and I obeyed, I found myself in a chamber of barbaric beauty and in the presence of the celebrated Sháhmaráh.

The apartment, save for one end being wholly occupied by a magnificent *mushrabîyeh* screen, was walled with what looked like Verde Antico marble or green serpentine. An ebony couch having feet shaped as those of a leopard and enriched with gleaming bronze, having the skins of leopards cast across it, and, upon the skins, silken soft cushions wrought in patterns of green and gold, stood upon the mosaic floor at the head of three shallow steps which descended to a pool where a fountain played, softly musical; wherein lurked gleaming shapes of silver and gold. Bright mats were strewn around, and at one corner of the pool a huge silver *mibkharah* sent up its pencilings of aromatic smoke.

Upon this couch Sháhmaráh reclined, and I perceived immediately that her reputation for beauty was richly deserved. There was something leopardine in her pliant shape, which seemed to harmonize with the fierce black and gold of the skins upon which she was stretched; she had the limbs of a Naiad and the eyes of an Egyptian Circe. Upon her head she wore a *rabtah,* or turban, of pure white, secured and decorated in front by a brooch of ancient Egyptian enamel-work probably fourteenth dynasty, and for whcih I would gladly have given her one hundred pounds. If I have forgotten what else she wore it may be because my senses were in somewhat of a turmoil as I stood before her in that opulent apartment—which I suddenly recognized, and not without discomfiture, to be the *meslakh* of the *hammám*. I can only relate, then, that the image left upon my mind was one of jewels and dusky peach-like loveliness. Jewels there were in a-bundance, clasped about the warm curves of her arms and overloading her fingers; she wore gold bands thickly encrusted with gems about her ankles (the slim ankles of a dancing girl); and a fiery ruby of the true pigeon's-blood color gleamed upon the first toe of her left foot, the nails of which were highly manicured and stained with henna.

Fixing her wonderful eyes upon me—

"You have brought the veil?" she said.

"The merchant Ali Mohammed ordered me to convey to him the price agreed upon, O jewel of Egypt," I mumbled, "ere I yielded up this a poor man's only treasure."

Sháhmaráh sat upright upon the couch. Her delicate brows were drawn together in a frown, and her eyes, rendered doubly luminous by the pigment with which they were surrounded, glared fiercely at me, whilst she stamped one bare foot upon a cushion lying on the mosaic floor.

"The veil!" she cried imperiously. "I will send the merchant Ali Mohammed an order on the treasury of the Bey."

"O moon of the Orient," I replied, "O ravisher of souls, I am but a poor ugly old woman basking in the radiance of beauty and loveliness. Would you ruin one so old and feeble and helpless? I must have the price agreed upon; let it be counted into this bag"—and concealing my tell-tale hands as much as possible, I bent humbly and placed a leather wallet upon a little table beside her which bore fruits, sweetmeats, and a long-necked gold flagon. "When it is done, the *yashmak* of pearls, which only thy dazzling perfection might dare to wear, shall be yielded up to thee, O daughter of musk and amber-gris."

There fell a short silence, wherein the fountain musically plashed and Sháhmaráh shot little inquiring glances laden with venom into the mists of my black veil, and others which held a query over my shoulder at her confidant.

"I might have you cast into a dungeon beneath this palace," she hissed at me, bending lithely forward and extending a jeweled forefinger. "No one would miss thee, O mother of afflictions."

"In that event," I crooned quaveringly, "O tree of pearls, the veil could never be thine; for the merchant Ali Mohammed, who awaits me at the gate, refuses to deliver it up until the price agreed upon has been placed in his hands."

"He is a Jew, and a son of Jews, who eats without washing! a devourer of pork, and an unclean insect," she cried.

She extended the jeweled hand towards the girl who stood behind me and who, having loosened her wraps, proved to be a comely but shrewd-looking Assyrian. "Let the money be counted into the bag," she ordered, "that we may be rid of the presence of this garrulous and hideous old hag."

"O fountain of justice," I exclaimed; "O peerless
houri, to behold whom is to swoon with delight
and rapture."

From a locked closet the Assyrian girl took a
wooden coffer, and before my gratified eyes began
to count out, upon the little table notes and gold
until a pile lay there to have choked a miser with
emotion. (The ready-money transactions of the East
have always delighted me.) But, with the chinking
of the last piece of gold upon the pile—

"There is no more," said the girl. "It is one
hundred pounds short."

"It is more than enough!" cried Sháhmaráh. "I
am ruined. Give me the veil and go."

"O vision of paradise," I exclaimed in anguish,
"the merchant Ali Mohammed would never consent.
In lieu of the remainder"—I pointed to the antique
enamel in her turban—"give me the brooch from
thy *rabtah.*"

"O sink of corruption!" was her response, her
whole body positively quivering with rage, "it is
not for thy filthy claws. Here!"—she pulled a ring
containing a fair-sized emerald from one of her
fingers and tossed it contemptuously upon the pile
of money—"thou art more than repaid. The veil!
the veil!"

I turned to the girl who had counted out the gold.

"O minor moon, whom even the glory of paradise
cannot dim," I said, "put the money in the wallet,
for my hands are old and infirm, and give it to me."

The Assyrian scooped the gold and notes into the leather bag with the utmost unconcern, and as though she had been shelling peas into a basket. The profound disregard for wealth exhibited in the *harêm* of Yûssuf Bey was extraordinary; and I mentally endorsed the opinion expressed by Abû Tabâh that the ruin of the Bey was imminent.

Securing the heavy wallet to the girdle which I wore beneath my veilings, I placed upon the table where the money had lain a small silken packet.

"Here is the veil," I said; "for my story of the merchant, Ali Mohammed, who had refused to yield it up, was but a stratagem to test the generosity of thy soul, as thy refusal to give me the price agreed upon was but a subterfuge to test my honesty."

Heedless of the words, Shâhmarâh snatched up the packet, tore off the wrappings, and in a trice was standing upright before me wearing the *yashmak* of pearls.

I think I had never seen a figure more barbarically lovely than that of this soulless Egyptian so adorned.

"My mirror, Sáfiyeh! my mirror!" she cried.

And the girl placing a big silver mirror in her hand, she stood there looking into its surface, her wonderful eyes swimming with ecstasy and her slim body swaying in a perfect rapture of admiration for her own beauty.

Suddenly she dropped the mirror upon the cushions and threw wide her arms.

"Am I not the fairest woman in Egypt?" she

exclaimed. "I tread upon the hearts of men and my power is above the power of kings!"

Then a subtle change crept over her features; and ere I could utter the first of the honeyed compliments ready upon my tongue—

"Send Amineh to warn Mahmûd that the old woman is about to depart," she directed her attendant; and, turning to me: "Wait in the outer room. Thy presence is loathsome to me, O mother of calamities."

"I hear and obey," I replied, "O pomegranate blossom"—and, following the direction of her rigidly extended finger, I shuffled back to the little octagonal apartment and the masked door was slammed almost upon my heels.

This room, which possessed no windows, was solely illuminated by a silken-shaded lantern, but I had not long to wait in that weird half-light ere my conductress, again closely muffled in her shawls, opened the door at the head of the steps and signed to me to descend.

"Lead the way, my beautiful daughter," I said; for I had no intention of submitting myself to the risk of a dagger in the back.

She consented without demur, which served to allay my suspicions somewhat, and in silence we went down the uncarpeted stairs and out into the trellis-covered walk. The shadow beneath the high wall had deepened and widened since we had last skirted the gardens, and I felt my way along with my hand cautiously outstretched.

At a point within sight of the flower-grown arbor beneath which I knew the gate to be concealed, my guide halted.

"I must return, mother," she said quickly. "There is the gate, and Mahmûd will open it for you."

"Farewell, O daughter of the willow branch," I replied. "May Allah, the Great, the Compassionate, be with thee, and may thou marry a prince of Persia."

Light of foot she sped away, and, my forebodings coming to a sudden climax, I crept forward with excessive caution, holding my clenched hand immediately in front of my face—a device which experience of the hospitable manners of the East had taught me.

It was well that I did so. Within three spaces of the gate a noose fell accurately over my head and was drawn tight with a strangling jerk!

But that it also encircled my upraised arm, its clasp must have terminated my wordly affairs.

My assailant had sprung upon me from behind; and, in the fleeting instant between the fall of the noose and its tightening, I turned about . . . and thrust the nose of my Colt repeater (which I grasped in that protective upraised hand) fully into the grinning mouth of the negro gate keeper!

There was a rattle and gleam of falling ivory, for several of the *bowwab's* teeth had been dislodged by the steel barrel. Keeping the weapon firmly thrust into the man's distended jaws, I circled around him, whilst his hands relaxed their hold upon the strangling-cord, and pushed him backward in the direction of the door.

"Open thou black son of offal!" I said, "or I will blow thee a cavity as wide as thy blubber mouth through the back of that fat and greasy neck! This was, no doubt, a stratagem of thy mistress to test my fitness to be entrusted with large sums of money?"

When, a few moments later, I stood in the lane outside the gardens of Yûssuf Bey, and felt with my hand the fat wallet at my waist, I experienced a thrill of professional satisfaction, for had I not successfully negotiated a duplicate veil, embroidered with imitation pearls which the excellent Suleyman Levi by dint of four days of almost ceaseless toil had made for me? . . .

From the shadows of the opposite wall Abû Tabâh stepped forth, stately.

"Quick!" I said. "I fear pursuit at any moment! Is the *arabîyeh* waiting?"

"You have it?" he demanded, some faint sign of human animation creeping over his impassive face.

"I have!" I replied. "I will give it to you in the *arabîyeh*."

Side by side we passed down the deserted thoroughfare to where, beside a solitary palm, a pair-horse carriage was waiting. Appreciating something of my companion's natural impatience, I pressed into his hand the famous sandalwood box which once had reposed in the *tarbûsh* of Ali

Mohammed. The carriage rolled around a corner and out into the lighted Shâria Mobâdayân. Abû Tabâh opened the sandalwood box, and then, reverently, the inner box of silver. Within shimmered the pearls of the sacred *burko*. He did not touch the relic with his hands, but reclosed the boxes and concealed the reliquary beneath his black robe. I heard the crackle of notes; and a little packet surrounded by a band of elastic was pressed into my hand.

"Three hundred pounds, English," said Abû Tabâh. "One hundred pounds in recompense for the commission you returned, and two hundred pounds for the recovery of the relic."

I thrust the wad into the bag beneath my robe containing the other spoils of the evening. A second and even more grateful glow of professional joy warmed my heart. For in the reliquary which I had handed to Abû Tabâh reposed the second product of Suleyman Levi's scientific toils; his four days' labor having resulted in the production of two quite passable duplicates; although neither were by any means up to the standard of Messrs. Moses, Murphy & Co.

Coming to the house wherein I had endued my disguise, Abû Tabâh left me to metamorphose myself into a decently dressed Englishman suitable for admission to an hotel of international repute.

"*Lîltâk sa'îda*, Abû Tabâh," I said.

In the open doorway he turned.

"*Lîltâk sa'îda*, Kernaby Pasha," he replied, and smiled upon me very sweetly.

VI

It was after midnight when I returned to Shepheard's, but I went straight to my room, and switching on the table-lamp, wrote a long letter to my principals. Something seemed to have gone wrong with the lock of my attaché-case, and my good humor was badly out of joint by the time that I succeeded in opening it. From underneath a mass of business correspondence I took out a large, sealed envelope, which I enclosed with a letter in one yet larger, to be registered to Messrs. Moses, Murphy & Co., Birmingham, in the morning. I turned in utterly tired but happy, to dream complacently of the smile of Abû Tabâh and of the party of holy men who had journeyed from Ispahân.

Exactly a fortnight later the following registered letter was handed to me as I was about to sit down to lunch—

The Hon. Neville Kernaby.
    Shepheard's Hotel,
        Cairo, Egypt.

Dear Mr. Neville Kernaby—

We are returning herewith the silken veil which you describe as "the authentic *burko* of the Seyyîdeh Nefîseh, stolen from her shrine in the Tombs of the Khalîfs." Your statement that you can arrange for its purchase at the cost of one thousand pounds does not interest us, nor do we expect so high-salaried an expert as yourself to send us palpable and very inferior forgeries. We are manufacturers of duplicates, not buyers of same.

Yours truly,
LLOYD LLEWELLYN.

(For Messrs. Moses, Murphy & Co.).

I was positively aghast. Tearing open the enclosed package, I glared like a madman at the *yashmak* which it contained. The silk, in comparison with that of which the real veil was compared, was coarse as cocoanut matting; the embroidery was crude; the pearls shrieked "imitation" aloud! At a glance I knew the thing for one of the pair made by Suleyman Levi!

The truth crashed in upon my mind. Following my visit to the *harêm* of Yûssuf Bey, I had bestowed no more than a glance upon the envelope wherein, early on the morning of the same day, I had lovingly sealed the authentic veil; and a full hour had elapsed between the time of parting with the sugar-lipped one and my return to my rooms at the hotel.

I understood, now, why the lock of my attaché-case had been out of order on that occasion . . . and I comprehended the sweet smile of Abû Tabâh!

II

THE DEATH-RING OF SNEFERU

I

THE orchestra had just ceased playing; and, taking advantage of the lull in the music, my companion leaned confidentially forward, shooting suspicious glances all around him, although there was nothing about the well-dressed after-dinner throng filling Shepheard's that night to have aroused misgiving in the mind of a cinema anarchist.

"I have a very big thing in view," he said, speaking in a husky whisper. "I shall be one up on you, Kernaby, if I pull it off."

He glanced sideways, in the manner of a pantomime brigand, at a party of New York tourists, our immediate neighbors, and from them to an elderly peer with whom I was slightly acquainted and who, in addition to his being stone deaf, had never noticed anything in his life, much less attempted so fatiguing an operation as intrigue.

"Indeed," I commented; and rang the bell with the purpose in view of ordering another cooling beverage.

True, I might be the Egyptian representative of a Birmingham commercial enterprise, but I did not

31

gladly suffer the society of this individual, whose
only claim to my acquaintance lay in the fact that
he was in the employ of a rival house. My lack of
interest palpably disappointed him; but I thought
little of the man's qualities as a connoisseur and less
of his company. His name was Theo Bishop and I
fancy that his family was associated with the tanning
industry. I have since thought more kindly of poor
Bishop, but at the time of which I write nothing
could have pleased me better than his sudden dissolution.

Perhaps unconsciously I had allowed my boredom
to become rudely apparent; for Bishop slightly
turned his head aside, and—

"Right-o, Kernaby," he said; "I know you think
I am an ass, so we will say no more about it.
Another cocktail?"

And now I became conscience-stricken; for
mingled with the disappointment in Bishop's tone
and manner was another note. Vaguely it occurred
to me that the man was yearning for sympathy of
some kind, that he was bursting to unbosom himself, and that the vanity of a successful rival was
by no means wholly responsible. I have since placed
that ambiguous note and recognized it for a note of
tragedy. But at the time I was deaf to its pleading.

We chatted then for some while longer on indifferent topics, Bishop being, as I have indicated, a
man difficult to offend; when, having correspondence
to deal with, I retired to my own room. I suppose
I had been writing for about an hour, when a servant

came to announce a caller. Taking an ordinary visiting-card from the brass salver, I read—

Abû Tabâh.

No title preceded the name, no address followed, but I became aware of something very like a nervous thrill as I stared at the name of my visitor. Personality is one of the profoundest mysteries of our being. Of the person whose card I held in my hand I knew little, practically nothing; his actions, if at times irregular, had never been wantonly violent; his manner was gentle as that of a mother to a baby and his singular reputation among the natives I thought I could afford to ignore; for the Egyptian, like the Celt, with all his natural endowments, is yet a child at heart. Therefore I cannot explain why, sitting there in my room in Shepheard's Hotel, I knew and recognized, at the name of Abû Tabâh, the touch of fear.

"I will see him downstairs," I said.

Then, as the servant was about to depart, recognizing that I had made a concession to that strange sentiment which the Imám Abû Tabâh had somehow inspired in me—

"No," I added; "show him up here to my room."

A few moments later the man returned again, carrying the brass salver, upon which lay a sealed envelope. I took it up in surprise, noting that it was one belonging to the hotel, and, ere opening it—

"Where is my visitor?" I said in Arabic.

"He regrets that he cannot stay," replied the man; "but he sends you this letter."

Greatly mystified, I dismissed the servant and tore open the envelope. Inside, upon a sheet of hotel notepaper I found this remarkable message—

KERNABY PASHA—

There are reasons why I cannot stay to see you personally, but I would have you believe that this warning is dictated by nothing but friendship. Grave peril threatens. It is associated with the hieroglyphic—

If you would avert it, and if you value your life, avoid all contact with anything bearing this figure.

ABÛ TABÂH.

The mystery deepened. There had been something incongruous about the modern European visiting-card used by this representative of Islam, this living illustration of the *Arabian Nights*; now, his incomprehensible "warning" plunged me back again into the mediæval Orient to which he properly belonged. Yet I knew Abû Tabâh, for all his romantic aspect, to be eminently practical, and I could not credit him with descending to the methods of melodrama.

As I studied the precise wording of the note, I seemed to see the slim figure of its author before me, black-robed, white-turbaned, and urbane, his delicate ivory hands crossed and resting upon the head of the ebony cane without which I had never seen him. Almost, I succumbed to a sort of subjective hallucination; Abû Tabâh became a veritable presence, and the poetic beauty of his face struck me anew, as, fixing upon me his eyes, which were like the eyes of a gazelle, he spoke the strange words cited above, in the pure and polished English which he held at command, and described in the air, with a long nervous forefinger, the queer device which symbolized the Ancient Egyptian god, Set, the Destroyer.

Of course, it was the aura of a powerful personality, clinging even to the written message; but there was something about the impression made upon me which argued for the writer's sincerity.

That Abû Tabâh was some kind of agent, recognized—at any rate unofficially—by the authorities, I knew or shrewdly surmised; but the exact nature of his activities, and how he reconciled them with his religious duties, remained profoundly mysterious. The episode had rendered further work impossible, and I descended to the terrace, with no more definite object in view than that of finding a quiet corner where I might meditate in the congenial society of my briar, and at the same time seek inspiration from the ever-changing throng in the Shâria Kâmel Pasha.

I had scarcely set my foot upon the terrace, however, ere a hand was laid upon my arm. Turning quickly I recognized, in the dusk, Hassan es-Sugra, for many years a trusted employee of the British Archæological Society.

His demeanor was at once excited and furtive, and I recognized with something akin to amazement that he, also, had a story to unfold. I mentally catalogued this eventful evening "the night of strange confidences."

Seated at a little table on the deserted balcony (for the evening was very chilly) and directly facing the shop of Philip, the dealer in Arab woodwork, Hassan es-Sugra told his wonder tale; and as he told it I knew that Fate had cast me, willy-nilly, for a part in some comedy upon which the curtain had already risen here in Cairo, and whereof the second act should be played in perhaps the most ancient setting which the hand of man has builded. As the narrative unrolled itself before me, I perceived wheels within wheels; I was wholly absorbed, yet half incredulous.

" . . . When the professor abandoned work on the pyramid, Kernaby Pasha," he said, bending eagerly forward and laying his muscular brown hand upon my sleeve, "it was not because there was no more to learn there."

"I am aware of this, O Hassan," I interrupted, "it was in order that they might carry on the work at the Pyramid of Illahûn, which resulted in a find of jewelery almost unique in the annals of Egyptology."

"Do I not know all this!" exclaimed Hassan impatiently; "and was not mine the hand that uncovered the golden uræus? But the work projected at the Pyramid of Méydûm was never completed, and I can tell you why."

I stared at him through the gloom; for I had already some idea respecting the truth of this matter.

"It was that the men, over two hundred of them, refused to enter the passage again," he whispered dramatically, "it was because misfortune and disaster visited more than one who had penetrated to a certain place therein." He bent further forward. "The Pyramid of Méydûm is the home of a powerful *Efreet*, Kernaby Pasha! But I who was the last to leave it, know what is concealed there. In a certain place, low down in the corner of the King's Chamber, is a ring of gold, bearing a cartouche. It is the royal ring of the Pharaoh who built the pyramid."

He ceased, watching me intently. I did not doubt Hassan's word, for I had always counted him a man of integrity; but there was much that was obscure and much that was mysterious in his story.

"Why did you not bring it away?" I asked.

"I feared to touch it, Kernaby Pasha; it is an evil talisman. Until to-day I have feared to speak of it."

"And to-day?"

Hassan extended his hands, palms upward.

"I am threatened with the loss of my house," he said simply, "if I do not find a certain sum of money within a period of twelve days."

I sat resting my chin on my hand and staring into the face of Hassan es-Sugra. Could it be that from superstitious motives such a treasure had indeed been abandoned? Could it be that Fate had deilvered into my hands a relic so priceless as the signet-ring of Sneferu, one of the earliest Memphite Pharaohs? Since I had recently incurred the displeasure of my principals, Messrs. Moses, Murphy & Co., of Birmingham, the mere anticipation of such a "find" was sufficient to raise my professional enthusiasm to white heat, and in those few moments of silence I had decided upon instant action.

"Meet me at Rikka Station, to-morrow morning at nine o'clock," I said, "and arrange for donkeys to carry us to the pyramid."

II

On my arrival at Rikka, and therefore at the very outset of my inquiry, I met with what one slightly prone to superstition might have regarded as an unfortunate omen. A native funeral was passing out of the town amid the wailing of women and the chanting by the *Yemeneeyeh*, of the Profession of the Faith, with its queer monotonous cadences, a performance which despite its familiarity in the

Near East never failed to affect me unpleasantly. By the token of the *tarbûsh* upon the bier, I knew that this was a man who was being hurried to his lonely resting-place on the fringe of the desert.

As the procession wound its way out across the sands, I saw to the removal of my baggage and joined Hassan es-Sugra, who awaited me by the wooden barrier. I perceived immediately that something was wrong with the man; he was palpably laboring under the influence of some strong excitement, and his dark eyes regarded me almost fearfully. He was muttering to himself like one suffering from an over-indulgence in *Hashish,* and I detected the words *"Allahu akbar!"* (God is most great) several times repeated.

"What ails you, Hassan, my friend?" I said; and noting how his gaze persistently returned to the melancholy procession wending its way towards the little Moslem cemetery:—"Was the dead man some relation of yours?"

"No, no, Kernaby Pasha," he muttered gutturally, and moistened his lips with his tongue; "I was but slightly acquainted with him."

"Yet you are much disturbed."

"Not at all, Kernaby Pasha," he assured me; "not in the slightest."

By which familiar formula I knew that Hassan es-Sugra would conceal from me the cause of his distress, and therefore, since I had no appetite for further mysteries, I determined to learn it from another source.

"See to the loading of the donkey," I directed him—for three sleek little animals were standing beside him, patiently awaiting the toil of the day.

Hassan setting about the task with a cheerful alacrity obviously artificial, I approached the native station master, with whom I was acquainted, and put to him a number of questions respecting his important functions—in which I was not even mildly interested. But to the Oriental mind a direct inquiry is an affront, almost an insult; and to have inquired bluntly the name of the deceased and the manner of his death would have been the best way to have learned nothing whatever about the matter. Therefore having discussed in detail the slothful incompetence of Arab ticket collectors and the lazy condition and innate viciousness of Egyptian porters as a class, I mentioned incidentally that I had observed a funeral leaving Rikka.

The station master (who was bursting to talk about this very matter, but who would have declined on principle to do so had I definitely questioned him) now unfolded to me the strange particulars respecting the death of one, Ahmed Abdulla, who had been a retired dragoman though some time employed as an excavator.

"He rode out one night upon his white donkey," said my informant, "and no man knows whither he went. But it is believed, Kernaby Pasha, that it was to the Haram el-Kaddâb" (the False Pyramid)—extending his hand to where, beyond the belt of fertility, the tomb of Sneferu up-reared its three platforms from the fringe of the desert. "To enter the pyramid even in day time is to court misfortune; to enter at night is to fall into the hands of the powerful *Efreet* who dwells there. His donkey returned without him, and therefore search was made for Ahmed Abdulla. He was found the next day"—again the long arm shot out towards the desert—"dead upon the sands, near the foot of the pyramid."

I looked into the face of the speaker; beyond doubt he was in deadly earnest.

"Why should Ahmed Abdulla have wanted to visit such a place at night?" I asked.

My acquaintance lowered his voice, muttered "*Sahâm Allah fee 'adoo ed—dîn!*" (May God transfix the enemies of the religion) and touched his forehead, his mouth, and his breast with the iron ring which he wore.

"There is a great treasure concealed there, Kernaby Pasha," he replied; "a treasure hidden from the world in the days of Suleyman the Great, sealed with his seal, and guarded by the servants of Gánn Ibn-Gánn."

"So you think the guardian *ginn* killed Ahmed Abdulla?"

The station master muttered invocations, and—

"There are things which may not be spoken of," he said; "but those who saw him dead say that he was terrible to look upon. A great *Welee*, a man of wisdom famed throughout Egypt, has been summoned to avert the evil; for if the anger of the *ginn* is aroused they may visit the most painful and unfortunate penalties upon all Rikka. . . ."

Half an hour later I set out, having confidentially informed the station master that I sought to obtain a fine turquoise necklet which I knew to be in the possession of the Sheikh of Méydûm. Little did I suspect how it was written that I should indeed visit the house of the venerable Sheikh. Out through the fields of young green corn, the palm groves and the sycamore orchards I rode, Hassan plodding silently behind me and leading the donkey who bore the baggage. Curious eyes watched our passage, from field, doorway, and *shadûf;* but nothing of note marked our journey save the tremendous heat of the sun at noon, beneath which I knew myself a fool to travel.

I camped on the western side of the pyramid, but well clear of the marshes, which are the home of countless wild-fowl. I had no idea how long it would take me to extract the coveted ring from its hiding-place (which Hassan had closely described to me); and, remembering the speculative glances of the villagers, I had no intention of exposing myself against the face of the pyramid until dusk should have come to cloak my operations.

Hassan es-Sugra, whose new taciturnity was remakable and whose behavior was dsitinguishod by an odd disquiet, set out with his gun to procure our dinner, and I mounted the sandy slope on the south-west of the pyramid, where from my cover behind a mound of rubbish, I studied through my field-glasses the belt of vegetation marking the course of the Nile. I could detect no sign of surveillance, but in view of the fact that the smuggling of relics out of Egypt is a punishable offence my caution was dictated by wisdom.

We dined excellently, Hassan the Silent and I, upon quail, tinned tomatoes, fresh dates, bread, and Vichy-water (to which in my own case was added a stiff three fingers of whisky).

When the newly risen moon cast an ebon shadow of the Pyramid of Sneferu upon the carpet of the sands, I made my way around the angle of the ancient building towards the mound on the northern side whereby one approaches the entrance. Three paces from the shadow's edge, I paused, transfixed, because of that which confronted me.

Outlined against the moon-bright sky upon a ridge of the desert behind and to the north of the great structure, stood the motionless figure of a man!

For a moment I thought that my mind had conjured up this phantasmal watcher, that he was a thing of moon-magic and not of flesh and blood. But as I stood regarding him, he moved, seemed to raise his head, then turned and disappeared beyond the crest.

How long I remained staring at the spot where he had been I know not; but I was aroused from my useless contemplation by the jingling of camel bells. The sound came from behind me, stealing sweetly through the stillness from a great distance. I turned in a flash, whipped out my glasses and searched the remote fringe of the Fáyûm. Stately across the jeweled curtain of the night moved a caravan, blackly marked against that wondrous background. Three walking figures I counted, three laden donkeys, and two camels. Upon the first of the camels a man was mounted, upon the second was a *shibreeyeh*, a sort of covered litter, which I knew must conceal a woman. The caravan passed out of sight into the palm grove which conceals the village of Méydûm.

I returned my glasses to their case, and stood for some moments deep in reflection; then I descended the slope, to the tiny encampment where I had left Hassan es-Sugra. He was nowhere to be seen; and having waited some ten minutes I grew impatient, and raising my voice:

"Hassan!" I cried; "Hassan es-Sugra!"

No answer greeted me, although in the desert stillness the call must have been audible for miles. A second and a third time I called his name . . . and the only reply was the shrill note of a pyramid bat that swooped low above my head; the vast solitude of the sands swallowed up my voice and the walls of the Tomb of Sneferu mocked me with their echo, crying eerily:

"Hassan! Hassan es-Sugra. . . . Hassan! . . ."

III

This mysterious episode affected me unpleasantly, but did not divert me from my purpose: I succeeded in casting out certain demons of superstition who had sought to lay hold upon me; and a prolonged scrutiny of the surrounding desert somewhat allayed my fears of human surveillance. For my visit to the chamber in the heart of the ancient building I had arrayed myself in rubber-soled shoes, an old pair of drill trousers, and a pyjama jacket. A Colt repeater was in my hip pocket, and, in addition to several instruments which I thought might be useful in extracting the ring from its setting, I carried a powerful electric torch.

Seated on the threshold of the entrance, fifty feet above the desert level, I cast a final glance backward towards the Nile valley, then, the lighted torch carried in my jacket pocket, I commenced the descent of the narrow, sloping passage. Periodically, when some cranny between the blocks offered a foothold, I checked my progress, and inspected the steep path below for snake tracks.

Some two hundred and forty feet of labored descent discovered me in a sort of shallow cavern little more than a yard high and partly hewn out of the living rock which formed the foundation of the pyramid. In this place I found the heat to be almost insufferable, and the smell of remote mortality which assailed my nostrils from the sand-strewn floor threatened to choke me. For five minutes or more I lay there, bathed in perspiration, my nerves at high tension, listening for the slightest sound within or without. I cannot pretend that I was entirely master of myself. The stuff that fear

is made of seemed to rise from the ancient dust; and
I had little relish for the second part of my journey,
which lay through a long horizontal passage rarely
exceeding fourteen inches in height. The mere
memory of that final crawl of forty feet or so is
sufficient to cause me to perspire profusely; therefore let it suffice that I reached the end of the second
passage, and breathing with difficulty the deathful,
poisonous atmosphere of the place, found myself at
the foot of the rugged shaft which gives access to the
King's Chamber. Resting my torch upon a con-
venient ledge, I climbed up, and knew myself to be
in one of the oldest chambers fashioned by human
handiwork.

The journey had been most exhausing, but, allowing myseh only a few moments' rest, I crossed to
the eastern corner of the place and directed a ray
of light upon the crevice which, from Hassan's description, I believed to conceal the ring. His account
having been detailed, I experienced little difficulty
in finding the cavity; but in the very moment of
success the light of the torch grew dim . . . and I
recognized with a mingling of chagrin and fear that
it was burnt out and that I had no means of re-
charging it.

Ere the light expired, I had time to realize two
things: that the cavity was empty . . . and that
someone or something was approaching the foot
of the shaft along the horizontal passage below!

Strictly though I have schooled my emotions, my
heart was beating in a most uncomfortable fashion,

as, crouching near the edge of the shaft, I watched
the red glow fade from the delicate filament of the
lamp. Retreat was impossible; there is but one
entrance to the pyramid; and the darkness which
now descended upon me was indescribable; it possessed horrific qualities; it seemed palpably to enfold
me like the wings of some monstrous bat. The air
of the King's Chamber I found to be almost unbear-
able, and it was no steady hand with which I gripped
my pistol.

The sounds of approach continued. The suspense
was becoming intolerable—when, into the Memphian
gloom below me, there suddenly intruded a faint
but ever-growing light. Between excitement and
insufficient air, I regarded suffocation as imminent.
Then, out into view beneath me, was thrust a slim
ivory hand which held an electric pocket lamp.
Fascinatedly I watched it, saw it joined by its fellow,
then observed a white-turbaned head and a pair of
black-robed shoulders follow. In my surprise I
almost dropped the weapon which I held. The new
arrival now standing upright and raising his head,
I found myself looking into the face of *Abû
Tabâh!*

"To Allah, the Great, the Compassionate, be all
praise that I have found you alive," he said simply.

He exhibited little evidence of the journey which
I had found so fatiguing, but an expression strongly
like that of real anxiety rested upon his ascetic face.

"If life is dear to you," he continued, "answer
me this, Kernaby Pasha; have you found the ring?"

"I have not," I replied; "my lamp failed me; but I think the ring is gone."

And now, as I spoke the words, the strangeness of his question came home to me, bringing with it an acute suspicion.

"What do you know of this ring, O my friend?" I asked.

Abû Tabâh shrugged his shoulders.

"I know much that is evil," he replied; "and because you doubt the purity of my motives, all that I have learned you shall learn also; for Allah the Great, the Merciful, this night has protected you from danger and spared you a frightful death. Follow me, Kernaby Pasha, in order that these things may be made manifest to you."

IV

A pair of fleet camels were kneeling at the foot of the slope below the entrance to the pyramid, and having recovered somewhat from the effect of the fatiguing climb out from the King's Chamber—

"It might be desirable," I said, "that I adopt a more suitable raiment for camel riding?"

Abû Tabâh slowly shook his head in that dignified manner which never deserted him. He had again taken up his ebony walking-stick and was now resting his crossed hands upon it and regarding me with his strange, melancholy eyes.

"To delay would be unwise," he replied. "You have mercifully been spared a painful and unfortunate end (all praise to Him who averted the peril); but the ring, which bears an ancient curse, is gone: for me there is no rest until I have found and destroyed it."

He spoke with a solemn conviction which bore the seal of verity.

"Your destructive theory may be perfectly sound," I said; "but as one professionally interested in relics of the past, I feel called upon to protest. Perhaps before we proceed any further you will enlighten me respecting this most obscure matter. Can you inform me, for example, what became of Hassan es-Sugra?"

"He observed my approach from a distance, and fled, being a man of little virtue. Respecting the other matters you shall be fully enlightened, to-night The white camel is for you."

There was a gentle finality in his manner to which I succumbed. My feelings towards this mysterious being had undergone a slight change; and whilst I cannot truthfully say that I loved him as a brother, a certain respect for Abû Tabâh was taking possession of my mind. I began to understand his reputation with the natives; beyond doubt his uncanny wisdom was impressive; his lofty dignity awed. And no man is at his best arrayed in canvas shoes, very dirty drill trousers, and a pyjama jacket.

As I had anticipated, the village of Méydûm proved to be our destination, and the gait of the magnificent creatures upon which we were mounted was exhausting. I shall always remember that moonlight ride across the desert to the palm groves of Méydûm. I entered the house of the Sheikh with misgivings; for my attire fell short of the ideal to which every representative of protective Britain looks up, but often fails to realize.

In a *mandarah,* part of it inlaid with fine mosaic and boasting a pretty fountain, I was presented to the imposing old man who was evidently the host of Abû Tabâh. Ere taking my seat upon the *dîwan,* I shed my canvas shoes, in accordance with custom, accepted a pipe and a cup of excellent coffee, and awaited with much curiosity the next development. A brief colloquy between Abû Tabâh and the Sheikh, at the further end of the apartment resulted in the disappearance of the Sheikh and the approach of my mysterious friend.

"Because, although you are not a Moslem, you are a man of culture and understanding," said Abû Tabâh, "I have ordered that my sister shall be brought into your presence."

"That is exceedingly good of you," I said, but indeed I knew it to be an honor which spoke volumes at once for Abû Tabâh's enlightenment and good opinion of myself.

"She is a virgin of great beauty," he continued; "and the excellence of her mind exceeds the perfection of her person."

"I congratulate you," I answered politely, "upon the possession of a sister in every way so desirable."

Abû Tabâh inclined his head in a characteristic gesture of gentle courtesy.

"Allah has indeed blessed my house," he ad-

mitted; "and because your mind is filled with conjectures respecting the source of certain information
which you know me to possess, I desire that the
matter shall be made clear to you."

How I should have answered this singular man
I know not; but as he spoke the words, into the
mandarah came the Sheikh, followed by a girl robed
and veiled entirely in white. With gait slow and
graceful she approached the *dîwan*. She wore a
white *yelek* so closely wrapped about her that it
concealed the rest of her attire, and a white *tarbar,*
or head-veil, decorated with gold embroidery, almost
entirely concealed her hair, save for one jet-black
plait in which little gold ornaments were entwined
and which hung down on the left of her forehead.
A white *yashmak* reached nearly to her feet, which
were clad in little red leather slippers.

As she approached me I was impressed, not so
much with the details of her white attire, nor with
the fine lines of a graceful figure which the gossamer
robe quite failed to conceal, but with her wonderful
gazelle-like eyes, which were uncannily like those
of her brother, save that their bordering of *kohl* lent
them an appearance of being larger and more
luminous.

No form of introduction was observed; with
modestly lowered eyes the girl saluted me and took
her seat upon a heap of cushions before a small
coffee table set at one end of the *dîwan*. The Sheikh
seated himself beside me, and Abû Tabâh, with a
reed pen, wrote something rapidly on a narrow strip

of paper. The Sheikh clapped his hands, a man entered bearing a brazier containing live charcoal, and, having placed it upon the floor, immediately withdrew. The *dîwan* was lighted by a lantern swung from the ceiling, and its light, pouring fully down upon the white figure of the girl, and leaving the other persons and objects in comparative shadow, produced a picture which I am unlikely to forget.

Amid a tense silence, Abû Tabâh took from a box upon the table some resinous substance. This he sprinkled upon the fire in the brazier; and the girl extending a small hand and round soft arm across the table, he again dipped his pen in the ink and drew upon the upturned palm a rough square which he divided into nine parts, writing in each an Arabic figure. Finally, in the centre he poured a small drop of ink, upon which, in response to words rapidly spoken, the girl fixed an intent gaze.

Into the brazier Abû Tabâh dropped one by one fragments of the paper upon which he had written what I presumed to be a form of invocation. Immediately, standing between the smoking brazier and the girl, he commenced a subdued muttering. I recognized that I was about to be treated to an exhibition of *darb el-mendel*, Abû Tabâh being evidently a *sahhar*, or adept in the art called *er-roohânee*. Save for this indistinct muttering, no other sound disturbed the silence of the apartment, until suddenly the girl began to speak Arabic and in a sweet but monotonous voice.

"Again I see the ring," she said, "a hand is

holding it before me. The ring bears a green scarab, upon which is written the name of a king of Egypt. . . . The ring is gone. I can see it no more."

"Seek it," directed Abû Tabâh in a low voice, and threw more incense upon the fire. "Are you seeking it?"

"Yes," replied the girl, who now began to tremble violently, "I am in a low passage which slopes downwards so steeply that I am afraid."

"Fear nothing," said Abû Tabâh; "follow the passage."

With marvelous fidelity the girl described the passage and the shaft leading to the King's Chamber in the Pyramid of Méydûm. She described the cavity in the wall where once (if Hassan es-Sugra was worthy of credence) the ring had been concealed.

"There is a freshly made hole in the stonework," she said. "The picture has gone; I am standing in some dark place and the same hand again holds the ring before me."

"Is it the hand of an Oriental," asked Abû Tabâh, "or of a European?"

"It is the hand of a European. It has disappeared; I see a funeral procession winding out from Rikka into the desert."

"Follow the ring," directed Abû Tabâh, a queer, compelling note in his voice.

Again he sprinkled perfume upon the fire and—

"I see a Pharaoh upon his throne," continued the monotonous voice, "upon the first finger of his left hand he wears the ring with the green scarab. A prisoner stands before him in chains; a woman pleads with the king, but he is deaf to her. He draws the ring from his finger and hands it to one standing behind the throne—one who has a very evil face. Ah!..."

The girl's voice died away in a low wail of fear or horror. But—

"What do you see?" demanded Abû Tabâh.

"The death-ring of Pharaoh!" whispered the soft voice tremulously; "it is the death-ring!"

"Return from the past to the present," ordered Abû Tabâh. "Where is the ring now?"

He continued his weird muttering, whilst the girl, who still shuddered violently, peered again into the pool of ink. Suddenly—

"I see a long line of dead men," she whispered, speaking in a kind of chant; "they are of all the races of the East, and some are swathed in mummy wrappings; the wrappings are sealed with the death-ring of Pharaoh. They are passing me slowly, on their way across the desert from the Pyramid of Méydûm to a narrow ravine where a tent is erected. They go to summon one who is about to join their company..."

I suppose the suffocating perfume of the burning incense was chiefly responsible, but at this point I realized that I was becoming dizzy and that immediate departure into a cooler atmosphere was imperative. Quietly, in order to avoid disturbing the séance, I left the *mandarah*. So absorbed were the three in their weird performance that my departure

was apparently unnoticed. Out in the coolness of
the palm grove I soon recovered. I doubt if I
possess the temperament which enables one to contemplate with equanimity a number of dead men
promenading in their shrouds.

v

"The truth is now wholly made manifest," said
Abû Tabâh; "the revelation is complete."

Once more I was mounted upon the white camel
and the mysterious *imám* rode beside me upon its
fellow, which was of less remarkable color.

"I hear your words," I replied.

"The poor Ahmed Abdulla," he continued, "who
was of little wisdom, knew, as Hassan es-Sugra
knew, of the hidden ring; for he was one of those
who fled from the pyramid refusing to enter it again.
Greed spoke to him, however, and he revealed the
secret to a certain Englishman, called Bishop, con-
tracting to aid him in recovering the ring."

At last enlightenment was mine . . . and it
brought in its train a dreadful premonition.

"Something I knew of the peril," said Abû Tabâh,
"but not, at first, all. The Englishman I warned,
but he neglected my warning. Already Ahmed
Abdulla was dead, having been despatched by his em-
ployer to the pyramid; and the people of Rikka had
sent for me. Now, by means known to you, I learned
that evil powers threatened your life also, in what
form I knew not at that time save that the sign of

Set had been revealed to me in conjunction with your death."

I shuddered.

"That the secret of the pyramid was a Pharaoh's ring I did not learn until later; but now it is made manifest that the thing of power is the death-ring of Sneferu. . . ."

The huge bulk of the Pyramid of Méydûm loomed above us as he spoke the words, for we were nearly come to our destination; and its proximity occasioned within me a physical chill. I do not think an open check for a thousand pounds would have tempted me to enter the place again. The death-ring of Sneferu possessed uncomfortable and supernatural properties. So far as I was aware, no example of such a ring (the *lettre de cachet* of the period) was included in any known collection. One dating much after Sneferu, and bearing the cartouche of Apepi II (one of the Hyksos, or Shepherd Kings) came to light late in the nineteenth century; it was reported to be the ring which, traditionally, Joseph wore as emblematical of the power vested in him by Pharaoh. Sir Gaston Maspero and other authorities considered it to be a forgery and it vanished from the ken of connoisseurs. I never learned by what firm it was manufactured.

A mile to the west of the pyramid we found Theo Bishop's encampment. I thought it to be deserted—until I entered the little tent. . . .

An oil-lamp stood upon a wooden box; and its rays made yellow the face of the man stretched upon the camp-bed. My premonition was realized; Bishop must have entered the pyramid less than an hour ahead of me; he it was who had stood upon the mound, silhouetted against the sky, when I had first approached the slope. He had met with the fate of Ahmed Abdulla.

He had been dead for at least two hours, and by the token of certain hideous glandular swellings, I knew that he had met his end by the bite of an Egyptian viper.

"Abû Tabâh!" I cried, my voice hoarsely unnatural—"the recess in the King's Chamber is a viper's nest!"

"You speak wisdom, Kernaby Pasha; the viper is the servant of the *ginn.*"

Upon the third finger of his swollen right hand Bishop wore the ring of ghastly history; and the mysterious significance of the Sign of Set became apparent. For added to the usual cartouche of the Pharaoh was the symbol of the god of destruction, thus:

We buried him deeply, piling stones upon the grave, that the jackals of the desert might never disturb the last holder of the death-ring of Sneferu.

III

THE LADY OF THE LATTICE

I

THE interior of the room was very dark, but with the aid of the electric torch which I carried I was enabled to form a fairly good impression of its general character, and having now surveyed the entire house I had concluded that it might possibly serve my purpose. The real ownership of many native houses in Cairo is difficult to establish, and the unveracious Egyptian from whom I had procured the keys may or may not have been entitled to let the premises. However, he had the keys; and that in the Near East is a sufficient evidence of ownership. My viewing the place at night was dictated by motives of prudence; for I did not propose unduly to impress my personality upon the inhabitants of the Darb el-Ahmar.

Curiosity respecting the outlook at the rear now led me to enter the deep recess at one end of the room, which boasted an imperfect but not unpicturesque *mushrabîyeh* window. Moonlight slanted down into the narrow lane which the window overhung and cast a quaint fretwork shadow upon the dusty floor at my feet. Idly I opened one of the little square lattices and peered down into the shadowy gully beneath. The lane was silent and empty, and I next directed my attention to a similar window which protruded from the adjoining house.

A panel corresponding to mine stood open also in the neighboring window; and by means of a soft light in the room I detected the head and shoulders of a woman, who, her arm resting upon the ledge, surveyed the vacant night.

By reason of her position, whilst her hand and arm lay fully in the moonlight, her face and figure were indistinct. I, on the contrary, was clearly visible to her, and although I knew that she must have seen me she made no effort to withdraw. On the contrary, she leaned artlessly forward as if to gaze upon the stars, permitting me a sight of her unveiled face and of a portion of her shapely neck.

Her eyes, as is usual with Egyptian women, were large and fine, and as is usual with all women, she was aware of the fact, casting glances upward and to the right and left calculated to exhibit their beauty.

The coquetry of her movements was unmistakable; and when, lifting a pretty arm, she brushed aside a lock of hair which overhung her brow and uttered a tremulous sigh, I perceived that I had found favor in her sight.

And indeed the graceful gesture had inclined my heart towards her; for it had served to reveal not only the symmetry of her shape but the presence upon her arm, immediately above the elbow, of a magnificent bangle in gold and lapis-lazuli, which, if I might trust my judgment, was fashioned no later than the XIXth dynasty! Clearly the house next door, and its occupant, were the property of some man of wealth and taste.

There is a maxim in the East—"Avoid the veil"; and to this hitherto I had paid the strictest attention. Soft glances from *harêm* windows usually leave me cold. But the presence of an armlet finer than anything in the Treasure of Zagazig placed a new complexion upon this affair, and the connoisseur within me took the matter out of my hands.

Across the intervening patch of darkness our glances met; the girl's dark lashes were lowered demurely, then raised again, and the boldness of my unfaltering gaze was rewarded by a smile. Thus encouraged:—

"O daughter of the moon," I whispered fancifully in Arabic, "condescend to speak to one whom the sight of thy beauty hath enslaved."

"I fear to be discovered, Inglîsi," came the soft reply; "or willingly would I converse with thee, for I am lonely and wretched."

She sighed again and directed upon me a glance that was less wretched than roguish. Evidently the adventure was much to her liking.

"Let me solace your loneliness," I replied; "for assuredly we can conceive some plan of meeting."

She lowered her eyes at that, and seemed to hesitate; then—

"In the roof of your house," she whispered, often glancing over her shoulder into the room beyond, "is a trap—which is bolted. . . ."

Footsteps sounded in the lane beneath—whereat the vision at the window vanished and the lattice was closed; but not before the girl had intimated by a gesture that I was to remain.

Discreetly withdrawing into my dusty apartment, I endeavored to make out the form of the intruder who now was passing underneath the window; but the density of the shadows in the lane rendered it impossible for me to do so. He seemed to pause for a time and I imagined that I could see him staring upward; then he passed on and silence again claimed that deserted quarter of Cairo.

For fully half an hour I waited, and was preparing to depart when a part of the shadows overlying the projecting window seemed to grow blacker, and I realized with joy that at last the lattice was reopening, but that the room within was now in darkness. Whilst I watched, remaining scrupulously invisible, a small parcel deftly thrown dropped upon the floor at my feet—and my neighbor's window was reclosed.

Closing my own, I picked up the parcel. It proved to be a small ivory box, which at some time had evidently contained *kohl*, wrapped in a piece of silk and containing a note. Returning to the lower floor I directed the light of my electric torch upon this charmingly romantic billet. It was conceived in English and characterized by the rather alarming *naiveté* of the Oriental woman. I give it in its entirety.

"To-morrow night, nine o'clock."

My cautious inquiries respecting the house in the Darb el-Ahmar led only to the discovery that it belonged to a mysterious personage whose real identity was unknown even to his servants; but this did not particularly intrigue me; for in the East the maintenance of two entirely self-contained establishments is not more uncommon than in countries less generously provided in the matter of marriage laws. After all the taking of a second wife does not so much depend on a man's religious convictions as upon his first wife.

Reflecting upon the probable history of the armlet of lapis-lazuli, I returned to Shepheard's in time to keep my appointment with Joseph Malaglou—a professed Christian who claimed to be of Greek parentage. I may explain here that it was necessary to provide for the safe conduct through the customs and elsewhere of those cases of "Sheffield cutlery" which actually contained the scarabs, necklaces, and other "antiques," the sale of which formed a part of the business of my firm. Joseph Malaglou had hitherto successfully conducted this matter for me, receiving the goods and storing them at his own warehouse; but for various reasons I had decided in future to lease an establishment of my own for this purpose.

He was waiting in the lounge as I entered, and had he been less useful to me I think I should have had him thrown out; for if ever a swarthy villain stepped forth from the pages of an illustrated "penny dreadful," that swarthy villain was Joseph Malaglou. He approached me with outstretched hand; he was perniciously polite; his ingratiating smile fired my soul with a lust of blood. Fortunately, our business was brief.

"The latest consignment is in the hands of my agent at Alexandria," he said, "and if you are still determined that the ten cases shall be despatched to you direct, I will instruct him; but you cannot very well have them sent *here*."

He shrugged and smiled, glancing all about the lounge.

"I have no intention of converting Shepheard's Hotel into a cutlery warehouse," I replied. "I will advise you in the morning of the address to which the cases should be despatched."

Joseph Malaglou was palpably disturbed—a mysterious circumstance, since, whilst I had made no mention of reducing his fees, under the new arrangement he would be saved trouble and storage.

"As delay in these matters is unwise," he urged, "why not have the goods despatched immediately, and consigned to you at my address?"

There was reason on the man's side, for I had not yet actually leased the house in the Darb el-Ahmar; therefore—

"I will sleep on the problem," I said, "and communicate my decision in the morning."

I stood on the steps watching him depart, a man palpably disturbed in mind; indeed his behavior was altogether singular, and could only portend one thing—knavery. I think it highly probable that the Ottoman Empire had a certain claim upon Joseph Malaglou. He was one of those nondescript brutes whose mere existence is a menace to our rule in the Near East. He openly applauded British methods, and was the worst possible advertisement for the cause he claimed to have espoused. Altogether he left me in an uneasy mood; so that shortly after the third, or daybreak, call to prayer had sounded from Cairo's minarets on the morrow, I had arranged to lease the house in the Darb el-Ahmar for a period of three months, in the name of one Ahmed Ben Tawwab, a mythical friend, and had instructed Joseph Malaglou accordingly.

Other affairs claimed my attention throughout the day; but dusk discovered me at my newly acquired house in the quaint street adjoining the Bâb ez-Zuwêla. I procured the keys from the venerable old thief who had leased me the premises and learned from him that a representative of Joseph Malaglou had been admitted to the house earlier in the evening, in accordance with my instructions, and had delivered a load of boxes there.

Thus, on opening the door, I was not surprised to find the ten cases from Alexandria lying within, neatly labelled:

To Ahmed Ben Tawwab,
Darb el-Ahmar,
Sukkarîya,
Cairo.

Ascending to the top floor, I mounted the rickety ladder and unbolted and opened the trap. A cautious glance to the right revealed the fact that little difficulty existed in passing from roof to roof; for in Egyptian houses these are flat and are used for various domestic purposes. I consulted my watch: the hour of the tryst was come.

And even as I learned the fact, from my neighbor's roof sounded the faint creaking of hinges ... and out into the moonlight stepped an odd figure—that of the lady of the lattice, dressed in a "European" blue serge costume which had obviously been purchased, ready made, in the bazaars! She wore high-heeled French shoes upon her pretty feet and her picturesque hair was concealed beneath a large Panama hat, from the brim of which floated one of those voluminous green veils dear to the heart of touring woman and so arranged as to hide her face. Only the gleam of her eyes and teeth was visible through the gauze.

I assisted her to step across, wondering since she was thus attired, to what crazy expedition I was committed.

"Please do not kiss me," she whispered, speaking in moderately good English, "Fatimah is listening!"

Such ingenuousness was rather alarming.

"But," I replied, "you have left the trap open."

"It is all right. Fatimah has locked the door of my room and will admit no one, because I have a headache and am sleeping!"

Resting her hand confidingly in mine, she descended the ladder into the adjoining house, and, removing the veil from her face, looked up at me.

"You will be kind to me, will you not?" she asked.

I suppose a lengthy essay upon the mentality of Oriental womanhood would serve no purpose here, therefore I refrain from inserting it. Seated upon the chests in the room below, Mizmûna—for this was her name—confided her troubles with perturbing frankness. She had conceived a characteristically Eastern and sudden infatuation for my society; nor am I prepared to maintain that she would have remained obdurate to anyone else who had been in a position to unbolt the door which offered the only chance of escape from her prison. The house of mystery, she informed me, belonged to a person styling himself Yûssuf of Rosetta (a name that sounded factitious) and she hated him. For two months, I gathered, she had been in Cairo, during which time she had never passed beyond the walls of the neighboring courtyard. And the object of her nocturnal adventure was innocent enough; she wanted to see the European shops and the tourists passing in and out of the big hotels in the Shâria Kâmel Pasha!

III

It was as we passed along the Shâria el-Maghribi, where I had pointed out the St. James's Restaurant, better known as "Jimmy's," I remember, that

Mizmûna uttered a little, suppressed cry, and clutched my arm sharply.

"Oh!" she whispered fearfully, "it is Hanna! and he has seen me!"

With frightened, fascinated eyes she was staring across the street, apparently at a group of curiously muffled natives—and her whole body was trembling.

"Quick!" she said, pulling me urgently, "take me back! if they find me they will kill me!"

"But if they have already seen you——"

"Oh! take me back," she entreated piteously. "Hanna must not find out where I live."

Here was mystery; but evidently my first dreadful theory that Hanna was Mizmûna's husband had been incorrect. Apparently he was not even acquainted with Yûssuf of Rosetta. But whoever or whatever he might be, I silently cursed the lapis armlet which had led me to involve myself in his affairs, as I hurried my companion across the Place de l'Opera and homeward. . . .

We were come indeed unmolested but breathless, as near our destination as that nameless street beside the Mosque of Muayyâd, when Mizmûna suddenly stopped, uttered a stifled shriek, and—

"Oh, save me!" she panted, winding her arms about my neck. "Look! Look! in the shadow of the mosque door!"

Panic threatened me for one fleeting moment; for this part of Cairo is utterly deserted at night and the mystery of the thing was taking toll of my nerves; then firmly unclasping the trembling arms,

I pushed Mizmûna behind me and snatched out my Colt automatic . . . as ·a group of muffled figures became magically detached from the shadows that had hidden them; and began silently to advance.

I raised the pistol.

"*Usbur!*" I cried "*âuz eh?*" (Stop! what do you want?)

They halted at once; but no answering voice broke the uncanny silence in which they regarded me. Mizmûna plucked at my arm.

"Quick! Quick!" she whispered tremulously, "the keys! the keys!"

I was swift to grasp her meaning.

"My right pocket!" I whispered in answer.

The girl's shaking hand groped for the keys, found them; and, uttering no parting word, Mizmûna darted off along the Sukkarîya, which here bisects the Darb el-Ahmar. An angry muttering arose from the little knot of oddly muffled figures, but not one of them had the courage to attempt a pursuit of the fugitive. Keeping my back to the wall of the mosque and feeling along it with one hand outstretched, I began to back away from the attacking party; intending to take to my heels along the first lane I came to.

This plan was sound enough; its weakness lay in the fact that I could make no proper survey of that which lay immediately behind me. The result was that I backed into someone who must have been stealthily approaching from the rear.

I knew nothing of his presence until he suddenly

threw himself upon from behind, and I was down on my face in the dust! My pistol was jerked out of my hand, and, still preserving that unbroken disconcerting silence, the muffled group bore down upon me.

I gave myself up for lost. My unseen assailant, who seemingly possessed wrists of steel, jerked my right hand up into the region of my shoulder-blades and pinioned my left arm so as to render me helpless as an infant. Then two of the muffled Nubians —for Nubians the moonlight now showed them to be —raised me to my feet, and the grip from behind was removed.

That I had unwittingly intruded upon the amours of some wealthy and unscrupulous pasha I no longer doubted; and knowing somewhat of the ways of outraged lovers of the East, the mental vision which arose before me was unpleasing to contemplate. Yet even the extravagant picture which my imagination had painted fell short of the ferocious reality. For even as I was lifted upright, in the grasp of my huge guards, a door in the side of the neighboring mosque burst open, and there sprang into view an excessively tall, excessively lean and hawk-faced old man carrying a naked scimitar in his hand.

He possessed eyes like the eyes of an eagle, and a thin, hooked nose having dilated, quivering nostrils. In three huge strides he reached me, towered over me like some evil *ginnee* of Arabian lore, and raised his gleaming scimitar with the unmistakable intention of severing my head from my trunk at a single blow!

I think I have never experienced an identical sensation in my life; my tongue clave to the roof of my mouth; my heart suspended its functions; and I felt my eyes start forward in their sockets. I had not thought my constitution capable of such profound and helpless fear, nor had I hitherto paid proper respect to the memory of Charles I. I would gladly have closed my eyes in order that I might not witness the downward sweep of the fatal blade, but the lids seemed to be paralysed. Never whilst memory serves me can I forget one detail of the appearance of that frightful old devil; and never can I forget my gratitude to that unseen captor, the man who had seized me from behind, and who now, alone, averted the blade from my neck.

Over my head he lunged—with an ebony stick —and skilfully; so that the pointed ferrule came well and truly into contact with the knuckles of my would-be executioner. The weapon fell, jingling, at my feet . . . and a slim, black-robed figure was suddenly interposed between myself and the furious old Arab.

It was Abû Tabâh!

Dignified, unruffled, his classically beautiful face composed and resembling, in the moonlight, beneath the snowy turban, that of some young prophet, he stood, one protective hand resting upon my shoulder, and confronted my assailant. His eyes were aglow with the eerie light of fanaticism.

"It is written that the wrath of fools is the joy of Iblees," * he declared.

Their glances met in conflict, the eagle eyes of my aged but formidable enemy glaring insanely into the fine, dark eyes of Abû Tabâh. The Arab was by no means quelled; yet presently his glance fell before the hypnotic stare of the mysterious *imám*.

"The Prophet (may God be kind to him) spared not the despoiler!" he said heavily. "With these, my two hands"—he extended the twitching, sinewy members before Abû Tabâh—"will I choke the life from the throat of the dog who wronged me."

Abû Tabâh raised his hand sternly.

"This matter has been entrusted to *me*," he said, staring down the enraged old man. "If you would have me abandon it, say so; if you would have me pursue it, be silent."

For five seconds the other sustained the strange gaze of those big, mysterious eyes, then folded his arms upon his breast, audibly gnashing his large and strong-looking teeth and averting his head from my direction in order that spleen might not consume him. Abû Tabâh turned and confronted me.

"Explain the cause of your presence here," he demanded, continuing to speak in Arabic, "and unfold to me the whole truth respecting your case."

* Satan.

"My friend," I replied, steadily regarding him, "I am eternally your debtor; but I decline to utter one word for explanation until these fellows unhand me and until I am offered some suitable excuse for the outrageous attack upon my person."

Abû Tabâh performed his curiously Gallic shrug of the shoulders—and pointed, with his ebony cane, to my pinioned arms. In a trice the Nubians fell back, and I was free. The infuriated old man directed upon me a glance that was bloodily ferocious, but—

"O persons of little piety," I said, "is it thus that a true Moslem rewards the generous impulse and the meritorious deed? To-night a damsel in distress, flying from a brutal captor, solicited my aid. I was treacherously assaulted ere I could escort her to a place of safety, and all but murdered by the man who would appear to be that damsel's natural protector. Alas, I fear to contemplate what may have befallen her as a result of such vile and foolish conduct."

Abû Tabâh slightly inclined his body resting his slim, ivory hands upon his cane; his face remained perfectly tranquil as he listened to this correct, though misleading statement; but—

"Ah!" cried the old man of the scimitar, adopting an unpleasant, crouching attitude, "perjured liar that thou art! Did I not see with mine own eyes how she embraced thee? O, son of a mange, that I should have lived to have witnessed so obscene a spectacle. Not content with despoiling

me of this jewel of my *harêm,* thou dost parade
her abandonment and my shame in the public
highways of Cairo! . . ."

In vain Abû Tabâh strove to check this tirade.
Step by step the Sheikh approached closer; syllable
by syllable his voice rose higher.

"What!" he shrieked, "is it for this that I have
offered five thousand English pounds to whomso-
ever shall restore her to me! Faugh! I spit upon
her memory!—and though I pursue thee to the
Mountains of the Moon, across the Bridge Es-
Sîrat, and through the valley of Gahennam, lo!
my hour will come to slay thee, noisome offal!"

He ceased from lack of breath, and stood quivering before me. But at last I had grasped the clue
to this imbroglio into which fate had thrust me.

"O misguided man," I replied, "grief hath up-
set thine intelligence. Again I tell thee that I
sought to deliver the damsel from her persecutor,
and, perceiving an ambush, she clung to me as her
only protector. Thou are demented. Let another
earn the paltry reward; I will have none of it."

I turned to Abû Tabâh, addressing him in English.

"Relieve me of the society of this infatuated old
ruffian," I said, "and accompany me to some place
where I can quietly explain what I know of the
matter."

"Assuredly I will accompany you to such a
spot," he answered suavely; "for whilst, knowing
your character, I do not believe you to be the
abductor of the damsel Mizmûna, a warrant to

search your house was issued an hour ago, on a charge of *hashish* smuggling!"

IV

There are certain shocks that numb the brain. This was one of them. My recollection of the period immediately following those words of Abû Tabâh is hazy and indistinct. My narrow escape from decapitation at the hands of the ferocious Arab assassin and the tangled love-affairs of that aged Othello became insignificant memories. (I seem to recollect that we left him in tears.)

My next clear-cut memory is that of walking beside the mysterious *imâm* along the Darb el-Ahmar and of stopping before the closed door of my newly acquired premises!

The street was quite deserted again. Those muffled Nubians who seemed to constitute a body-guard for my inscrutable companion had disappeared in company with the bereaved Sheikh.

"This is your house?" said Abû Tabâh sweetly.

My habit of thinking before I speak or act asserted itself automatically.

"I recently leased it on another's behalf," I replied.

"In that event," continued the *imâm*, "unless the information lodged with me to-night prove to be inaccurate, that other must speedily proclaim himself."

He tested the cumbersome lock, and, as I knew would be the case, since Mizmûna had recently entered, found it to be unfastened, opened the door and stepped in.

"Have you a pocket lamp?" he asked.

I pressed the button of my electric torch and directed its rays fully upon the stack of boxes. It was the great sage, Apollonius of Tyana, who said "loquacity has many pitfalls, but silence none"; therefore I silently watched Abû Tabâh consulting the label on the topmost chest. Presently—

"Ahmed Ben Tawwab," he read aloud; "is that the name of the friend on whose behalf you secured a lease of this house?"

"It is," I answered.

"If you will rest the light upon this box and assist me to open one of the others, I shall be obliged to you," said Abû Tabâh.

Knowing, as I did, that this strange man was in some way connected with the native police and with the guardianship of Egyptian morals, I recognized refusal to be impolitic if not impossible. But, as we set to work to raise the lid of the chest, my mind was more feverishly busy than my fingers.

Ere long our task was successful, and the contents of the chest lay exposed. These were: two hundred Osiris statuettes, twelve one-pound tins of mummy heads . . . *and fifty packets of hashish.*

Silence was no effort to me now; I was dumbfounded. The musical voice of my companion broke in upon my painful reverie.

"The information upon which I now am acting," he said, "reached me to-night in the form of a letter, bearing no address and no signature. The suppression of this vile *hashish* traffic is so near to my heart that I immediately secured the necessary powers to search the premises named, and was on my way hither when I observed you (although I did not at once recognize you) in the act of escaping from a group of my servants who had been detailed, some weeks ago, to trace a missing damsel known to be in Cairo. Concerning your share in that affair I await a full statement from your own lips; concerning your share in this I can only say that unless Ahmed Ben Tawwab comes forward by to-morrow and admits his guilt, I must apply to the British agent for a formal inquiry. Is there anything that you would wish to say, or any action you desire that I should take?"

I turned to him in the dim light. Habitually I am undemonstrative, especially with natives. But there was a nobility and an implacable sense of justice about this singular *religieux* which conquered me completely.

"Abû Tabâh," I said, "I thank you for your friendship. I have committed a grave folly; but I am neither an abductor nor a *hashish* dealer. This is the work of an unknown enemy, and already I have a theory respecting his identity."

"Can I aid you— or do you prefer that I leave you to pursue this clue in your own way?" he asked tactfully.

"I prefer to work alone."

"The affair is truly mysterious," he admitted,

"and I purpose to spend the night in meditation respecting it. After the hour of morning prayer, therefore, I will visit you. *Lîltâk sa'îda*, Kernaby Pasha."

"*Lîltâk sa'îda*, Abû Tabâh," I said, as he stepped out of the door.

Slowly and stately the *imâm* passed down the street; and the *ginnee* of solitude reclaimed that deserted spot. A night watchman, *nebbut* on shoulder, passed along the distant Sukkarîya. A dog howled.

I re-entered the doorway conscious of a sudden mental excitement; for an explanation of the anonymous letter had just presented itself to my mind. The owner of the neighboring house must have detected my rendezvous with his lady-love, have investigated the contents of the cases, and denounced me from motives of revenge! That the villainous Joseph Malaglou had been in the habit of smuggling *hashish* into Egypt in my cases of "cutlery" was evident enough and accounted for his reluctance to fall in with the new arrangement; but my bemused brain utterly failed to grapple with the problem of why, knowing their damning contents, he had permitted these ten cases to be delivered at *my* address. Moreover, how my worthy neighbor—who had evidently abducted Mizmûna from the old man of the scimitar—had learned my real name was another mystery which I found no leisure to examine. For I had but just set foot again within the ill-omened place when there came a patter of swift, light footsteps—and out from behind the fatal stack of boxes ran Mizmûna, and threw herself into my arms!

"Oh, my friend, my protector!" she cried distractedly, "what shall I do? Yûssuf has discovered our plot! Fatimah, that mother of calamities, has betrayed me, and I dare not return! I am an outcast; for although I was stolen from the Sheikh Ismail without my consent, how can I hope for his forgiveness?"

Such a flood of sorrows and confidences overwhelmed me, and I placed a silent but deathless curse upon the lapis armlet which had brought me to this pass. Mizmûna sobbed upon my shoulder.

"Yûssuf has planned your ruin as well as mine," she said brokenly. "For it was he who denounced you to the Magician." (As "the Magician" Abû Tabâh was known and feared throughout Lower Egypt.) "Oh that I might return to the house of Ismail where I lived in luxury in a marble pavilion, guarded by Hanna and a hundred negroes, where I possessed the robes of a princess and was laden with costly jewels!"

So very human and natural an ambition met with my hearty approval, and, upon consideration of the word-picture of his domestic state, the old man of the scimitar rose immensely in my esteem. How my malevolent neighbor had succeeded in abducting Mizmûna from such a fortress I failed to imagine. But I began to see my way more clearly, and hope was reborn in my bosom.

"Fear nothing, child," I said to the weeping girl. "You shall return to your marble pavilion and to the care of that worthy, if somewhat hasty man, from whose arms you were torn. And now inform me—where is Yûssuf?"

Mizmûna raised her face and looked up at me, her long lashes wet with tears, but the slow, childish smile of the Eastern woman already curving her red lips.

"He is in his own room destroying papers," she said.

"Who told you this?"

"Ali, the *bowwab,* who is faithful to me—and who hates Fatimah."

"Is the trap rebolted?"

"I know not."

"Remain here until I return," I said, seating her upon one of the boxes. "Where are my keys?"

"I hid them upon the ledge of the window, beside the door yonder."

Taking them from this simple "hiding-place," I locked the door to give Mizmûna courage, and, taking the lamp with me, began to mount the stairs, first assuring myself of the presence in my pocket of my Colt automatic, which Abû Tabâh had restored to me.

The ray of my lamp shining out ahead, I came to the crazy ladder giving access to the trap. I climbed up, raising the trap, and gazed upon the jeweled dome of midnight Egypt. Dire necessity spurred me, and I walked across to the adjoining trap, carefully inserted two fingers in the iron ring and pulled.

It was not fastened below! Inch by inch I raised it, and, finding the room beneath it to be in darkness, opened the trap fully and descended the ladder.

I flashed the light quickly about the place; then stood staring at what it revealed. My heart began to beat rapidly, for in that dirty attic I had found salvation . . . and a further clue to the mystery of all my misfortunes.

It was a *hashish* warehouse!

Taking off my shoes, I thrust one into either pocket of my jacket, and, perceiving that the house was constructed on a plan identical with that adjoining it, I crept downstairs to the apartment of the *mushrabîyeh* window. A heavy curtain was draped in the doorway, but I could see that the room within was illuminated.

I drew the curtains slowly aside and peeped in. I saw an apartment that had evidently been furnished very luxuriantly, but which now was partially dismantled. In the recess formed by the window a low table was placed, bearing a shaded lamp. The table was littered with papers, account books and ledgers; and, seated thereat, his back towards the door, was a man who figured feverishly. I stepped into the room.

"Good evening, Yûssuf of Rosetta," I said; "you do well to set your affairs in order."

V

Swiftly as though a serpent had touched him, the man in the recess leaped to his feet and twisted about to confront me.

I found myself looking into a hideous, swarthy face—blanched now to the lips, so that the cunning black eyes glared out as from a mask—into the hideous swarthy face of *Joseph Malaglou!*

The store of *hashish* in the upper room had somewhat prepared me for this discovery; yet, momentarily, the consummate villainy of the Greek had me bereft of speech. As I stood there glaring at him, he began furtively to grope with one hand along the edge of the *diwan* behind him. Then, suddenly, he became aware of the pistol which I carried—and abandoned the quest of whatever weapon he had sought, swallowing audibly.

"So, my good Malaglou," I said, "you sought to make me responsible for your sins, my friend? I perceive now how the Fates have played with me. My very first conversation with your charming protégée——"

He bit savagely at his black moustache, advanced upon me; then, his gaze set upon the Colt, he stood still again.

" . . . was reported to you by the traitorous Fatimah," I continued evenly; "and, when, on the morrow, I advised you of my new address, the identity of the hitherto unknown Romeo who had raised his eyes to your Juliet became apparent. You doubtless had designed to unpack my boxes for me as you have been in the habit of doing; but green-eyed jealousy suggested how, by the sacrifice of only one consignment of *hashish*, you might wreak my ruin. I disapprove of your morals, Malaglou. My own code may be peculiar, but it does not embrace *hashish* dealing; therefore, Malaglou, you are about to take a sheet of note-paper—bearing your office heading—and write from my dictation. . . ."

"And suppose I refuse? You dare not shoot me!"

"You little know my true character, Malaglou. But I should not shoot you, as you say; I should introduce you to a gentleman who is very anxious to make your acquaintance—the venerable Sheikh Ismail."

The effect of this remark greatly exceeded my most sanguine expectations. I think I have never seen a man so pitiably frightened.

"The Sheikh . . . Ismail!" gasped Joseph Malaglou. "He is in Cairo?"

"He has generously offered me five thousand pounds for your name and address."

"Ah, my God!" whispered Malaglou. "Kernaby, you will not betray me to that fiend! You are an Englishman and you will not soil your hands with such a deed!"

To my dismay—for it was a disgusting sight—Malaglou fell trembling upon his knees before me. The threat of shooting had had no such effect as the mere name of the Sheikh Ismail. My respect for that really remarkable old ruffian rose by leaps and bounds.

"Get up," I said harshly, "and, if you can, write."

He obeyed me; the man was almost hysterical. And, very shakily, this is what he wrote:

"I, Joseph Malaglou, also known as *Ahmed Ben Tawwab*, confess that I am a dealer in *hashish* and spurious antiques, which I have been in the habit of storing at my warehouse in Cairo, and also in my private residence in the Darb el Ahmar. Finding it desirable to enlarge the facilities of the latter, I induced the Hon. Neville Kernaby, who is ignorant of my real business, to lease for me a house which adjoins my own, as I did not desire it to be known that I was the lessee. Subsequently, learning that the suspicions of the authorities had been aroused, I anonymously denounced Kernaby, thus hoping to avert suspicion from myself and cause his arrest as the consignee of the cases which had been delivered at the new premises."

"Very good," I said, when this precious document had been completed. "You understand that you will now accompany me to the central police station in the Place Bâb el-Khalk and sign this confession in the presence of suitable witnesses? You will doubtless be detained; therefore in the interests of your safety, we must arrange that Mizmûna be hidden securely until the case is settled. Oh! set your evil mind at rest! I shall not betray you to

the Sheikh; unless—" I looked him squarely in the
eyes—"any whisper of my name appears in this
matter!"

"But where is she?" he said hoarsely.

"She is hiding in the adjoining house."

"I have a small place at Shubra where I can conceal her."

"Very well. I will bring her here and permit
you to make suitable arrangements, but let them
be complete; for if Ismail should find the girl and
thus discover your identity, nothing could save you
—and you will be unable to leave Cairo (I shall see
to that) until the case is settled."

VI

It was on the following evening, as I sat smoking
upon the terrace of the hotel and reflecting upon
the execrably bad luck which pursued me, that I
observed Abû Tabâh mounting the carpeted steps
with slow and stately carriage. He saluted me
gravely and accepted the seat which I offered him.

My plan had run smoothly; Malaglou had given
himself up to the authorities, but had been released
upon payment of a substantial bail. Mizmûna was
concealed at Shubra, and I was flogging my brain
in a vain endeavor to conjure up a plan whereby,
without betraying the villainous Greek and thus
causing him to betray *me*, I might secure the
Sheikh's reward—or, at least, the lapis armlet.

"Alas," said Abû Tabâh, "that the wicked should
prosper."

"To whose prosperity," I inquired, "do you more especially refer?"

He regarded me with his fine melancholy eyes.

"You have an English adage," he continued, "which says, 'set a thief to catch a thief.'"

"Quite so. But might I inquire what bearing this crystallized wisdom has upon our present conversation?"

"The man, Joseph Malaglou," he replied, "learning of the hue-and-cry after a certain missing damsel——"

I remember I was about to light a cigar as he uttered those words, but a dawning perception of the iniquitous truth crept poisonously into my mind, and I threw both cigar and matches over the rail into the Shâra Kâmel and clutched fiercely at the little table between us.

"And of the reward offered for her recovery," pursued the *imám*, "denounced to us, one Yûssuf of Rosetta, a man owning a small house at Shubra. Yûssuf had fled, and the only occupant of the place was the missing damsel Mizmûna. Alas that fortune should so favor the sinful. The abductor, the despoiler, escapes retribution; and the traitor, the informer, the dealer in *hashish* is rewarded."

The Turk has signally failed to rule Egypt; but there are certain Ottoman institutions which are not without claims, as I realized at that moment in regard to Joseph Malaglou: I was thinking, particularly, of the bow-string.

"Already," said Abû Tabâh, with his sweet but

melancholy smile, "the heart of the Sheikh Ismail inclined toward the damsel, for whom his soul yearned; and has not it been written that he who heals the breach betwixt man and wife shall himself be blessed? Behold the reward of the peacemaker—which I design as a gift to my sister."

I was unable to speak, but I became aware of a bitter taste upon my palate as, from beneath his robe, the smiling *imám* took out the armlet of gold and lapis-lazuli!

IV
OMAR OF ISPAHAN

I

"**I** HEAR that the Harêm Suit is occupied," said Sir Bertram Collis, bustling up to me as I sat smoking in the gardens of a certain Cairo hotel, which I shall not name because of the matters that befell there. "Daphne is full of curiosity respecting the romantic occupant."

"Don't let Lady Collis be too sure," put in Chundermeyer, "that there is anything romantic about the occupant."

"Your definition of romance, Chundermeyer," I interrupted, "would probably be 'a diamond the size of a Spanish onion.'"

Chundermeyer smiled, but it was a smile in which his dark eyes, twinkling through the pebbles of horn-rimmed spectacles, played no part. I must confess that the society of this unctuous partner in the well-known Madras firm of Isaacs and Chundermeyer palled somewhat at times. He, on the other hand, was eternally dropping into a chair beside me, and proffering huge and costly cigars from a huge and costly case. This sort of parvenu persecution is one of the penalties of being recognized by Debrett.

"As a matter of fact," I continued, "the occupant

of the Harêm Suite is no less romantic a personage
than the daughter of the Mudîr (Governor) of the
Fayûm."

"Really!" said Chundermeyer, with that sudden
interest which mention of a title always aroused in
him. "Surely it is most unusual for so highly
placed a Moslem lady to reside at an hotel?"

"Most unusual," I replied. "Of course such a
thing would be inconceivable in India; but the
management of this establishment, who cater almost
exclusively to tourists, find, I am told, that a 'harêm
suite' is quite a good advertisement. The reason
of the presence of this lady in the hotel is a diplomatic one. She is visiting Cairo in order to witness
the procession of Ashûra, peculiarly sacred to
Egyptian women, and it appears that, having no
blood relations here, she could not accept the hospitality of any one of the big families without
alienating the others."

"By Jove!" said Sir Bertram, "I must tell
Daphne this yarn. She'll be delighted! Come along,
Kernaby; if we're to have tea at Mena House, it is
high time we were off."

I left Chundermeyer to his opulent cigar without
regret. That he was an astute man of affairs and
an expert lapidary I did not doubt, for he had offered
to buy my Hatshepsu scarab ring at a price exactly
ten per cent below its trade value; but to my mind
there is something almost as unnatural about a
Hindu-Hebrew as about a Græco-Welshman or a
griffin.

Of course, Daphne Collis was not ready; and, Sir
Bertram going up to their apartments to induce her
to hurry, I strolled out again into the gardens for
a quiet cigarette and a cocktail. As I approached
a suitable seat in a sort of charming little arbor
festooned with purple blossom, a man who had been
waiting there rose to greet me.

With a certain quickening of the pulse, I recognized Abû Tabâh, arrayed, as was his custom, in
black, only releived by a small snowy turban, which
served to enhance the ascetic beauty of his face and
the mystery of the wonderful, liquid eyes.

He inclined his head in that gesture of gentle
dignity which I knew; and:

"I have been awaiting an opportunity of speech
with you, Kernaby Pasha," he said, in his flawless,
musical English, "upon a matter in which I hope
you will consent to aid me."

Since this mysterious man, variously known as
"the *imám*" and "the Magician," but whom I knew
to be some kind of secret agent of the Egyptian
Government, had recently saved me from assassina-
tion, to decline to aid him was out of the question.
We seated ourselves in the arbor.

"I should welcome an opportunity of serving you,
my friend," I assured him, "since your services to
me can never be repaid."

His lips moved slightly in the curiously tender
smile which a poor physiognomist might have mistaken for evidence of effeminacy, bending towards
me with a cautious glance about.

"You are staying at this hotel throughout the Christmas festivities?" he asked.

"Yes; I have temporarily deserted Shepheard's in order to accept the hospitality of Sir Bertram Collis, a very old friend. I shall probably return on the Tuesday following Christmas Day."

"There is to be a carnival and masquerade ball here to-morrow. You shall be present?"

"I hope so," I replied in surprise. "To what does all this tend?"

Abû Tabâh bent yet closer.

"Many of your friends and acquaintances possess valuable jewels?"

"They do."

"Then warn them—individually, in order to occasion no general alarm—to guard these with the utmost care."

My surprise increased. "You alarm me," I said. "Are there rogues in our midst?"

"No," answered the *imâm*, fixing his melancholy gaze upon my face; "so far as my knowledge bears me, there is but one, yet that one is worse than a host of others."

"Do you mean that he is here—in the hotel?"

Abû Tabâh shrugged his slim shoulders.

"If I knew his exact whereabouts," he replied, "there would be no occasion to fear him. All that I know is that he is in Cairo; and since many richly attired women of Europe and America will be here to-morrow night, of a surety Omar Ali Khân will be here also!"

I shook my head in perplexity.

"Omar Ali Khân?"——I began.

"Ah," continued Abû Tabâh, "to you that name conveys nothing, but to me it signifies Omar of Ispahân, 'the Father of Thieves.' Do you remember," fixing his strange eyes hypnotically upon me, "the theft of the sacred *burko* of Nefîseh?"

"Quite well," I replied hastily; since the incident represented an unpleasant memory.

"It was Omar of Ispahân who stole it from the shrine. It was Omar of Ispahân who stole the blue diamond of the Rajah of Bagore from the treasure-room at Jullapore, and Omar of Ispahân"—lowering his voice almost to a whisper—"who stole the Holy Carpet ere it reached Mecca!"

"What!" I cried. "When did that happen? I never heard of such an episode!"

Abû Tabâh raised his long, slim hand warningly.

"Be cautious!" he whispered; "the flowers of the garden, the palms in the grove, the very sands of the desert have ears! The lightest word spoken in the *harêm* of the Khedive, or breathed from a minaret of the Citadel, is heard by Omar of Ispahân! The holy covering for the Kaaba was restored, on payment of a ruinous ransom by the Sherîf of Mecca, and none save the few ever knew of its loss."

For a time I was silent; words failed me; for the veil of the Kaaba, miscalled "the Carpet," is about the size of a bowling-green; then—

"In what manner does this affair concern you, Abû Tabâh?" I asked.

"In this way: the daughter of the Mudîr el-Fáyûm is here, in order that she may be present on the Night of Ashûra in the Mûski. For a Moslem lady to stay in such a place as this"—there was a faint note of contempt in the speaker's voice—"is without precedent, but the circumstances are peculiar. The *khân* near the Mosque of Hosein is full, and it is not seemly that the Mudîr's daughter should live at any lesser establishment. Therefore, as she brings her two servants, it has been possible for her to remain here. But"—his voice sank again—" her ornaments are famed throughout Islâm."

I nodded comprehendingly.

"To me," Abû Tabâh whispered, "has been entrusted the task of guarding them; to you, I entrust that of guarding the possessions of the other guests!"

I started.

"But, my friend," I said, "this is a dreadful responsibility which you impose upon me."

"Other precautions are being taken," he replied calmly; "but you, observing great circumspection, can speak to the guests, and, being forewarned of his presence, can even watch for the coming of Omar of Ispahân."

II

The effect of my news upon Lady Collis was truly dramatic.

"Oh," she cried, "my rope of pearls. Mr. Chundermeyer only told me last week that it was worth at least two hundred pound more than I gave for it."

Mr. Chundermeyer had made himself popular with many of the ladies in the hotel by similar diplomatic means, but I think that if he had been compelled to purchase at his own flattering valuations Messrs. Isaacs and Chundermeyer would have been ruined.

"You need not wear it, my dear," said her husband tactlessly.

"Don't be so ridiculous!" she retorted. "You know I have brought my Queen of Sheba costume for to-morrow night."

That, of course, settled the matter, so that beyond making one pretty woman extremely nervous, my campaign against the dreaded Omar of Ispahân had opened—blankly. Later in the day I circulated my warning right and left, and everywhere sowed consternation without reaping any appreciable result.

"One naturally expects thieves on these occasions," said a little Chicago millionairess, "and if I only wore my diamonds when no rogues were about, I might as well have none. There are crooks in America I'd back against your Persian thief any day."

On the whole, I think, the best audience for my dramatic recitation was provided by Mr. Chundermeyer, whom I found in the American bar, just before the dinner hour. His yellow skin perceptibly blanched at my first mention of Omar Ali Khân, and one hand clutched at a bulging breast pocket of the dinner-jacket he wore.

"Good heavens, Mr. Kernaby," he said, "you alarm me—you alarm me, sir!"

"The reputation of Omar is not unknown to you?"

"By no means unknown to me," he responded in the thick, unctuous voice which betrayed the Semitic strain in his pedigree. "It was this man who stole the pair of blue diamonds from the Rajah of Bagore."

"So I am told."

"But have you been told that it was my firm who bought those diamonds for the Rajah?"

"No; that is news to me."

"It was my firm, Mr. Kernaby, who negotiated the sale of the blue diamonds to the Rajah; therefore the particulars of their loss, under most extraordinary circumstances, are well known to me. You have made me very nervous. Who is your informant?"

"A member of the native police with whom I am acquainted."

Mr. Chundermeyer shook his head lugubriously.

"I am conveying a parcel of rough stones to Amsterdam," he confessed, glancing warily about him over the rims of his spectacles, "and I feel very much disposed to ask for more reliable protection than is offered by your Egyptian friend."

"Why not lodge the stones in a bank, or in the manager's safe?"

He shook his head again, and proffered an enormous cigar.

"I distrust all safes but my own," he replied. "I prefer to carry such valuables upon my person, foolish though the plan may seem to you. But do you observe that squarely built, military looking person standing at the bar, in conversation with M. Balabas, the manager?"

"Yes; an officer, I should judge."

"Precisely; a *police* officer. That is Chief Inspector Carlisle of New Scotland Yard."

"But he is a guest here."

"Certainly. The management sustained a severe loss last Christmas during the progress of a ball at which all Cairo was present, and as the inspector chanced to be on his way home from India, where official business had taken him, M. Balabas induced him to break his journey and remain until after the carnival."

"Wait a moment," I said; "I will bring him over."

Crossing to the bar, I greeted Balabas, with whom I was acquainted, and—

"Mr. Chundermeyer and I have been discussing the notorious Omar of Ispahân, who is said to be in Cairo," I remarked.

Inspector Carlisle, being introduced, smiled broadly.

"Mr. Balabas is very nervous about this Omar man," he replied, with a slight Scottish accent; "but, considering that everybody has been warned,

I don't see myself that he can do much damage."

"Perhaps you would be good enough to reassure Mr. Chundermeyer," I suggested, "who is carrying valuables."

Chief Inspector Carlisle walked over to the table at which Chundermeyer was seated.

"I have met your partner, sir," he said, "and I gathered that you were on your way to Amsterdam with a parcel of rough stones; in fact, I supposed that you had arrived there by now."

"I am fond of Cairo during the Christmas season," explained the other, "and I broke my journey. But now I sincerely wish I were elsewhere."

"Oh, I shouldn't worry!" said the detective cheerily. "There are enough of us on the look-out."

But Mr. Chundermeyer remained palpably uneasy.

III

The gardens of the hotel on the following night presented a fairy-like spectacle. Lights concealed among the flower-beds, the bloom-covered arbors, and the feathery leafage of the acacias, suffused a sort of weird glow, suggesting the presence of a million fire-flies. Up beneath the crowns of the lofty palms little colored electric lamps were set, producing an illusion of supernatural fruit, whilst the fountain had been magically converted into a cascade of fire.

In the ball-room, where the orchestra played, and

a hundred mosque lamps bathed the apartment in soft illumination, a cosmopolitan throng danced around a giant Christmas tree, their costumes a clash of color to have filled a theatrical producer with horror, outraging history and linking the ages in startling fashion. Thus, St. Antony of the Thebäid danced with Salome, the luresome daughter of Herodias; Nero's arm was about the waist of Good Queen Bess; Charles II cantered through a two-step with a red-haired Vestal Virgin; and the Queen of Sheba (Daphne Collis) had no less appropriate a partner than Sherlock Holmes.

Doubtless it was all very amusing, but, personally, I stand by my commonplace dress-suit, having, perhaps, rather a ridiculous sense of dignity. Inspector Carlisle also was soberly arrayed, and we had several chats during the evening; he struck me as being a man of considerable culture and great shrewdness.

For Abû Tabâh I looked in vain. Following our conservation on the previous afternoon, he had vanished like a figment of a dream. I several times saw Chundermeyer, who had elected to disguise himself as Al-Mokanna, the Veiled Prophet of Khorassan. He seemed to be an enthusiastic dancer, and there was no lack of partners.

But of these mandarins, pierrots, Dutch girls, monks, and court ladies I speedily tired, and sought refuge in the gardens, whose enchanted aspect was completed by that wondrous inverted bowl, jewel-studded, which is the nightly glory of Egypt. In the floral, dim-lighted arbors many romantic couples shrank from the peeping moon; but quiet and a hushful sense of peace ruled there beneath the stars more in harmony with my mood.

One corner of the gardens, in particular, seemed to be quite deserted, and it was the most picturesque spot of all. For here a graceful palm upstood before an outjutting *mushrabiyeh* window, dimly lighted, over which trailed a wealth of bougainvillia blossom, whilst beneath it lay a floral carpet, sharply bisected by the shadow of the palm trunk. It was like some gorgeous illustration to a poem by Hafiz, only lacking the figure at the window.

And as I stood, enchanted, before the picture, the central panels of the window were thrown open, and, as if conjured up by my imagination, a woman appeared, looking out into the gardens—an Oriental woman, robed in shimmering, moon-kissed white, and wearing a white *yashmak*. Her arms and fingers were laden with glittering jewels.

I almost held my breath, drawing back into the sheltering shadow, for I had not hitherto suspected myself of being a sorcerer. For perhaps a minute, or less, she stood looking out, then the window closed, and the white phantom disappeared. I recovered myself, recognizing that I stood before the isolated wing of the hotel known as the Harêm Suite, and that Fate had granted me a glimpse of the daughter of the Mudîr of the Fáyûm.

Recollecting, in the nick of time, an engagement to dance with Lady Collis, I hurried back to the ball-room. On its very threshold I encountered

Chundermeyer. I could see his spectacles glittering through the veil of his ridiculous costume, and even before he spoke I detected about him an aura of tragedy.

"Mr. Kernaby," he gasped, "for Heaven's sake help me to find Inspector Carlisle! I have been robbed!"

"What?"

"My diamonds!"

"You don't mean——"

"Find the inspector, and come to my rooms. I am nearly mad!"

Daphne Collis, who had seen me enter, joined us at this moment, and, overhearing the latter part of Chundermeyer's speech:

"Oh, whatever is the matter?" she whispered.

As for Chundermeyer the effect upon him of her sudden appearance was positively magical. He stared through his veil as though her charming figure had been that of some hideous phantom. Then slowly, as if he dreaded to find her intangible, he extended one hand and touched her rope of pearls.

"Ah, heavens!" he gasped. "I am really going mad, or is there a magician amongst us?"

Daphne Collis's blue eyes opened very widely, and the color slowly faded from her cheeks.

"Mr. Chundermeyer," she began. But—

"Let us go into this little recess, where there is a good light," mumbled Chundermeyer shakily, "and I will make sure."

The three of us entered the palm-screened alcove,

Chundermeyer leading. He stood immediately under a lamp suspended by brass chains from the roof.

"Permit me to examine your pearls for one moment," he said.

Her hands trembling, Daphne Collis took off the costly ornament and placed it in the hands of the greatly perturbed expert. Chundermeyer ran the pearls through his fingers, then lifted the largest of the set towards the light and scrutinized it closely. Suddenly he dropped his arms, and extended the necklace upon one open palm.

"Look for yourself," he said slowly. "It does not require the eyes of an expert."

Daphne Collis snatched the pearls and stared at them dazedly. Her pretty face was now quite colorless.

"This is not my rope of pearls," she said, in a monotonous voice; "it is a very poor imitation!"

Ere I could frame any kind of speech—

"Look at this," groaned Chundermeyer, "as you talk of a poor imitation!"

He was holding out a leather-covered box, plush-lined, and bearing within the words, "Isaacs and Chundermeyer, Madras." Nestling grotesquely amid the blue velvet were six small pieces of coal!

Chundermeyer sank upon the cushions of the settee, tossing the casket upon a little coffee table.

"I am afraid I feel unwell," he said feebly. "Mr. Kernaby, I wonder if you would be so kind as to find Inspector Carlisle, and ask a waiter to bring me some cognac."

"Oh, what shall I do, what shall I do?" whispered poor Daphne Collis.

"Just remain here," I said soothingly, "with Mr. Chundermeyer." And I induced her to sit in a big cane rest-chair. "I will return in a moment with Bertram and the inspector."

Desiring to avoid a panic, I walked quietly into the ball-room and took stock of the dancers, for a waltz was in progress. The inspector I could not see, but Sir Bertram I observed at the further end of the floor, dancing with Mrs. Van Heysten, the Chicago lady whom I had warned to keep a close watch upon her diamonds.

I managed to attract Collis's attention, and the pair, quitting the floor, joined me where I stood. A few words sufficed in which to inform them of the catastrophe, and, pointing out the alcove wherein I had left Chundermeyer and Lady Collis, I set off in search of Inspector Carlisle.

Ten minutes later, having visited every likely spot, I came to the conclusion that he was not in the hotel, and with M. Balabas I returned to the alcove adjoining the ball-room. Dancing was in full swing, and I thought as we passed along the edge of the floor how easily I could have checked the festivities by announcing that Omar of Ispahân was present.

The first sight to greet me upon entering the little palm-shaded alcove was that of Mrs. Van Heysten in tears. She had discovered herself to be wearing a very indifferent duplicate of her famous diamond tiara.

I think it was my action of soothingly patting her upon the shoulder that drew Chundermeyer's attention to my Hatshepsu scarab.

"Mr. Kernaby!" he cried—"Mr. Kernaby!" And pointed to my finger.

I had had the scarab set in a revolving bezel, and habitually wore it with the beetle uppermost and the cartouche concealed. As I glanced down at the ring, Chundermeyer stretched out his hand and detached it from my finger. Approaching the light, he turned the bezel.

The flat part of the scarab was quite blank, bearing no inscription whatever. Like Lady Collis's rope of pearls, Mrs. Van Heysten's tiara, and Chundermeyer's diamonds, it was a worthless and very indifferent duplicate!

IV

Never can I forget the scene in that crowded little room—poor M. Balabas all anxiety respecting the reputation of his establishment, and vainly endeavoring to reason with the victims of the amazing Omar Khân. Finally—

"I will search for Inspector Carlisle myself," said Mr. Chundermeyer; "and if I cannot find him, I shall be compelled to communicate with the local police authorities."

M. Balabas still volubly protesting, the unfortunate Veiled Prophet made his way from the alcove. I cannot say if the inspiration came as the result of a sort of auto-hypnosis induced by staring at the worthless ring in my hand—the stone was not even real lapis-lazuli—but a theory regarding the manner in which these ingenious substitutions had been effected suddenly entered my mind.

Three minutes later I was knocking at the door of Chundermeyer's room. I received no invitation to enter, and the door was locked. I sought M. Balabas; and, without confiding to him the theory upon which I was acting, I urged the desirability of gaining access to the apartment. As a result, a master key was procured, and we entered.

At the first glance the room seemed to be empty, though it showed evidence of having recently been occupied, for it was in the utmost disorder. Perhaps we should have quitted it unenlightened, if I had not detected the sound of a faint groan proceeding from the closed wardrobe. Stepping across the room, I opened the double doors, and out into my arms fell a limp figure, bound hand and foot, and having a bath-towel secured tightly around the head to act as a gag. It was Mr. Chundermeyer!

I think, as I helped to unfasten him, I was the most surprised man in the land of Egypt. He was arrayed only in a bath-robe and slippers, and his bare wrists and ankles were cruelly galled by the cords which had bound him. For some minutes he was unable to utter a word, and when at last he achieved speech, his first utterance constituted a verbal thunderbolt.

"I have been robbed!" he cried huskily. "I was

sand-bagged as I came from my bath, and look—
everyone of my cases is gone!''

It was M. Balabas who answered him.

"As you returned from your *bath*, Mr. Chundermeyer?" he said. "At what time was that?"

"About a quarter-past seven," was the amazing
reply.

"But, good Heaven!" cried M. Balabas, "I was
speaking to you less than ten minutes ago!"

"You are mad!" groaned Chundermeyer, rubbing
his bruised wrists. "Have I not been locked in the
wardrobe all night!"

"Ah, merciful saints," cried M. Balabas, dramatically raising his clenched fists to heaven, "I see it
all! You understand, Mr. Kernaby. It is *not* Mr.
Chundermeyer with whom we have been conversing,
in whose hands you have been placing your valuables,
it is that devil incarnate who three years ago im-
personated the Emîr al-Hadj, in order to steal the
Holy Carpet; who can impersonate anyone; who, it
is said, can transform himself at will into an old
woman, a camel, or a fig tree; it is the conjuror, the
wizard—Omar of Ispahân!"

My own ideas were almost equally chaotic; for
although, as I now recalled, I had never throughout
the evening obtained a thoroughly good view of the
features of the veiled Prophet, I could have sworn
to the voice, to the carriage, to the manner of Mr.
Chundermeyer.

The puzzling absence of Chief Inspector Carlisle
now engaged everybody's attention; and, acting upon

the precedent afforded by the finding of Mr. Chunder-meyer, we paid a visit to the detective's room.

Inspector Carlisle, fully dressed, and still wearing a soft felt hat, as though he had but just come in, lay on the floor, unconscious, with the greater part of a cigar, which examination showed to be drugged, close beside him.

* * * * * *

As I entered my room that night and switched on the light, in through the open window from the balcony stepped Abû Tabâh.

His frequent and mysterious appearances in my private apartments did not surprise me in the least, and I had even ceased to wonder how he accomplished them; but—

"You are too late, my friend," I said. "Omar of Ispahân has outwitted you."

"Omar of Ispahân has outwitted men wiser than I," he replied gravely; "but covetousness is a treacherous master, and I am not without hope that we may yet circumvent the father of thieves."

"You are surely jesting," I replied. "In all probability he is now far from Cairo."

"I, on the contrary, have reason to believe," replied Abû Tabâh calmly, "that he is neither far from Cairo, far from the hotel, nor far from this very apartment."

His manner was strange and I discoverd excitement to be growing within me.

"Accompany me on the balcony," he said; "but first extinguish the light."

A moment later I stood looking down upon the moon-bathed gardens, and Abû Tabâh, beside me, stretched out his hand.

"You see the projecting portion of the building yonder?"

"Yes," I replied; "the Harêm Suite."

"Immediately before the window there is a palm tree."

"I have observed it."

"And upon the opposite side of the path there is an acacia."

"Yes; I see it."

"The moon is high, and whilst all the side of the hotel is in shadow the acacia is in the moonlight. Its branches would afford concealment, however; and one watching there could see what would be hidden from one on this balcony. I request you, Kernaby Pasha, to approach that *lebbekh* tree from the further side of the fountain, in order to remain invisible from the hotel. Climb to one of the lower branches, and closely watch four windows."

I stared at him in the darkness.

"Which are the four windows that I am to watch?"

"They are—one, that immediately below your own; two, that to the right of it; three, the window above the Harêm Suite; and, four, the extreme east window of this wing, on the first floor."

Now, my state of mystification grew even denser. For the windows specified were, in the order of mention, that of Inspector Carlisle, who had not yet recovered consciousness; of Mr. Chundermeyer; of Major Redpath, a retired Anglo-Indian who had been confined to his room for some time with an attack of malaria; and of M. Balabas, the manager.

"For what," I inquired, "am I to watch?"

"For a man to descend."

"And then?"

"You will hold your open watch case where it is clearly visible from this spot. Instant upon the man's appearance you will cover it up, and then uncover it, either once, twice, thrice, or four times."

"After which?"

"Remain scrupulously concealed. Have the collar of your dinner jacket turned up in order to betray as little whiteness as possible. Do not interfere with the man who descends; but if he enters the Harêm Suite, see that he does not come out again! There is no time for further explanation, Kernaby Pasha; it is Omar of Ispahân with whom we have to deal!"

v

Perched up amid the foliage of the acacia, I commenced that singular guard imposed upon me by Abû Tabâh. Did he suspect one of these four persons of being the notorious Omar? Or had his mysterious instructions some other significance? The problem defied me; and, recognizing that I was hopelessly at sea, I abandoned useless conjecture and merely watched.

Nor was my vigil a long one. I doubt if I had been at my post for ten minutes ere a vague figure appeared upon the shadow-veiled balcony of one of the suspected windows—that of Major Redpath, above the Harêm Suite!

Scarcely daring to credit my eyes, I saw the figure throw down on to the projecting top of the *mushrabîyeh* window below a slender rope ladder. I covered the gleaming gold of my watch-case with my hand, and gave the signal—*three*.

The spirit of phantasy embraced me; and, unmoved to further surprise, I watched the unknown swarm down the ladder with the agility of an ape. He seemed to wear a robe, surely that of *the Veiled Prophet!* He silently manipulated one of the side-panels of the window, opened it, and vanished within the Harêm Suite.

Raising my eyes, I beheld a second figure—that of Abû Tabâh—descending a similar ladder to the balcony of Inspector Carlisle's room. He gained the balcony and entered the room. Four seconds elapsed; he reappeared, unfurled a greater length of ladder, and came down to the flower-beds. Lithely as a cat he came to the projecting *mushrabîyeh*, swung himself aloft, and as I watched breathlessly, expecting him to enter in pursuit of the intruder, climbed to the top and began to mount the ladder descending from Major Redpath's room!

He had just reached the major's balcony, and was stepping through the open window, when a most alarming din arose in the Harêm Suite; evidently a

fierce struggle was proceeding in the apartments of
the Mudîr's daughter!

I scrambled down from the acacia and ran to the
spot immediately below the window, arriving at the
very moment that the central lattice was thrown
open, and a white-veiled figure appeared there and
prepared to spring down! Perceiving my approach:

"Oh, help me, in the name of Allah!" cried the
woman, in a voice shrill with fear. "Quick—catch
me!"

Ere I could frame any reply, she clutched at the
palm tree and dropped down right into my extended
arms, as a crashing of overturned furniture came
from the room above.

"Help them!" she entreated. "You are armed,
and my women are being murdered."

"Help, Kernaby Pasha!" now reachèd my ears,
in the unmistakable voice of Abû Tabâh, from somewhere within. "See that he does not escape from
the window!"

"Coming!" I cried.

And, by means of the palm trunk, I began to
mount towards the open lattice.

Gaining my objective, I stumbled into a room
which presented a scene of the wildest disorder. It
was a large apartment, well but sparsely furnished
in the Eastern manner, and lighted by three hanging
lamps. Directly under one of these, beside an overturned cabinet of richly carven wood inlaid with
mother-o'-pearl, lay a Nubian, insensible, and
arrayed only in shirt and trousers. There was no

one else in the room, and, not pausing to explore those which opened out of it, I ran and unbolted the heavy door upon which Abû Tabâh was clamoring for admittance.

The *imám* leaped into the room, rebolted the door, and glanced to the right and left; then he ran into the adjoining apartments, and finally, observing the insensible Nubian upon the floor, he stared into my face, and I read anger in the eyes that were wont to be so gentle.

"Did I not enjoin you to prevent his escape from the window?" he cried.

"No one escaped from the window, my friend," I retorted, "except the lady who was occupying the suite."

Abû Tabâh fixed his weird eyes upon me in a hypnotic stare of such uncanny power that I was angrily conscious of much difficulty in sustaining it; but gradually the quelling look grew less harsh, and finally his whole expression softened, and that sweet smile, which could so transform his face, disturbed the severity of the set lips.

"No man is infallible," he said. "And wiser than you or I have shown themselves the veriest fools in contest with Omar Ali Khân. But know, O Kernaby Pasha, that the lady who occupied this suite secretly left it at sunset to-night, bearing her jewels with her, and he"—pointing to the insensible Nubian on the floor—"took her place and wore her raiment——"

"Then the Mudîr's daughter——"

"Is my sister Ayesha!"

I looked at him reproachfully, but he met my gaze with calm pride.

"Subterfuge was permitted by the Prophet, (on whom be peace)," he continued; "but not lying! My sister *is* the daughter of the Mudîr el-Fáyûm."

It was a rebuke, perhaps a merited one; and I accepted it in silence. Although, from the moment that I had first set eyes on him, I had never doubted Abû Tabâh to be a man of good family, this modest avowal was something of a revelation.

"Her presence here, which was permitted by my father," he said, "was a trap; for it is well known throughout the Moslem world that she is the possessor of costly ornaments. The trap succeeded. Omar of Ispahân, at great risk of discovery, remained to steal her jewels, although he had already amassed a choice collection."

Someone had begun to bang upon the bolted door, and there was an excited crowd beneath the window.

"You supposed, no doubt," the *imám* resumed calmly, "that I suspected Major Redpath and M. Balabas, as well as Mr. Chundermeyer and the English detective? It was not so. But I regarded the room of M. Balabas as excellently situated for Omar's purpose, and I knew that M. Balabas rarely retired earlier than one o'clock. Even more suitable was that of Major Redpath, whose illness I believe to have been due to some secret art of Omar's."

"But he is down with chronic malaria!"

"It may even be so; yet I believe the attack to have been induced by Omar of Ispahân."

"But why?"

"Because, as I learned to-night, Major Redpath is the only person in Cairo who has ever met Mr. Chundermeyer! I will confess that until less than an hour ago I did not know if Inspector Carlisle was *really* an inspector! Oh, it is a seeming absurdity; but Omar of Ispahân is a wizard! Therefore I entered the inspector's room, and found him to be still unconscious. Major Redpath was in deep slumber, and Omar had entered and quitted his room without disturbing him. I did likewise, and visited Mr. Chundermeyer's—the door was ajar—on my way downstairs."

"But, my friend," I said amazedly, "with my own eyes I beheld Mr. Chundermyer gagged and bound in his wardrobe! I saw his bruised wrists!"

"He gagged, bound, and bruised himself!" replied Abû Tabâh calmly. "With my own eyes I once beheld a blind mendicant hanging by the neck from a fig tree, a bloody froth upon his lips. I cut him down and left him for dead. Yet was he neither dead nor a blind mendicant; he was Omar Ali Khân! Oblige me by opening the door, Kernaby Pasha."

I obeyed, and an excited throng burst in, headed by M. Balabas and Inspector Carlisle, the latter looking very pale and haggard!

"Where is the man posing as Chundermeyer?" began the detective hoarsely. "By sheer sleight-of-hand, and under ye're very noses"—excitement rendered him weirdly Caledonian—"he has robbed ye! I cabled Madras to-day, and the real Chundermeyer arrived at Amsterdam last Friday! As I returned with the reply cable in my pocket to-night I became so dizzy I was only just able to get to my room. He'd doctored every smoke in my case! Where is he?"

"I assisted him to escape, disguised as a woman. some ten minutes ago," I replied feebly. "I should be sincerely indebted to you if you would kick me."

"Escaped!" roared Inspector Carlisle. "Then what are ye doing here? Pursue him, somebody! Are ye all mad?"

"We should be," said Abû Tabâh, "to attempt pursuit. As well pursue the shadow of a cloud, the first spear of sunrise, or the phantom heifer of Pepi-Ankh, as pursue Omar of Ispahân! He is gone— but empty-handed. Behold what I recovered from 'Mr. Chundermeyer's' room."

From beneath his black *gibbeh* he took out a leather bag, opened it, and displayed to our startled eyes the tiara of Mrs. Van Heysten, the rope of pearls, and—my Hatshepsu scarab!

Ere anyone could utter a word, Abû Tabâh inclined his head in dignified salutation, turned, and walked stately from the room.

BREATH OF ALLAH

I

OR close upon a week I had been haunting the purlieus of the Mûski, attired as a respectable dragoman, my face and hands reduced to a deeper shade of brown by means of a water-color paint (I had to use something that could be washed off and grease-paint is useless for purposes of actual disguise) and a neat black moustache fixed to my lip with spirit-gum. In his story *Beyond the Pale,* Rudyard Kipling has trounced the man who inquires too deeply into native life; but if everybody thought with Kipling we should never have had a Lane or a Burton and I should have continued in unbroken scepticism regarding the reality of magic. Whereas, because of the matters which I am about to set forth, for ten minutes of my life I found myself a trembling slave of the unknown.

Let me explain at once that my undignified masquerade was not prompted by mere curiosity or the quest of the pomegranate, it was undertaken as the natural sequel to a letter received from Messrs. Moses, Murphy and Co., the firm which I represented in Egypt, containing curious matters affording much food for reflection. "We would ask you," ran the communication, "to renew your inquiries into the

partciular compositoin of the perfume 'Breath of
Allah,' of which you obtained us a sample at a cost
which we regarded as excessive. It appears to con-
sist in the blending of certain obscure essential oils
and gum-resins; and the nature of some of these has
defied analysis to date. Over a hundred experi-
ments have been made to discover substitutes for
the missing essences, but without success; and as we
are now in a position to arrange for the manufacture
of Oriental perfume on an extensive scale we
should be prepared to make it *well worth your while*
(the last four words characteristically underlined
in red ink) if you could obtain for us a correct
copy of the original prescription."

The letter went on to say that it was proposed
to establish a separate company for the exploita-
tion of the new perfume, with a registered address
in Cairo and a "manufactory" in some suitably
inaccessible spot in the Near East.

I pondered deeply over these matters. The scheme
was a good one and could not fail to reap considerable profits; for, given extensive advertising, there
is always a large and monied public for a new smell.
The particular blend of liquid fragrance to which the
letter referred was assured of a good sale at a high
price, not alone in Egypt, but throughout the capitals
of the world, provided it could be put upon the
market; but the proposition of manufacture was
beset with extraordinary difficulties.

The tiny vial which I had despatched to Birmingham nearly twelve months before had cost me close

upon £100 to procure, for the reason that "Breath of Allah" was the secret property of an old and aristocratic Egyptian family whose great wealth and exclusiveness rendered them unapproachable. By dint of diligent inquiry I had discovered the *attár* to whom was entrusted certain final processes in the preparation of the perfume—only to learn that he was ignorant of its exact composition. But although he had assured me (and I did not doubt his word) that not one grain had hitherto passed out of the possession of the family, I had succeeded in procuring a small quantity of the precious fluid.

Messrs. Moses, Murphy and Co. had made all the necessary arrangements for placing it upon the market, only to learn, as this eventful letter advised me, that the most skilled chemists whose services were obtainable had failed to analyse it.

One morning, then, in my assumed character, I was proceeding along the Shâria el-Hamzâwi seeking for some scheme whereby I might win the confidence of Mohammed er-Rahmân the *attár*, or perfumer. I had quitted the house in the Darb el-Ahmar which was my base of operations but a few minutes earlier, and as I approached the corner of the street a voice called from a window directly above my head: "Saïd! Saïd!"

Without supposing that the call referred to myself, I glanced up, and met the gaze of an old Egyptian of respectable appearance who was regarding me from above. Shading his eyes with a gnarled hand—

"Surely," he cried, "it is none other than Saïd the nephew of Yûssuf Khalig! *Es-selâm 'aleykûm, Saïd!*"

"*Aleykûm, es-selâm,*" I replied, and stood there looking up at him.

"Would you perform a little service for me, Saïd?" he continued. "It will occupy you but an hour and you may earn five piastres."

"Willingly," I replied, not knowing to what the mistake of this evidently half-blind old man might lead me.

I entered the door and mounted the stairs to the room in which he was, to find that he lay upon a scantily covered *diwan* by the open window.

"Praise be to Allah (whose name be exalted)!" he exclaimed, "that I am thus fortunately enabled to fulfil my obligations. I sometimes suffer from an old serpent bite, my son, and this morning it has obliged me to abstain from all movement. I am called Abdûl the Porter, of whom you will have heard your uncle speak; and although I have long retired from active labor myself, I contract for the supply of porters and carriers of all descriptions and for all purposes; conveying fair ladies to the *hammâm,* youth to the bridal, and death to the grave. Now, it was written that you should arrive at this timely hour."

I considered it highly probable that it was also written how I should shortly depart if this garrulous old man continued to inflict upon me details of his absurd career. However—

"I have a contract with the merchant, Mohammed er-Rahmân of the Sûk el-Attârin," he continued, "which it has always been my custom personally to carry out."

The words almost caused me to catch my breath; and my opinion of Abdul the Porter changed extraordinary. Truly my lucky star had guided my footsteps that morning!

"Do not misunderstand me," he added. "I refer not to the transport of his wares to Suez, to Zagazig, to Mecca, to Aleppo, to Baghdad, Damascus, Kandahar, and Pekin; although the whole of these vast enterprises is entrusted to none other than the only son of my father: I speak, now, of the bearing of a small though heavy box from the great magazine and manufactory of Mohammed er-Rahmân at Shubra, to his shop in the Sûk el-Attârin, a matter which I have arranged for him on the eve of the Molid en-Nebi (birthday of the Prophet) for the past five-and-thirty years. Every one of my porters to whom I might entrust this special charge is otherwise employed; hence my observation that it was written how none other than yourself should pass beneath this window at a certain fortunate hour."

Fortunate indeed had that hour been for me, and my pulse beat far from normally as I put the question: "Why, O Father Abdul, do you attach so much importance to this seemingly trivial matter?"

The face of Abdul the Porter, which resembled that of an intelligent mule, assumed an expression of low cunning.

"The question is well conceived," he said, raising a long forefinger and wagging it at me. "And who in all Cairo knows so much of the secrets of the great as Abdul the Know-all, Abdul the Taciturn! Ask me of the fabled wealth of Karafa Bey and I will name you every one of his possessions and entertain you with a calculation of his income, which I have worked out in *nûss-faddah!** Ask me of the amber mole upon the shoulder of the Princess Azîza and I will describe it to you in such a manner as to ravish your soul! Whisper, my son"—he bent towards me confidentially—"once a year the merchant Mohammed er-Rahmân prepares for the Lady Zuleyka a quantity of the perfume which impious tradition has called 'Breath of Allah.' The father of Mohammed er-Rahmân prepared it for the mother of the Lady Zuleyka and his father before him for the lady of that day who held the secret—the secret which has belonged to the women of this family since the reign of the Khalîf el-Hakîm from whose favorite wife they are descended. To her, the wife of the Khalîf, the first *dirhem* (drachm) ever distilled of the perfume was presented in a gold vase, together with the manner of its preparation, by the great wizard and physician Ibn Sina of Bokhara" (Avicenna).

"You are well called Abdul the Know-all!" I cried in admiration. "Then the secret is held by Mohammed er-Rahmân?"

"Not so, my son," replied Abdul. "Certain of

* A *nûss-faddah* equals a quarter of a farthing.

the essences employed are brought, in sealed vessels, from the house of the Lady Zuleyka, as is also the brass coffer containing the writing of Ibn Sina; and throughout the measuring of the quantities, the secret writing never leaves her hand.''

"What, the Lady Zuelyka attends in person?"

Abdul the Porter inclined his head serenely.

"On the eve of the birthday of the Prophet, the Lady Zuelyka visits the shop of Mohammed er-Rahmân, accompanied by an *imám* from one of the great mosques."

"Why by an *imám*, Father Abdul?"

"There is a magical ritual which must be observed in the distillation of the perfume, and each essence is blessed in the name of one of the four archangels; and the whole operation must commence at the hour of midnight on the eve of the Molid en-Nebi."

He peered at me triumphantly.

"Surely," I protested, "an experienced *attár* such as Mohammed er-Rahmân would readily recognize these secret ingredients by their smell?"

"A great pan of burning charcoal," whispered Abdul dramatically, "is placed upon the floor of the room, and throughout the operation the attendant *imám* casts pungent spices upon it, whereby the nature of the secret essences is rendered unrecognizable. It is time you depart, my son, to the shop of Mohammed, and I will give you a writing making you known to him. Your task will be to carry the materials necessary for the secret operation (which takes place to-night) from the magazine of

Mohammed er-Rahmân at Shubra, to his shop in the
Sûk el-Attârin. My eyesight is far from good, Saïd.
Do you write as I direct and I will place my name to
the letter.''

II

The words "well worth your while" had kept
time to my steps, or I doubt if I should have survived the odious journey from Shubra. Never can
I forget the shape, color, and especially the weight,
of the locked chest which was my burden. Old
Mohammed er-Rahmân had accepted my service on
the strength of the letter signed by Abdul, and of
course, had failed to recognize in "Saïd" that Hon.
Neville Kernaby who had certain confidential dealings with him a year before. But exactly how I was
to profit by the fortunate accident which had led
Abdul to mistake me for someone called "Saïd"
became more and more obscure as the box grew
more and more heavy. So that by the time that I
actually arrived with my burden at the entrance to
the Street of the Perfumers, my heart had hardened
towards Abdul the Know-all; and, setting my box
upon the ground, I seated myself upon it to rest and
to imprecate at leisure that silent cause of my
present exhaustion.

After a time my troubled spirit grew calmer, as I
sat there inhaling the insidious breath of Tonquin
musk, the fragrance of attár of roses, the sweetness
of Indian spikenard and the stinging pungency of

myrrh, opoponax ,and ihlang-ylang. Faintly I could detect the perfume which I have always counted the most exquisite of all save one—that delightful preparation of Jasmine peculiarly Egyptian. But the mystic breath of frankincense and erotic fumes of ambergris alike left me unmoved; for amid these odors, through which it has always seemed to me that that of cedar runs thematically, I sought in vain for any hint of "Breath of Allah."

Fashionable Europe and America were well represented as usual in the Sûk el-Attârin, but the little shop of Mohammed er-Rahmân was quite deserted, although he dealt in the most rare essences of all. Mohammed, however, did not seek Western patronage, nor was there in the heart of the little white-bearded merchant any envy of his seemingly more prosperous neighbors in whose shops New York, London, and Paris smoked amber-scented cigarettes, and whose wares were carried to the uttermost corners of the earth. There is nothing more illusory than the outward seeming of the Eastern merchant. The wealthiest man with whom I was acquainted in the Muski had the aspect of a mendicant; and whilst Mohammed's neighbors sold phials of essence and tiny boxes of pastilles to the patrons of Messrs. Cook, were not the silent caravans following the ancient desert routes laden with great crates of sweet merchandise from the manufactory at Shubra? To the city of Mecca alone Mohammed sent annually perfumes to the value of two thousand pounds sterling; he manufactured three kinds of incense ex-

clusively for the royal house of Persia; and his wares
were known from Alexandria to Kashmîr, and prized
alike in Stambûl and Tartary. Well might he watch
with tolerant smile the more showy activities of his
less fortunate competitors.

The shop of Mohammed er-Rahmân was at the
end of the street remote from the Hamzâwi (Cloth
Bazaar), and as I stood up to resume my labors
my mood of gloomy abstraction was changed as
much by a certain atmosphere of expectancy—I cannot otherwise describe it—as by the familiar smells
of the place. I had taken no more than three paces
onward into the Sûk ere it seemed to me that all
business had suddenly become suspended; only the
Western element of the throng remained outside
whatever influence had claimed the Orientals. Then
presently the visitors, also becoming aware of this
expectant hush as I had become aware of it, turned
almost with one accord, and following the direction
of the merchants' glances, gazed up the narrow
street towards the Mosque of el-Ashraf.

And here I must chronicle a curious circumstance.
Of the Imám Abû Tabâh I had seen nothing· for
several weeks, but at this moment I suddenly found
myself thinking of that remarkable man. Whilst
any mention of his name, or nickname—for I could
not believe ''Tabâh'' to be patronymic—amongst
the natives led only to pious ejaculations indicative
of respectful fear, by the official world he was tacitly
disowned. Yet I had indisputable evidence to show
that few doors in Cairo, or indeed in all Egypt, were

closed to him; he came and went like a phantom. I should never have been surprised, on entering my private apartments at Shepheard's, to have found him seated therein, nor did I question the veracity of a native acquaintance who assured me that he had met the mysterious *imám* in Aleppo on the same morning that a letter from his partner in Cairo had arrived mentioning a visit by Abû Tabâh to el-Azhar. But throughout the native city he was known as the Magician and was very generally regarded as a master of the *ginn*. Once more depositing my burden upon the ground, then, I gazed with the rest in the direction of the mosque.

It was curious, that moment of perfumed silence, and my imagination, doubtless inspired by the memory of Abû Tabâh, was carried back to the days of the great *khalîfs*, which never seem far removed from one in those mediæval streets. I was transported to the Cairo of Harûn al Raschîd, and I thought that the Grand Wazîr on some mission from Baghdad was visiting the Sûk el-Attârin.

Then, stately through the silent group, came a black-robed, white-turbaned figure outwardly similar to many others in the bazaar, but followed by two tall muffled negroes. So still was the place that I could hear the tap of his ebony stick as he strode along the centre of the street.

At the shop of Mohammed er-Rahmân he paused, exchanging a few words with the merchant, then resumed his way, coming down the Sûk towards me. His glance met mine, as I stood there beside the box; and, to my amazement, he saluted me with smiling dignity and passed on. Had he, too, mistaken me for Saïd—or had his all-seeing gaze detected beneath my disguise the features of Neville Kernaby?

As he turned out of the narrow street into the Hamzâwi, the commercial uproar was resumed instantly, so that save for this horrible doubt which had set my heart beating with uncomfortable rapidity, by all the evidences now about me his coming might have been a dream.

III

Filled with misgivings, I carried the box along to the shop; but Mohammed er-Rahmân's greeting held no hint of suspicion.

"By fleetness of foot thou shalt never win Paradise," he said.

"Nor by unseemly haste shall I thrust others from the path," I retorted.

"It is idle to bandy words with any acquaintance of Abdul the Porter's," sighed Mohammed; "well do I know it. Take up the box and follow me."

With a key which he carried attached to a chain about his waist, he unlocked the ancient door which alone divided his shop from the outjutting wall marking a bend in the street. A native shop is usually nothing more than a double cell; but descending three stone steps, I found myself in one of those cellar-like apartments which are not uncommon in this part of Cairo. Windows there were none, if I

except a small square opening, high up in one of the
walls, which evidently communicated with the narrow
courtyard separating Mohammed's establishment
from that of his neighbor, but which admitted scanty
light and less ventilation. Through this opening I
could see what looked like the uplifted shafts of a
cart. From one of the rough beams of the rather
lofty ceiling a brass lamp hung by chains, and a
quantity of primitive chemical paraphernalia littered
the place; old-fashioned alembics, mysterious looking jars, and a sort of portable furnace, together
with several tripods and a number of large, flat brass
pans gave the place the appearance of some old
alchemist's den. A rather handsome ebony table,
intricately carved and inlaid with mother-o'-pearl
and ivory, stood before a cushioned *dîwan* which
occupied that side of the room in which was the
square window.

"Set the box upon the floor," directed Mohammed,
"but not with such undue dispatch as to cause thyself to sustain an injury."

That he had been eagerly awaiting the arrival of
the box and was now burningly anxious to witness
my departure, grew more and more apparent with
every word. Therefore—

"There are asses who are fleet of foot," I said,
leisurely depositing my load at his feet; "but the
wise man regulateth his pace in accordance with
three things: the heat of the sun; the welfare of
others; and the nature of his burden."

"That thou hast frequently paused on the way

from Shubra to reflect upon these three things,"
replied Mohammed, "I cannot doubt; depart, therefore, and ponder them at leisure, for I perceive that
thou art a great philosopher."

"Philosophy," I continued, seating myself upon
the box, "sustaineth the mind, but the activity of
the mind being dependent upon the welfare of the
stomach, even the philosopher cannot afford to labor
without hire."

At that, Mohammed er-Rahmân unloosed upon me
a long pent-up torrent of invective—and furnished
me with the information which I was seeking.

"O son of a wall-eyed mule!" he cried, shaking
his fists over me, "no longer will I suffer thy idiotic
chatter! Return to Abdul the Porter, who employed
thee, for not one *faddah* will I give thee, calamitous
mongrel that thou art! Depart! for I was but this
moment informed that a lady of high station is about
to visit me. Depart! lest she mistake my shop for
a pigsty."

But even as he spoke the words, I became aware
of a vague disturbance in the street, and—

"Ah!" cried Mohammed, running to the foot of
the steps and gazing upwards, "now am I utterly
undone! Shame of thy parents that thou art, it
is now unavoidable that the Lady Zuleyka shall find
thee in my shop. Listen, offensive insect—thou art
Saïd, my assistant. Utter not one word; or with
this"—to my great alarm he produced a dangerous-
looking pistol from beneath his robe—"will I blow
a hole through thy vacuous skull!"

Hastily concealing the pistol, he went hurrying up the steps, in time to perform a low salutation before a veiled woman who was accompanied by a Sûdanese servant-girl and a negro. Exchanging some words with her which I was unable to detect, Mohammed er-Rahmân led the way down into the apartment wherein I stood, followed by the lady, who in turn was followed by her servant. The negro remained above. Perceiving me as she entered, the lady, who was attired with extraordinary elegance, paused, glancing at Mohammed.

"My lady," he began immediately, bowing before her, "it is Saïd my assistant, the slothfulness of whose habits is only exceeded by the impudence of his conversation."

She hesitated, bestowing upon me a glance of her beautiful eyes. Despite the gloom of the place and the *yashmak* which she wore, it was manifest that she was good to look upon. A faint but exquisite perfume stole to my nostrils, whereby I knew that Mohammed's charming visitor was none other than the Lady Zuleyka.

"Yet," she said softly, "he hath the look of an active young man."

"His activity," replied the scent merchant, "resideth entirely in his tongue."

The Lady Zuleyka seated herself upon the *dîwan*, looking all about the apartment.

"Everything is in readiness, Mohammed?" she asked.

"Everything, my lady."

Again the beautiful eyes were turned in my direction, and, as their inscrutable gaze rested upon me, a scheme—which, since it was never carried out, need not be described—presented itself to my mind. Following a brief but eloquent silence—for my answering glances were laden with significance:—

"O Mohammed," said the Lady Zuleyka indolently, "in what manner doth a merchant, such as thyself, chastise his servants when their conduct displeaseth him?"

Mohammed er-Rahmân seemed somewhat at a loss for a reply, and stood there staring foolishly.

"I have whips for mine," murmured the soft voice. "It is an old custom of my family."

Slowly she cast her eyes in my direction once more.

"It seemed to me, O Saïd," she continued, gracefully resting one jeweled hand upon the ebony table, "that thou hadst presumed to cast love-glances upon me. There is one waiting above whose duty it is to protect me from such insults. Miska!"—to the servant girl—"summon El-Kimri (The Dove)."

Whilst I stood there dumbfounded and abashed the girl called up the steps:

"El-Kimri! Come hither!"

Instantly there burst into the room the form of that hideous negro whom I had glimpsed above; and—

"O Kimri," directed the Lady Zuleyka, and languidly extended her hand in my direction, "throw this presumptuous clown into the street!"

My discomfiture had proceeded far enough, and I recognized that, at whatever risk of discovery, I must act instantly. Therefore, at the moment that El-Kimri reached the foot of the steps, I dashed my left fist into his grinning face, putting all my weight behind the blow, which I followed up with a short right, utterly outraging the pugilistic proprieties, since it was well below the belt. El-Kimri bit the dust to the accompaniment of a human discord composed of three notes—and I leaped up the steps, turned to the left, and ran off around the Mosque of el-Ashraf, where I speedily lost myself in the crowded Ghurîya.

Beneath their factitious duskiness my cheecks were burning hotly: I was ashamed of my execrable artistry. For a druggist's assistant does not lightly make love to a duchess !

IV

I spent the remainder of the forenoon at my house in the Darb el-Ahmar heaping curses upon my own fatuity and upon the venerable head of Abdul the Know-all. At one moment it seemed to me that I had wantonly destroyed a golden opportunity, at the next that the seeming oportunity had been a mere mirage. With the passing of noon and tho approach of evening I sought desperately for a plan, knowing that if I failed to conceive one by midnight, another chance of seeing the famous prescription would probably not present itself for twelve months.

At about four o'clock in the afternoon came the dawn of a hazy idea, and since it necessitated a visit to my rooms at Shepheard's, I washed the paint off my face and hands, changed, hurried to the hotel, ate a hasty meal, and returned to the Darb el-Ahmar, where I resumed my disguise.

There are some who have criticized me harshly in regard to my commercial activities at this time, and none of my affairs has provoked greater acerbitude than that of the perfume called "Breath of Allah." Yet I am at a loss to perceive wherein my perfidy lay; for my outlook is sufficiently socialistic to cause me to regard with displeasure the conserving by an individual of something which, without loss to himself, might reasonably be shared by the community. For this reason I have always resented the way in which the Moslem veils the faces of the pearls of his *harêm*. And whilst the success of my present enterprise would not render the Lady Zuleyka the poorer, it would enrich and beautify the world by delighting the senses of men with a perfume more exquisite than any hitherto known.

Such were my reflections as I made my way through the dark and deserted bazaar quarter, following the Shâria el-Akkadi to the Mosque of el-Ashraf. There I turned to the left in the direction of the Hamzâwi, until, coming to the narrow alley opening from it into the Sûk el-Attârin, I plunged into its darkness, which was like that of a tunnel, although the upper parts of the houses above were silvered by the moon.

I was making for that cramped little courtyard
adjoining the shop of Mohammed er-Rahmân in
which I had observed the presence of one of those
narrow high-wheeled carts peculiar to the district,
and as the entrance thereto from the Sûk was closed
by a rough wooden fence I anticipated little difficult in gaining access. Yet there was one difficulty
which I had not foreseen, and which I had not met
with had I arrived, as I might easily have arranged
to do, a little earlier. Coming to the corner of the
Street of the Perfumers, I cautiously protruded my
head in order to survey the prospect.

Abû Tabâh was standing immediately outside the
shop of Mohammed er-Rahmân!

My heart gave a great leap as I drew back into
the shadow, for I counted his presence of evil omen
to the success of my enterprise. Then, a swift
revelation, the truth burst in upon my mind. He
was there in the capacity of *imám* and attendant
magician at the mystical "Blessing of the perfumes"! With cautious tread I retraced my steps,
circled round the Mosque and made for the narrow
street which runs parallel with that of the Perfumers
and into which I knew the courtyard beside
Mohammed's shop must open. What I did not know
was how I was going to enter it from that end.

I experienced unexpected difficulty in locating the
place, for the height of the buildings about me rendered it impossible to pick up any familiar land-
mark. Finally, having twice retraced my steps, I
determined that a door of old but strong workman-

ship set in a high, thick wall must communicate with the courtyard; for I could see no other opening to the right or left through which it would have been possible for a vehicle to pass.

Mechanically I tried the door, but, as I had anticipated, found it to be securely locked. A profound silence reigned all about me and there was no window in sight from which my operations could be observed. Therefore, having planned out my route, I determined to scale the wall. My first foothold was offered by the heavy wooden lock which projected fully six inches from the door. Above it was a crossbeam and then a gap of several inches between the top of the gate and the arch into which it was built. Above the arch projected an iron rod from which depended a hook; and if I could reach the bar it would be possible to get astride the wall.

I reached the bar successfully, and although it proved to be none too firmly fastened, I took the chance and without making very much noise found myself perched aloft and looking down into the little court. A sigh of relief escaped me; for the narrow cart with its disproportionate wheels stood there as I had seen it in the morning, its shafts pointing gauntly upward to where the moon of the Prophet's nativity swam in a cloudless sky. A dim light shone out from the square window of Mohammed er-Rahmân's cellar.

Having studied the situation very carefully, I presently perceived to my great satisfaction that whilst the tail of the cart was wedged under a crossbar, which retained it in its position, one of the shafts was in reach of my hand. Thereupon I entrusted my weight to the shaft, swinging out over the well of the courtyard. So successful was I that only a faint creaking sound resulted; and I descended into the vehicle almost silently.

Having assured myself that my presence was undiscovered by Abû Tabâh, I stood up cautiously, my hands resting upon the wall, and peered through the little window into the room. Its appearance had changed somewhat. The lamp was lighted and shed a weird and subdued illumination upon a rough table placed almost beneath it. Upon this table were scales, measures, curiously shaped flasks, and odd-looking chemical apparatus which might have been made in the days of Avicenna himself. At one end of the table stood an alembic over a little pan in which burnt a spirituous flame. Mohammed er-Rahmân was placing cushions upon the *dîwan* immediately beneath me, but there was no one else in the room. Glancing upward, I noted that the height of the neighboring building prevented the moonlight from penetrating into the courtyard, so that my presence could not be detected by means of any light from without; and, since the whole of the upper part of the room was shadowed, I saw little cause for apprehension within.

At this moment came the sound of a car approaching along the Shâria esh-Sharawâni. I heard it stop, near the Mosque of el-Ashraf, and in the almost perfect stillness of those tortuous streets from which

by day arises a very babel of tongues I heard approaching footsteps. I crouched down in the cart,
as the footsteps came nearer, passed the end of the
courtyard abutting on the Street of the Perfumers,
and paused before the shop of Mohammed er-Rahmân. The musical voice of Abû Tabâh spoke and
that of the Lady Zuleyka answered. Came a loud
rapping, and the creak of an opening door: then—

"Descend the steps, place the coffer on the table,
and then remain immediately outside the door," continued the imperious voice of the lady. "Make sure
that there are no eavesdroppers."

Faintly through the little window there reached
my ears a sound as of some heavy object being placed
upon a wooden surface, then a muffled disturbance
as of several persons entering the room; finally, the
muffled bang of a door closed and barred . . . and
soft footsteps in the adjoining street!

Crouching down in the cart and almost holding my
breath, I watched through a hole in the side of the
ramshackle vehicle that fence to which I have already
referred as closing the end of the courtyard which
adjoined the Sûk el-Attârin. A spear of moonlight,
penetrating through some gap in the surrounding
buildings, silvered its extreme edge. To an accompaniment of much kicking and heavy breathing, into
this natural limelight arose the black countenance of
"The Dove." To my unbounded joy I perceived
that his nose was lavishly decorated with sticking-
plaster and that his right eye was temporarily off
duty. Eight fat fingers clutching at the top of the

woodwork, the bloated negro regarded the apparent
ly empty yard for a space of some three seconds,
ere lowering his ungainly bulk to the level of the
street again. Followed a faint "pop" and a gurgling quite unmistakable. I heard him walking bacl
to the door, as I cautiously stood up and again sur·
veyed the interior of the room.

▼

Egypt, as the earliest historical records show, has
always been a land of magic, and according to native
belief it is to-day the theater of many super-natural
dramas. For my own part, prior to the episode
which I am about to relate, my personal experiences
of the kind had been limited and unconvincing. That
Abû Tabâh possessed a sort of uncanny power akin
to second sight I knew, but I regarded it merely as
a form of telepathy. His presence at the preparation of the secret perfume did not surprise me, for
a belief in the efficacy of magical operations prevailed, as I was aware, even among the more cultured
Moslems. My scepticism, however, was about to be
rudely shaken.

As I raised my head above the ledge of the window
and looked into the room, I perceived the Lady
Zuleyka seated on the cushioned *dîwan*, her hands
resting upon an open roll of parchment which lay
upon the table beside a massive brass chest of antique native workmanship. The lid of the chest was
raised, and the interior seemed to be empty, but

near it upon the table I observed a number of gold-stoppered vessels of Venetian glass and each of which was of a different color.

Beside a brazier wherein glowed a charcoal fire, Abû Tabâh stood; and into the fire he cast alternately strips of paper bearing writing of some sort and little dark brown pastilles which he took from a sandalwood box set upon a sort of tripod beside him. They were composed of some kind of aromatic gum in which benzoin seemed to predominate, and the fumes from the brazier filled the room with a blue mist.

The *imám*, in his soft, musical voice, was reciting that chapter of the Korân called "The Angel." The weird ceremony had begun. In order to achieve my purpose I perceived that I should have to draw myself right up to the narrow embrasure and rest my weight entirely upon the ledge of the window. There was little danger in the maneuver, provided I made no noise; for the hanging lamp, by reason of its form, cast no light into the upper part of the room. As I achieved the desired position I became painfully aware of the pungency of the perfume with which the apartment was filled.

Lying there upon the ledge in a most painful attitude, I wriggled forward inch by inch further into the room, until I was in a position to use my right arm more or less freely. The preliminary prayer concluded, the measuring of the perfumes had now actually commenced, and I readily perceived that without recourse to the parchment, from which the

Lady Zuleyka never once removed her hands, it would indeed be impossible to discover the secret. For, consulting the ancient prescription, she would select one of the gold-stoppered bottles, unscrew it, direct that so many grains should be taken from it, and never removing her gaze from Mohammed er-Rahmân whilst he measured out the correct quantity, would restopper the vessel and so proceed. As each was placed in a wide-mouthed glass jar by the perfumer, Abû Tabâh, extending his hands over the jar, pronounced the names:

"Gabraîl Mikaîl, Israfîl, Israîl."

Cautiously I raised to my eyes the small but powerful opera-glasses to procure which I had gone to my rooms at Shepheard's. Focussing them upon the ancient scroll lying on the table beneath me, I discovered, to my joy, that I could read the lettering quite well. Whilst Abû Tabâh began to recite some kind of incantation in the course of which the names of the Companions of the Prophet frequently occurred, I commenced to read the writing of Avicenna.

"In the name of God, the Compassionate, the Merciful, the High, the Great. . . ."

So far had I proceeded and no further when I became aware of a curious change in the form of the Arabic letters. They seemed to be moving, to be cunningly changing places one with another as if to trick me out of grasping their meaning!

The illusion persisting, I determined that it was due to the unnatural strain imposed upon my vision, and although I recognized that time was precious I found myself compelled temporarily to desist, since nothing was to be gained by watching these letters which danced from side to side of the parchment, sometimes in groups and sometimes singly, so that I found myself pursuing one slim Arab A (*'Alif*) entirely up the page from the bottom to the top where it finally disappeared under the thumb of the Lady Zuleyka!

Lowering the glasses I stared down in stupefaction at Abû Tabâh. He had just cast fresh incense upon the flames, and it came home to me, with a childish and unreasoning sense of terror, that the Egyptians who called this man the Magician were wiser than I. For whilst I could no longer hear his voice, I now could *see* the words issuing from his mouth! They formed slowly and gracefully in the blue clouds of vapour some four feet above his head, revealed their meaning to me in letters of gold, and then faded away towards the ceiling!

Old-established beliefs began to totter about me as I became aware of a number of small murmuring voices within the room. They were the voices of the perfumes burning in the brazier. Said one, in a guttural tone:

"I am Myrrh. My voice is the voice of the Tomb."

And another softly: "I am Ambergris. I lure the hearts of men."

And a third huskily: "I am Patchouli. My promises are lies."

My sense of smell seemed to have deserted me

and to have been replaced by a sense of hearing. And now this room of magic began to expand before my eyes. The walls receded and receded, until the apartment grew larger than the interior of the Citadel Mosque; the roof shot up so high that I knew there was no cathedral in the world half so lofty. Abû Tabâh, his hands extended above the brazier, shrank to minute dimensions, and the Lady Zuleyka, seated beneath me, became almost invisible.

The project which had led me to thrust myself into the midst of this feast of sorcery vanished from my mind. I desired but one thing: to depart, ere reason utterly deserted me. But, to my horror, I discovered that my muscles were become rigid bands of iron! The figure of Abû Tabâh was drawing nearer; his slowly moving arms had grown serpentine and his eyes had changed to pools of flame which seemed to summon me. At the time when this new phenomenon added itself to the other horrors, I seemed to be impelled by an irresistible force to jerk my head downwards: I heard my neck muscles snap metallically: I *saw* a scream of agony spurt forth from my lips . . . and I saw upon a little ledge immediately below the square window a little *mibkharah*, or incense burner, which hitherto I had not observed. A thick, oily brown stream of vapor was issuing from its perforated lid and bathing my face clammily. Sense of smell I had none; but a chuckling, demoniacal voice spoke from the *mibkharah*, saying—

"I am *Hashish!* I drive men mad! Whilst thou

hast lain up there like a very fool, I have sent my vapors to thy brain and stolen thy senses from thee. It was for this purpose that I was set here beneath the window where thou couldst not fail to enjoy the full benefit of my poisonous perfume. . . ."

Slipping off the ledge, I fell . . . and darkness closed about me.

VI

My awakening constitutes one of the most painful recollections of a not uneventful career; for, with aching head and tortured limbs, I sat upright upon the floor of a tiny, stuffy, and uncleanly cell! The only light was that which entered by way of a little grating in the door. I was a prisoner; and, in the same instant that I realized the fact of my incarceration, I realized also that I had been duped. The weird happenings in the apartment of Mohammed er-Rahmân had been hallucinations due to my having inhaled the fumes of some preparation of *hashish,* or Indian hemp. The characteristic sickly odor of the drug had been concealed by the pungency of the other and more odoriferous perfumes; and because of the position of the censer containing the burning *hashish,* no one else in the room had been affected by its vapor. Could it have been that Abû Tabâh had known of my presence from the first?

I rose, unsteadily, and looked out through the grating into a narrow passage. A native constable stood at one end of it, and beyond him I obtained a glimpse of the entrance hall. Instantly I recognized that I was under arrest at the Bâb el-Khalk police station!

A great rage consumed me. Raising my fists I banged furiously upon the door, and the Egyptian policeman came running along the passage.

"What does this mean, *shawêsh?*" I demanded. "Why am I detained here? I am an Englishman. Send the superintendent to me instantly."

The policeman's face expressed alternately anger, surprise, and stupefaction.

"You were brought here last night, most disgustingly and speechlessly drunk, in a cart!" he replied.

"I demand to see the superintendent."

"Certainly, certainly, *effendim!*" cried the man, now thoroughly alarmed. "In an instant, *effendim!*"

Such is the magical power of the word "Inglîsi" (Englishman).

A painfully perturbed and apologetic native official appeared almost immediately, to whom I explained that I had been to a fancy dress ball at the Gezira Palace Hotel, and, injudiciously walking homeward at a late hour, had been attacked and struck senseless. He was anxiously courteous, sending a man to Shepheard's with my written instructions to bring back a change of apparel and offering me every facility for removing my disguise and making myself presentable. The fact that he palpably disbelieved my story did not render his concern one whit the less.

I discovered the hour to be close upon noon, and, once more my outward self, I was about to depart from the Place Bâb el-Khalk, when, into the superintendent's room came Abû Tabâh! His handsome ascetic face exhibited grave concern as he saluted me.

"How can I express my sorrow, Kernaby Pasha," he said in his soft faultless English, "that so unfortunate and unseemly an accident should have befallen you? I learned of your presence here but a few moments ago, and I hastened to convey to you an assurance of my deepest regret and sympathy."

"More than good of you," I replied. "I am much indebted."

"It grieves me," he continued suavely, "to learn that there are footpads infesting the Cairo streets, and that an English gentleman may not walk home from a ball safely. I trust that you will provide the police with a detailed account of any valuables which you may have lost. I have here"—thrusting his hand into his robe—"the only item of your property thus far recovered. No doubt you are somewhat short-sighted, Kernaby Pasha, as I am, and experience a certain difficulty in discerning the names of your partners upon your dance programme."

And with one of those sweet smiles which could so transfigure his face, Abû Tabâh handed me my opera-glasses!

VI

THE WHISPERING MUMMY

I

FELIX BRÉTON and I were the only occupants of the raised platform at the end of the hall; and the inartistic performance of the bulky dancer who occupied the stage promised to be interminable. From motives of sheer boredom I studied the details of her dress—a white dress, fitting like a vest from shoulder to hip, and having short, full sleeves under which was a sort of blue gauze. Her hair, wrists, and ankles glittered with barbaric jewelery and strings of little coins.

A deafening orchestra consisting of tambourines, shrieking Arab viols, and the inevitable *daràbukeh*, surrounded the performer in a half-circle; and three other large-sized *ghawâzi* mingled their shrill voices with the barbaric discords of the musicians. I yawned.

"As a quest of local color, Bréton," I said, "this evening's expedition can only be voted a dismal failure."

Felix Bréton turned to me, with a smile, resting his elbows upon the dirty little marble-topped table. He looked sufficiently like an artist to have been merely a painter; yet his gruesome picture "Le Roi S'Amuse" had proved the salvation of the previous Salon.

"Have patience," he said; "it is Shejeret ed-Durr (Tree of Pearls) that we have come to see, and she has not yet appeared."

"Unless she appears shortly," I replied, stifling another yawn, "I shall disappear."

But even as I spoke, there arose a hum of excitement throughout the crowded room; the fat dancer, breathless from her unpleasing exertions, resumed her seat; and all the performers turned their heads towards a door at the side of the stage. A veiled figure entered, with slow, lithe step; and her appearance was acclaimed excitedly. Coming to the centre of the stage, she threw off her veil with a swift movement, and confronted the audience, a slim, barbaric figure. I glanced at Felix Bréton. His eyes were glittering with excitement. Here at last was the *ghazîyeh* of romance, the *ghazîyeh* of the Egyptian monuments; a true daughter of that mysterious tribe who, in the remote past of the Nile-land, wove spells of subtle moon-magic before the golden Pharaoh.

A monstrous crash from the musicians opened the music of the dance—the famous Gazelle dance —which commenced to a measure of long, monotonous cadences. Shejeret ed-Durr began slowly to move her arms and body in that indescribable manner which, like the stirring of palm fronds, speaks the veritable language of the voluptuous Orient. The attendant dancers clashing their miniature cymbals, the measure quickened, and swift passion informed the languorous body, which magically became transformed into that of a leaping nymph, a bacchante, a living illustration of Keats' wonder-words:

> "Like to a moving vintage, down they came,
>   Crown'd with green leaves, and faces all aflame;
> All madly dancing through the pleasant valley,
>   To scare thee, Melancholy!"

At the conclusion of her dance, Shejeret ed-Durr, resuming her veil, descended to the floor of the hall and passed from table to table, exchanging light badinage with those patrons known to her.

"Do you think you could induce her to come up here, Kernaby?" said Bréton excitedly; "she is simply the ideal model for my 'Danse Funébre.'"

"Any inducement other than our presence in this select part of the establishment," I replied, offering him a cigarette, "is unnecessary. She will present herself with all reasonable despatch."

Indeed, I had seen the dark eyes glance many times towards us, as we sat there in distinguished isolation; and, even as I spoke, the girl was ascending the steps, from whence she approached our table, smiling in friendly fashion. Bréton's surprise was rather amusing when she confidently seated herself, giving an order to the cross-eyed waiter in close attendance. It would be our privilege, of course, to pay the bill. Of its being a privilege, no one could doubt who had observed the envious glances cast in our direction by less favored patrons.

As Bréton spoke no Arabic, the task of interpreter devolved upon me; and I was carrying on quite

mechanically when my attention was drawn to a
peculiarly sinister-looking person seated alone at a
table close beside the corner of the stage. I remembered having observed him address some remark to
Shejeret ed-Durr, and having noted that she seemed
to avoid him. Now, he was directing upon us a glare
so electrically baleful that when I first detected it
I was conscious of a sort of shock. The man was
rather oddly dressed, wearing a black turban and a
sort of loose robe not unlike the *burnûs* of the desert
Arabs. I concluded that he belonged to some religious order, and that his bosom was inflamed with
a hatred of a most murderous character towards
myself, Felix Bréton, and the dancer.

I endeavored, without attracting the girl's notice
to indicate to Bréton the presence of the Man of the
Glare; but the artist was so engrossed in contemplation of Shejeret ed-Durr and kept me so busy in-
terpreting, that I abandoned the attempt in despair.
Having made his wishes evident to her, the girl
readily consented to pose for him; and when next I
glanced at the table near the stage, the Man of the
Glare had disappeared.

What induced me to look towards the rear of the
platform upon which we were seated I know not,
unless I did so in obedience to a species of hypnotic
suggestion; but something prompted me to glance
over my shoulder. And, for the second time that
night, I encountered the gaze of mysterious eyes.
From a little square window these compelling eyes
regarded me fixedly, and presently I distinguished

the outline of a head surmounted by a white turban.

The second watcher was Abû Tabâh!

What business could have brought the mysterious *imám* to such a place was a problem beyond my powers of conjecture, but that he was silently directing me to depart with all speed I presently made out. Having signified, by a gesture, that I had grasped the purport of his message, I turned again to Bréton, who was struggling to carry on a conversation with Shejeret ed-Durr in his native French.

I experienced some difficulty in inducing him to leave, but my arguments finally prevailed, and we passed out into the dimly lighted street. About us in the darkness pipes wailed, and there was the dim throbbing of the eternal *darábukeh*. We were in that part of El-Wasr adjoining the notorious Square of the Fountain. Discordant woman voices filled the night, and strange figures flitted from the shadows into the light streaming from the open doorways. It was the centre of secret Cairo, the midnight city; and three paces from the door of the dance hall, a slim, black-robed figure suddenly appeared at my elbow, and the musical voice of Abû Tabâh spoke close to my ear:

"Be on the terrace of Shepheard's in half an hour."

The mysterious figure melted again into the shadows about us.

II

On the deserted hotel balcony, Abû Tabâh awaited me.

"It was indeed fortunate, Kernaby Pasha," he said, "that I observed you this evening."

"I am greatly obliged to you," I replied, "for watching over me with such paternal solicitude. May I inquire what danger I have incurred?"

I was angrily conscious of feeling like a school-boy suffering reproof.

"A very great danger," Abî Tabâh assured me, his gentle, musical voice expressing real concern. "Ahmad es-Kebîr is the lover of the dancer called Shejeret ed-Durr, alhtough she who is of the *ghawâzi*, of Keneh does not return his affections."

"Ahmad es-Kebîr?—do you refer to a malignant looking person in a black turban?" I inquired.

Abû Tabâh gravely inclined his head.

"He is one of the *Rifa'îyeh*, the Black *Darwîshes*. They practise strange rites and are by some accredited with supernatural powers. For you the danger is not so great as for your friend, who seemed to be speaking words of love to the *ghazîyeh*."

I laughed shortly.

"You are mistaken, Abû Tabâh," I replied; "his interest was not of the character which you suppose. He is an artist and merely desired the girl to pose for him."

Abû Tabâh shrugged his shoulders.

"She is an unveiled woman," he said contemptuously, "but love in the heart of such a one as Ahmad is a terrible passion, consuming the vitals and rendering whom it afflicts either a partaker of Paradise or as one of the evil *ginn*."

"In the particular case under consideration," I said, "it would seem distinctly to have produced the latter and less agreeable symptoms."

"Let your friend step warily," advised Abû Tabâh; "for some who have aroused the enmity of the Black *Darwîshes* have met with strange ends, nor has it been possible to fix responsibility upon any member of the order."

"You think my poor friend, Felix Bréton, may be discovered some morning in an unpleasantly messy condition?"

"The Black *Darwîshes* do not employ the knife," answered Abû Tabâh; "they employ strange and more subtle weapons."

I stared hard at him in the darkness. I thought I knew my Cairo, but this sounded unpleasantly mysterious. However—

"I am indebted to you, Abû Tabâh," I said, "for your timely warning. As you know, I always personally avoid any possibility of misunderstanding in regard to my relations with Egyptian women-folk."

"With some rare exceptions," agreed Abû Tabâh, "particulars of which escape my memory at the moment, you have always been a model of discretion, Kernaby Pasha."

"I will warn my friend," I said hastily, "of the view of his conduct mistakenly taken by the gentleman in the black turban."

"It is well," replied Abû Tabâh; "we shall meet again ere long."

With that and the customary dignified salutations
he departed, leaving me wondering what hidden
significance lay in his words, "we shall meet again
ere long."

Experience had taught me that Abû Tabâh's warn-
ings were not to be lightly dismissed, and I knew
enough of the fanaticism of those strange Eastern
sects whereof the *Rifa'îyeh*, or Black *Darwîshes*,
was one, to realize that it would prove an unhealthy
amusement to interfere with their domestic affairs.
Felix Bréton, who possessed the rare gift of captur-
ing and transferring to canvas the atmosphere of the
East with the opulent colorings and vivid contrasts
which constitute its charm, had nevertheless but little
practical experience of the manners and customs of
the golden Orient. He had leased a large studio
situated on the roof of a fine old Cairene palace
hidden away behind the Street of the Booksellers
and almost in the shadow of the Mosque of el-Azhar.
His romantic spirit had prompted him after a time
to give up his rooms at the Continental and to take
up his abode in the apartment adjoining the studio;
that is to say, completely to cut himself off from
European life and to become an inhabitant of the
Oriental city. With his imperfect knowledge of the
practical side of native life in the East, I did not
envy him; but I was fully alive to his danger, isolated
as he was from the European community, indeed
from modernity; for out of the boulevards of modern
Cairo into the streets of the *Arabian Nights* is but
a step, yet a step that bridges the gulf of centuries.

As I entered his studio on the folowing morning, I discovered him at work upon the extraordinary picture "Danse Funébre." Shejeret ed-Durr was posing in the dress of an ancient priestess of Isis. Bréton briefly greeted me, waving his hand towards a cushioned *dìwan* before which stood a little coffee-table bearing decanters, siphons, cigarettes, and other companionable paraphernalia. Making myself comfortable, I studied the picture and the model.

"Danse Funébre" was an extraordinary conception, representing an elaborately furnished modern room, apparently that of an antiquary or Egyptologist; for a multitude of queer relics decorated the walls, cabinets, and the large table at which a man was seated. Boldly represented immediately to the left of his chair stood a mummy in an ornate sarcophagus, and forth from the swathed figure into the light cast downwards from an antique lamp, floated a beautiful spirit shape—that of an Egyptian priestess. Upon her face was an expression of intense anger, as, her fingers crooked in sinister fashion, she bent over the man at the table.

The mummy and sarcophagus depicted on the canvas stood before me against the wall of the studio, the lid resting beside the case. It was moulded, as is sometimes seen, to represent the face and figure of the occupant and was as fine an example of the kind as I had met with. The mummy was that of a priestess and dancer of the Great Temple at Philæ, and it had been lent by the museum authorities for the purpose of Bréton's picture.

His enthusiasm at first seeing Shejeret ed-Durr was explainable by the really uncanny resemblance which the girl bore to the modeled figure. Studying her, from my seat on the *diwan,* as she posed in that gauzy raiment depicted upon the lid of the sarcophagus, it seemed indeed that the ancient priestess was reborn in the form of Shejeret ed-Durr the *ghazîyeh.* Bréton had evidently tabooed make-up, with the exception of the characteristic black bordering to the eyes (which appeared in the presentment of the servant of Isis); and seen now in its natural coloring the face of the dancing-girl had undoubted beauty.

Presently, whilst the model rested, I informed Bréton of my conversation with Abû Tabâh; but, as I had anticipated, he was sceptical to the point of derision.

"My dear Kernaby," he said, "is it likely that I am going to interrupt my work now that I have found such an inspiring model, because some ridiculous *darwîsh* disapproves?"

"It is highly unlikely," I admitted; "but do not make the mistake of treating the matter lightly. You are right off the map here, and Cairo is not Paris."

"It is a great deal safer!" he cried in his boisterous fashion, "and infinitely more interesting."

But my mind was far from easy; for in the dark eyes of the model, when their glance rested upon Felix Bréton, there was that to have aroused poisonous sentiments in the bosom of the Man of the Glare.

III

During the course of the following month I saw
Felix Bréton two or three times, and he was enthusiastic about the progress of his picture and the
beauty of his model. The first hint that I received
of the strange idea which was to lead to stranger
happenings came one afternoon when he had called
upon me at Shepheard's.

"Do you believe in reincarnation, Kernaby?" he
asked suddenly.

I stared at him in surprise.

"Regardless of my personal views on the matter,"
I replied, "in what way does the subject interest
you?"

Momentarily he hesitated; then—

"The resemblance between Yâsmîna" (this was
the real name of Shejeret ed-Durr) "and the
priestess of Isis," he said, "appears to me too
marked to be explainable by mere coincidence. If
the mummy were my personal property I should
unwrap it——"

"Do you seriously desire me to believe that you
regard Yâsmîna as a reincarnation of the elder
lady?"

"That or a lineal descendant," he answered. "The
tribe of the *Ghawâzi* is of unknown antiquity and
may very well be descended from those temple
dancers of the days of the Pharaohs. If you have
studied the ancient wall paintings, you cannot have
failed to observe that the dancing girls represented

have entirely different forms from those of any other women depicted and from those of the ordinary Egyptian women of to-day.''

His enthusiasm was tremendous; he was one of those uncomfortable fanatics who will ride a theory to the death.

"I cannot say that I have noticed it," I replied. "Your knowledge of the female form divine is doubt-less more extensive than mine.''

"My dear Kernaby," he cried excitedly, "to the trained eye the difference is extraordinary. Until I saw Yâsmîna I had believed the peculiar form to which I refer to be extinct like the blue enamel and the sacred lotus. If it is not reincarnation it is heredity.''

I could not help thinking that it more closely re-sembled insanity than either; but since Bréton had made no reference to the wearer of the black turban, I experienced less anxiety respecting his physical than his mental welfare.

Three days later there was a dramatic develop-ment. Drifting idly into Bréton's studio one morn-ing I found him pacing the place in despair and glar-ing at his unfinished canvas like a man distraught.

"Where is Shejeret ed-Durr?" I inquired.

"Gone!" he replied. "She disappeared yester-day and I can find no trace of her.''

"Surely the excellent Suleyman, proprietor of the dancing establishment, can assist you?''

"I tell you," cried Bréton savagely, "that she has disappeared. No one knows what has become of her.''

I looked at him in dismay. He presented a mournful spectacle. He was unshaven and his dark hair was wildly disordered. His despair was more acute than I should have supposed possible in the circumstances; and I concluded that his interest in Yâsmîna was deeper than I had assumed or that I was incapable of comprehending the artistic temperament. I suppose the Gallic blood in him had something to do with it, but I was unspeakably distressed to observe that the man was on the verge of tears.

Consolation was impossible, and I left him pacing his empty studio distractedly. That night at an unearthly hour, long after I had retired to my own apartments, he came to Shepheard's. Being shown into my room, and the servant having departed—

"Yâsmîna is dead!" he burst out, standing there, a disheveled figure, just within the doorway.

"What!" I exclaimed, standing up from the table at which I had been writing and confronting him. "Dead? Do you mean——"

"He has murdered her!" said Bréton, in a dull monotonous voice—"that fiend of whom you warned me."

I was appalled; for I had been utterly unprepared for such a tragedy.

"Who discovered her?"

"No one discovered her; she will never be discovered! He has buried her body in some secret spot in the desert."

My amazement grew with every word that he uttered, and presently—

"Then how in Heaven's name did you learn of her murder?" I asked.

Felix Bréton, who had begun to pace up and down the room, a truly pitiable figure, paused and looked at me wildly.

"You will think that I am mad, Kernaby," he said; "but I must tell you—I must tell someone. I could see that you were incredulous when I spoke to you of reincarnation, but I was right, Kernaby, I was right! Either that or my reason is deserting me."

My opinion inclined distinctly in the direction of the latter theory, but I remained silent, watching Bréton's haggard face.

"To-night," he continued, "as I sat looking at my unfinished picture and trying to imagine what could have become of Yâsmîna, the mummy—the mummy of the priestess—*spoke to me!*"

I slowly sank back into my chair. I was now assured that Felix Bréton had formed a sudden and intense infatuation for Yâsmîna and that her mysterious disappearance had deranged his sensitive mind. Words failed me; I could think of nothing to say; and bending towards me his haggard face—

"It whispered to me," he said, "in *her* voice—in my own language, French, as I have taught it to her; just a few imperfect words, but sufficient to convey to me the story of the tragedy. Kernaby, what does it mean? Is it possible that her spirit, released from the body of Yâsmîna, has returned to that which I firmly believe it formerly inhabited? . . ."

I had had the misfortune to be a party to some distressing scenes, but few had affected me so unpleasantly as this. That poor Felix Bréton was raving I could not doubt, but having persuaded him to spend the night at Shepheard's and having seen him safely to bed, I returned to my own room to endeavor to work out the problem of what steps I should take regarding him on the morrow.

In the morning, however, he seemed more composed, having shaved and generally rendered himself more presentable; but the wild look still lingered in his eyes and I could see that the strange obsession had secured a firm hold upon him. He discussed the matter quite calmly during breakfast, and invited met to visit the scene of this supernatural happening. I assented, and hailing *arabîyeh* we drove together to the studio.

There was nothing abnormal in the appearance of the place, but I examined the mummy and the mummy case with a new curiosity; for if Felix Bréton was not mad (and this was a point upon which I recognized my incompetence to decide) the phantom voice was clearly the product of some trick. However, I was unable to discover anything to account for it. The sarcophagus stood against the outer wall of the studio and near to a large lattice window before which was draped a heavy tapestry curtain for the purpose of excluding undesirable light upon that side of the model's throne. There was no balcony outside the window, which was fully, thirty feet from the street below; therefore unless someone had been hiding in the window recess beside the sarcophagus, trickery appeared to be out of the question. Turning to Bréton, who was watching me haggardly—

"You searched the recess last night?" I said.

"I did—immediately. There was no one there. There was no one anywhere in the studio; and when I looked out of the open window, the street below was deserted from end to end."

Naturally, I took it for granted that he would avoid the place, at any rate by night; and I said as much, as we passed along the Mûski together. I can never forget the wildness in his eyes as he turned to me.

"I *must* go back, Kernaby," he said. "It seems like desertion, base and cowardly."

IV

Bréton did not join me at dinner that evening as we had arranged that he should do, and towards the hour of ten o'clock, growing more and more uneasy on his behalf, I set out for the studio, half hoping that I should meet him. I saw nothing of him, however, as I crossed the Ezbekîyeh Gardens and the Atabet el-Khadrâ into the Mûski. From thence onward to the Rondpoint the dark and narrow streets were almost deserted, and from the corner of the Shâria el-Khordâgîya to the Street of the Bookbinders I met with no living thing save a lean and furtive cat.

My footsteps echoed hollowly from wall to wall of the overhanging buildings, as I approached the door giving acess to the courtyard from which a stair communicated with the studio above. The moonlight, slanting down into the ancient place, left more than half of it in densest shadow, but just touched the railing of the balcony and the lower part of the *mushrabîyeh* screen masking what once had been the *harêm* apartments from the view of one entering the courtyard. Far above me, through an open lattice, a dim light shone out, though vaguely. This part of the house was bathed in the radiance of the moon, which dimmed that of the studio lamp; for the open window was the window of Bréton's studio.

The door at the foot of the stairs was partly open, and I ascended slowly, since the place was quite dark and I was forced to feel my way around the eccentric turnings introduced by an Arab architect to whom simplicity had evidently been an abomination.

A modern door had been fitted to the studio; and although this door was also unfastened, I rapped loudly, but, receiving no answer, entered the studio. It was empty. The lamp was lighted, as I had observed from below, and a faint aroma of Turkish tobacco smoke hung in the air. Clearly, Bréton had left but a few moments earlier; and I judged it probable that he would be returning very shortly, for had he set out for Shepheard's he would not have left his door unlocked, and in any event I should have met him on the way. Therefore, having glanced into the inner room, which, latterly, Bréton had been using as a bedroom, I sat down on the *dîwan* and prepared to await his return.

The lamp whose light I had seen shining through the window was that which hung before the model's throne, and the curtain which usually draped the window recess had been partially pulled aside, so that from where I sat I could see part of the centre lattice, which was open. My mind at this time was entirely occupied with uneasy speculations regarding Bréton, and although I had glanced more than once at the large unfinished picture on the easel, from which the face of Shejeret ed-Durr peered out across the shoulder of the seated man, and several times had looked at the mummy set upright in its painted sarcophagus, no sense of the uncanny had touched me or in any way prepared me for the amazing manifestation which I was about to witness.

How long I had sat there I cannot say exactly; possibly for ten minutes or a quarter of an hour: when, suddenly, an eerie whisper crept through the stillness of the big room!

Since I had more than once been temporarily tricked into belief in the supernatural, by means of certain ingenious devices, I did not readily fall a victim to the mysterious nature of the present occurrence. Yet I must confess that my heart gave a great leap and I was forced to exert all my will to control my nerves. I sat quite still, listening intently for a repetition of that evil whisper. Then, in the stillness, it came again.

"Felix," it breathed, "because of you I lie dead in a grave in the desert. . . . I died for you, Felix, and now I am so lonely. . . ."

The whispering voice offered no clue to the age or the sex of the speaker; for a true whisper is toneless. But the words, as Bréton had declared, were uttered in broken French and spoken with a curious accent.

It ceased, that ghostly whispering; and I realized that my nerves could stand no more of it; for that it came or seemed to come from the mummy of the priestess was a fact as undeniable as it was horrible.

Resorting to action, I sprang up and leaped across the room, grasping first at the curtain draped in the window on the right of the sarcophagus. I jerked it fully aside. The recess was empty. All three lattices were open, on the right, left, and in the centre of the window; but, craning out from the latter, I saw the street below to be vacant from end to end.

Stepping back into the room, and metaphorically clutching my courage with both hands, I approached the sarcophagus, peered behind it, all around it, and, finally, into the swathed face of the mummy itself. Nothing rewarded my search. But the studio of Felix Bréton seemed to have become icily cold; at any rate I found myself to be shivering; and walking deliberately, although it cost me a monstrous effort to do so, I descended the dark winding stairway into the courtyard, and, on regaining the street, discovered to my intense annoyance that my brow was wet with cold perspiration.

I had taken no more than ten paces in the direction of the Sûk es-Sûdan when I heard the sound of approaching footsteps, and for some reason (I can only suppose as a result of my highly strung condition) I stepped into the shelter of a narrow gateway, where I could see without being seen, and there awaited the appearance of the one who approached.

It was Felix Bréton, his face showing ghastly in the moonlight as he turned the corner. I could not be certain if a mere echo had deceived me, but I thought I could detect faintly the softer footfalls of someone who was following him. From my cover I had an uninterrupted view of the entrance to the house which I had just left; and without showing myself I watched Bréton approach the door. At its threshold he seemed to hesitate; and in that brief hesitancy were illustrated the conflicting emotions driving the man. I recalled the words he had spoken to me that morning. "I must go back, Kernaby; it seems like desertion, base and cowardly." He opened the door and disappeared.

As he did so, a second figure crossed from the shadows on the opposite side of the street—that is, the side upon which I was concealed; and in turn advanced towards the door. As he passed my hiding-place I acted. Without an instant's hesitation I hurled myself upon him.

How he avoided that furious attack—if he did avoid it—or whether in the darkness I miscalculated my spring, I do not know to this day: I only know that I missed my objective, stumbled, recovered my-

self . . . and turned with clenched fists to find *Abû
Tabâh* confronting me!

"Kernaby Pasha!" he cried.

"Abû Tabâh!" said I dazedly.

"I perceive that I am not alone in my anxiety
for the welfare of M. Felix Bréton."

"But why were you following him? I narrowly
missed assaulting you."

"Very narrowly," he agreed in his gentle manner;
"but you ask me why I was following M. Bréton.
I was following him because I have seen so many
of those who have crossed the path of the Black
Darwîshes meet with violent and inexplicable
deaths."

"Murder?" I whispered.

"Not murder—suicide. Therefore, observing, as
I had anticipated, a strangeness in your friend's
behavior, I have watched him."

"The strangeness of his behavior is easily accounted for," I said. And excitedly, for the horror
of the episode in the studio was still strongly upon
me, I told him of the whispering mummy.

"These are very dreadful things of which you
speak, Kernaby Pasha," he admitted, "but I warned
you that it was ill to incur the enmity of the Black
Darwîshes. That there is a scheme afoot to com-
pass the self-destruction or insanity of your friend
is now evident to me; and he has brought this calamity upon himself; for the words which he believed to
be spoken by the spirit of the girl Yâsmîna would not
have affected him so unpleasantly if his attitude

towards her had been marked by proper restraint
and the affair confined within suitable limitations.''

"Quite so.   But although the Black *Darwîshes*
may be both malignant and clever, that uncanny
whispering is beyond the control of natural forces.''

"Such is not my opinion," replied Abû Tabâh.
"A spirit does not mistake one person for another;
and the whispering voice addressed itself to 'Felix'
when Felix was not present.   I believe, Kernaby
Pasha, that you are the possessor of a pair of excellent opera-glasses?   May I suggest that you return
to Shepheard's and procure them.''

v

The platform of the minaret seemed very cold to
the touch of my stockinged feet; for I had left my
shoes at the entrance to the mosque below in accordance with custom; and now, from the wooden
balcony, I overlooked the neighboring roofs of Cairo,
and Abû Tabâh, beside me, pointed to where a vague
patch of light broke the darkness beneath us to the
left.

"The window of M. Felix Bréton's studio," he
said.

Raising the glasses to his eyes, he gazed in that
direction, whilst I also peered thither and succeeded
in making out the well of the courtyard and the
roofs of the buildings to right and left of it.   It was
not evident to me for what Abû Tabâh was looking,
and when presently he lowered the glasses and turned
to me I expressed my doubts in words.

"It is surely evident," I said, speaking, as I now almost invariably did to the *imám*, in English, of which he had a perfect mastery, "that we have little chance of discovering anything from here, since nothing was visible from the studio window. Furthermore, who save Yâsmîna could have spoken in the manner which I have related and in broken French?"

"An eavesdropper," he replied, " might have profited by the lessons which Yâsmîna received from M. Bréton; and all vocal characteristics are lost in a whisper. In the second place, Yâsmîna is not dead."

"What!" I cried.

Although, when Bréton had informed me of her death, I myself had doubted him, for some reason the ghostly whisper had convinced me as it had convinced him.

"She has been kept a prisoner during the past week in a house belonging to one of the Black *Darwîshes*," continued Abû Tabâh; "but my agents succeeded in tracing her this morning. By my orders, however, she has not been allowed to return to her home."

"And what was the object of those orders?"

"That I might learn for what purpose she had been made to disappear," replied Abû Tabâh; "and I have learned it to-night."

"Then you think that the whispering mummy——"

He suddenly clutched my arm.

"Quick! raise your glasses!" he said softly. "On the roof of the house to the left of the light. There is the whispering mummy!"

Strung up to a high pitch of excitement, I gazed through the glasses in the direction indicated by my companion. Without difficulty I discerned him —a man wearing a black turban—who crept like some ungainly cat along the flat roof, carrying in his hand what looked like one of those sugar canes which pass for a delicacy among the natives, but which to European eyes appear more suitable for curtain-poles than sweetmeats. Springing perilously across a yawning gulf, the wearer of the black turban gained the roof of the studio, crept along for some little distance further, and then, lying prone, began slowly to lower the bamboo rod in the direction of the lighted window.

I found that unconsciously I had suspended my respiration, and now, breathlessly, as the truth came home to me—

"It is a speaking-tube!" I cried, "I cannot see the end of it, but no doubt it is curved so as to protrude through the side of the lattice window. Do you look ,Abû Tabâh: *I* propose to act."

Thrusting the glasses into the *imám's* hand, I took my Colt repeater from my pocket, and, having peered for some seconds steadily in the direction of the dimly visible *Darwîsh,* I opened fire! I had fired five shots in the heat of my anger at that sinister crouching figure, ere Abû Tabâh seized my wrist.

"Stop!" he cried; "do you forget where you stand?"

Truly I had forgotten in my indignation, or I should not have outraged his feelings by firing from the minaret of a mosque. But sufficient of my wrath remained to occasion me a thrill of satisfaction, when, peering through the dusk, I saw the *Darwîsh* throw up his arms and disappear from view.

* * * * * *

"There is blood in the courtyard," said Abû Tabâh; "but Ahmad es-Kebîr has fled. Therefore he still lives, and his anger will be not the less but the greater. Depart from Cairo, M. Bréton: it is my counsel to you."

"But," cried Felix Bréton, glaring wildly at the big canvas on the easel, "I must finish my picture. As Yâsmîna is alive, she must return, and I must finish my picture!"

"Yâsmîna cannot return," replied Abû Tabâh, fixing his weird eyes upon the speaker. "I have caused her to be banished from Cairo." He raised his hand, checking Bréton's hot words ere they were uttered. "Recriminations are unavailing. Her presence disturbs the peace of the city, and the peace of the city it is my duty to maintain."

PART II

OTHER TALES

I

LORD OF THE JACKALS

IN those days, of course (said the French agent, looking out across the sea of Yûssuf Effendis which billowed up against the balcony to where, in the moonlight, the minarets of Cairo pointed the way to God), I did not occupy the position which I occupy to-day. No, I was younger, and more ambitious; I thought to carve in the annals of Egypt a name for myself such as that of De Lesseps.

I had a scheme—and there were those who believed in it—for extending the borders of Egypt. Ah! my friends, Egypt after all is but a double belt of mud following the Nile, and terminated east and west by the desert. The desert! It was the dream of my life to exterminate that desert, that hungry gray desert; it was my plan—a foolish plan as I know now—to link the fertile Fáyûm to the Oases! How was this to be done? Ah!

Why should I dig up those buried skeletons? It was not done; it never could be done; therefore, let me not bore you with how I had proposed to do it. Suffice it that my ambitions took me far off the beaten tracks, far, even, from the caravan roads— far into the gray heart of the desert.

But I was ambitious, and only nineteen—or scarcely twenty. At nineteen, a man who comes from St. Rémy fears no obstacle which Fate can place in his way, and looks upon the world as a grape-fruit to be sweetened with endeavor and sucked empty.

It was in those days, then, that I learned as your Rudyard Kipling has also learned that "East is East"; it was in those days that I came face to face with that "mystery of Egypt" about which so much is written, has always been written, and always will be written, but concerning which so few people, so very few people, know anything whatever.

Yes, I, René de Flassans, saw with my own eyes a thing that I knew to be magic, a thing whereat my reason rebelled—a thing which my poor European intelligence could not grapple, could not begin to explain.

It was this which you asked me to tell you, was it not? I will do so with pleasure, because I know that I speak to men of honor, and because it is good for me, now that I cannot count the gray hairs in my beard, to confess how poor a thing I was when I could count every hair upon my chin—and how grand a thing I thought myself.

One evening, at the end of a dreadful day in the saddle—beneath a sky which seemed to reflect all the fires of hell, a day passed upon sands simply smoking in that merciless sun—I and my native companions came to an encampment of Arabs.

They were Bedouins*—the tribe does not matter

* This incorrect but familiar spelling is retained throughout.

at the moment—and, as you may know, the Bedouin is the most hospitable creature whom God has yet created. The tent of the Sheikh is open to any traveller who cares to rest his weary limbs therein. Freely he may partake of all that the tribe has to offer, food and drink and entertainment; and to seek to press payment upon the host would be to insult a gentleman.

That is desert hospitality. A spear that stands thrust upright in the sand before the tent door signifies that whosoever would raise his hand against the guest has first to reckon with the Sheikh. Equally it would be an insult to erect one's own tent in the neighborhood of a Bedouin encampment.

Well, my friends, I knew this well, for I was no stranger to the nomadic life, and accordingly, without fear of the fierce-eyed throng who came forth to meet us, I made my respects to the Sheikh Saïd Mohammed, and was reckoned by him as a friend and a brother. His tent was placed at my disposal and provisions were made for the suitable entertainment of those who were with me.

You know how dusk falls in Egypt? At one moment the sky is a brilliant canvas, glorious with every color known to art, at the next the curtain—the wonderful veil of deepest violet—has fallen; the stars break through it like diamonds through the finest gauze; it is night, velvet, violet night. You see it here in this noisy modern Cairo. In the lonely desert it is ten thousand times grander, ten thousand times more impressive; it speaks to the soul with the voice of the silence. Ah, those desert nights!

So was the night of which I speak; and having partaken of the fare which the Sheikh caused to be set before me—and Bedouin fare is not for the squeamish stomach—I sipped that delicious coffee which, though an acquired taste, is the true nectar, and looked out beyond the four or five palm trees of this little oasis to where the gray carpet of the desert grew black as ebony and met the violet sweep of the sky.

Perhaps I was the first to see him; I cannot say; but certainly he was not perceived by the Bedouins, although one stood on guard at the entrance to the camp.

How can I describe him? At the time, as he approached in the moonlight with a shambling, stooping gait, I felt that I had never seen his like before. Now I know the reason of my wonder, and the reason of my doubt. I know what it was about him which inspired a kind of horror and a revulsion—a dread.

Elfin locks he had, gray and matted, falling about his angular face, shading his strange, yellow eyes. His was dressed in rags, in tatters; he was furtive, and he staggered as one who is very weak, slowly approaching out of the vastness.

Then it appeared as though every dog in the camp knew of his coming. Out from the shadows of the tents they poured, those yapping mongrels. Never have I seen such a thing. In the midst of the yellow-ish, snarling things, at the very entrance to the camp, the wretched old man fell, uttering a low cry.

But now, snatching up a heavy club which lay close to my hand, I rushed out of the tent. Others were thronging out too, but, first of them all, I burst in among the dogs, striking, kicking, and shouting. I stooped and raised the head of the stranger.

Mutely he thanked me, with half-closed eyes. A choking sound issued from his throat, and he clutched with his hands and pointed to his mouth.

An earthenware jar, containing cool water, stood beside a tent but a few yards away. Hurling my club at the most furious of the dogs, which, with bared fangs, still threatened to attack the recumbent man, I ran and seized the *dorak*, regained his side, and poured water between his parched lips.

The throng about me was strangely silent, until, as the poor old man staggered again to his feet, supported by my arm, a chorus arose about me—one long, vowelled word, wholly unfamiliar, although my Arabic was good. But I noted that all kept a respectful distance from myself and the man whom I had succored.

Then, pressing his way through the throng came the Sheikh Saïd Mohammed. Saluting the ragged stranger with a sort of grim respect, he asked him if he desired entertainment for the night.

The other shook his head, mumbling, pointed to the water jar, and by dint of gnashing his yellow and pointed teeth, intimated that he required food.

Food was brought to him hurriedly. He tied it up in a dirty cloth, grasped the water jar, and, with never a glance at the Arabs, turned to me. With his hand he touched his brow, his lips, and his breast in salute; then, although tottering with weakness, he made off again with that queer, loping gait.

The camp dogs began to howl, and a strange silence fell upon the Arabs about me. All stood watching the departing figure until it was lost in a dip of the desert, when the watchers began to return again to their tents.

Saïd Mohammed took my hand, and in a few direct and impressive words thanked me for having spared him and his tribe from a grave dishonor. Need I say that I was flattered? Had you met him, my friends, that fine Bedouin gentleman, polished as any noble of old France, fearless as a lion, yet gentle as a woman, you would know that I rejoiced in being able to serve him even so slightly.

Two of the dogs, unperceived by us, had followed the weird old man from the camp; for suddenly in the distance I heard their savage growls. Then, these growls were drowned in such a chorus of howling—the howling of jackals—as I had never before heard in all my desert wanderings. The howling suddenly subsided . . . but the dogs did not return.

I glanced around, meaning to address the Sheikh, but the Sheikh was gone.

Filled with wonder, then, respecting this singular incident, I entered the tent—it was at the farther end of the camp—which had been placed at my disposal, and lay down, rather to reflect than to sleep. With my mind confused in thoughts of yellow-eyed wanderers, of dogs, and of jackals, sleep came.

How long I slept I cannot say; but I was awakened
as the cool fingers of dawn were touching the crests
of the sand billows. A gray and dismal light filled
the tent, and something was scratching at the flap.

I sat up immediately, quite wide awake, and taking
my revolver, ran to the entrance and looked out.

A slinking shape melted into the shadows of the
tent adjoining mine, and I concluded that a camp
dog had aroused me. Then, in the early morning
silence, I heard a faint call, and peering through the
gloom to the east saw, in black silhouette, a solitary
figure standing near the extremity of the camp.

In those days, my friends, I was a brave fellow—
we are all brave at nineteen—and throwing a cloak
over my shoulders I strode intrepidly towards this
figure. I was within ten paces when a hand was
raised to beckon me.

It was the mysterious stranger! Again he
beckoned to me, and I approached yet nearer, asking
him if it was he who had aroused me.

He nodded, and by means of a grotesque kind of
pantomine ultimately made me understand that he
had caused me to be aroused in order to communicate
something to me. He turned, and indicated that we
were to walk away from the camp. I accompanied
him without hesitation.

Although the camp was never left unguarded, no
one had challenged us; and, a hundred yards beyond
the outermost tent, this strange old man stopped
and turned to me.

First, he pointed back to the camp, then to myself,

then out along the caravan road towards the Nile.

"Do you mean," I asked him—for I perceived that he was dumb or vowed to silence—"that I am to leave the camp?"

He nodded rapidly, his strange yellow eyes gleaming.

"Immediately?" I demanded.

Again he nodded.

"Why?"

Pantomimically he made me understand that death threatened me if I remained—that I must leave the Bedouins before sunrise.

I cannot convey to you any idea of the mad earnestness of the man. But, alas! youth regards the counsels of age with nothing but contempt; moreover, I thought this man mad, and I was unable to choke down a sort of loathing which he inspired in me.

I shook my head then, but not unkindly; and, waving my hand, prepared to leave him. At that, with a sorrow in his strange eyes which did not fail to impress me, he saluted me with gravity, turned, and passed out of sight.

Although I did not know it at the time, I had chosen of two paths the one that led through fire.

I slept little after this interview—if it was a real interview and not a dream—and feeling tired and unrefreshed, I saw the sun rise purple and angry over the distant hills.

You know what *khamsîn* is like, my friends? But you cannot know what *simoom* is like—*simoom* in the heart of the desert! It came that morning—a

wall of sand so high as to shut out the sunlight, so
dense as to turn the day into night, so suffocating
that I thought I should never live through it!

It was apparent to me that the Bedouins were
prepared for the storm. The horses, the camels and
the asses were tethered in an enclosure specially
strengthened to exclude the choking dust, and with
their cloaks about their heads the men prepared
for the oncoming of this terror of the desert.

My God! it was a demon which sought to blind
me, to suffocate me, and which clutched at my throat
with strangling fingers of sand! This, I told myself,
was the danger which I might have avoided by quitting the camp before sunrise.

Indeed, it was apparent to me that if I had taken
the advice so strangely offered, I might now have
been safe in the village of the Great Oasis for which
I was bound. But I have since seen that the *simoom*
was a minor danger, and not the real one to which
this weird being had referred.

The storm passed, and every man in the
encampment praised the merciful God who had
spared us all. It was in the disturbance attendant
upon putting the camp in order once more that I
saw her.

She came out from the tent of Saïd Mohammed,
to shake the sand from a carpet; the newly come
sunlight twinkled upon the bracelets which clasped
her smooth brown arms as she shook the gaily
colored mat at the tent door. The sunlight shone
upon her braided hair, upon her slight robe, upon

her silver anklets, and upon her tiny feet. Transfixed I stood watching—indeed, my friends, almost
holding my breath. Then the sunlight shone upon
her eyes, two pools of mysterious darkness into
which I found myself suddenly looking.

The face of this lovely Arab maiden flushed,
and drawing the corner of her robe across those
bewitching eyes, she turned and ran back into the
tent.

One glance—just one glance, my friends! But
never had Ulysses' bow propelled an arrow more
sure, more deadly. I was nineteen, remember, and
of Provence. What do you foresee! You who have
been through the world, you who once were nineteen.

I feigned a sickness, a sickness brought about by
the sandstorm, and taking base advantage of that
desert hospitality which is unbounded, which knows
no suspicion, and takes no count of cost, I remained
in the tent which had been vacated for me.

In this voluntary confinement I learned little of
the doings of the camp. All day I lay dreaming of
two dark eyes, and at night when the jackals
howled I thought of the wanderer who had counseled
me to leave. One day, I lay so; a second; a third
again; and the women of Saïd Mohammed's household tended me, closely veiled of course. But in
vain I waited for that attendant whose absence was
rendering my feigned fever a real one—whose eyes
burned like torches in my dreams and for the coming
of whose little bare feet across the sand to my tent

door I listened hour by hour, day by day, in vain—always in vain.

But at nineteen there is no such thing as despair, and hope has strength to defy death itself. It was in the violet dusk of the fourth day, as I lay there with a sort of shame of my deception struggling for birth in my heart, that she came.

She came through the tent door bearing a bowl of soup, and the rays of the setting sun outlined her fairy shape through the gossamer robe as she entered.

At that my poor weak little conscience troubled me no more. How my heart leaped, leaped so that it threatened to choke me, who had come safe through a great sandstorm.

There is fire in the Southern blood at nineteen, my friends, which leaps into flame beneath the glances of bright eyes.

With her face modestly veiled, the Bedouin maid knelt beside me, placing the wooden bowl upon the ground. My eager gaze pierced the *yashmak,* but her black lashes were laid upon her cheek, her glorious eyes averted. My heart—or was it my vanity?—told me that she regarded me at least with interest, that she was not at ease in my company; and as, having spoken no word, having ventured no glance, she rose again to depart, I was emboldened to touch her hand.

Like a startled gazelle she gave me one rapid glance, and was gone!

She was gone—and my very soul gone with her!

For hours I lay, not so much as thinking of the food beside me—dreaming of her eyes. What were my plans? Faith! Does one have plans at nineteen where two bright eyes are concerned?

Alas, my friends, I dare not tell you of my hopes, yet upon those hopes I lived. Oh, it is glorious to be nineteen and of Provence; it is glorious when all the world is young, when the fruit is ripe upon the trees and the plucking seems no sin. Yet, as we look back, we perceive that at nineteen we were scoundrels.

The Bedouin girl is a woman when a European woman is but a child, and Sakîna, whose eyes could search a man's soul, was but twelve years of age— twelve! Can you picture that child of twelve squeezing a lover's heart between her tiny hands, entwining his imagination in the coils of her hair?

You, my friend, may perhaps be able to conceive this thing, for you know the East, and the women of the East. At ten or eleven years of age many of them are adorable; at twenty-one most of them are *passé;* at twenty-six all of them—with rare exceptions—are shrieking hags.

But to you, my other friends, who are strangers to our Oriental ways, who know not that the peach only attains to perfect ripeness for one short hour, it may be strange, it may be horrifying, that I loved, with all the ardor which was mine, this little Arab maiden, who, had she been born in France, would not yet have escaped from the nursery. But I digress.

The Arabs were encamped, of course, in the neighborhood of a spring. It lay in a slight depression amid the tiny palm-grove. Here, at sunset, came the women with their pitchers on their heads, graceful of carriage, veiled, mysterious.

Many peaches have ripened and have rotted since those days of which I speak, but now—even now—I am still enslaved by the mystery of Egypt's veiled women. Untidy, bedraggled, dirty, she may be, but the real Egyptian woman when she bears her pitcher upon her head and glides, stately, sinuously, through the dusk to the well, is a figure to enchain the imagination.

Very soon, then, the barrier of reserve which, like the screen of the *harêm*, stands between Eastern women and love, was broken. My trivial scruples I had cast to the winds, and feigning weakness, I would sally forth to take the air in the cool of the evening; this two days later.

My steps, be assured, led me to the spring; and you who are men of the world will know that Sakîna, braving the reproaches of the Sheikh's household, neglectful of her duties, was last of all the women who came to the well for water.

I taught her to say my name—René! How sweet it sounded from her lips, as she strove in vain to roll the 'ʀ' in our Provençal fashion. Some *ginnee* most certainly presided over this enchanted fountain, for despite the nearness of the camp our rendezvous was never discovered, our meetings were never detected.

With her pitcher upon the ground beside her, she would sit with those wistful, wonderful eyes upraised to mine, and sway before the ardor of my impassioned words as a young and tender reed sways in the Nile breeze. Her budding soul was a love lute upon which I played in ecstasy; and when she raised her red lips to mine. . . . Ah! those nights in the boundless desert! God is good to youth, and harsh to old age!

Next to Saïd Mohammed, her father, Sakîna's brother was the finest horseman of the tribe, and his white mare their fleetest steed. I had cast covetous eyes upon this glorious creature, my friends, and secretly had made such overtures as were calculated to win her confidence.

Within two weeks, then, my plans were complete —up to a point. Since they were doomed to failure, like my great scheme, I shall not trouble you with their details, but an hour before dawn on a certain night I cut the camel-hair tethering of the white mare, and, undetected, led the beautiful creature over the silent sands to a cup-like depression, a thousand yards distant from the camp.

The Bedouin who was upon guard that night had with him a gourd of 'erksoos. This was customary, and I had chosen an occasion when the duty of filling the sentinel's gourd had fallen upon Sakîna; to his 'erksoos I had added four drops of dark brown fluid from my medicine chest.

It was an hour before dawn, then, when I stood beside the white mare, watching and listening; it

was an hour before dawn when she for whom my
great scheme was forgotten, for whom I was about
to risk the anger, the just anger, of men amongst
the most fierce in the known world, came running
fleetly over the hillocks down into the little valley,
and threw herself into my arms. . . .

When dawn burst in gloomy splendor over the
desert, we were still five hours' ride from the spot
where I had proposed temporarily to conceal myself,
with perhaps an hour's start of the Arabs. I knew
the desert ways well enough, but the ghostly and
desolate place in which I now found myself nevertheless filled me with foreboding.

A seam of black volcanic rock split the sands for
a great distance, forming a kind of natural wall of
forbidding aspect . In places this wall was pierced
by tunnel-like openings; I think they may have been
prehistoric tombs. There was no scrap of verdure
visible, north, south, east or west; only desolation,
sand, grayness, and this place, ghostly and wan with
that ancient sorrow, that odor of remote mortality
which is called "the dust of Egypt."

Seated before me in the saddle, Sakîna looked up
into my face with a never-changing confidence, having her little brown fingers interlocked about my
neck. But her strength was failing. A short rest
was imperative.

Thus far I had detected no evidence of pursuit
and, descending from the saddle, I placed my weary
companion upon a rock over which I had laid a rug,
and poured out for her a draught of cool water.

Bread and dates were our breakfast fare; but bread and dates and water are nectar and ambrosia when they are sweetened with kisses. Oh! the glorious madness of youth! Sometimes, my friends, I am almost tempted to believe that the man who has never been wicked has never been happy!

Picture us, then, if you can, set amid that desolation, which for us was a rose-garden, eating of that unpalatable food—which for us was the food of the gods!

So we remained awhile, deliriously happy, though death might terminate our joys ere we again saw the sun, when something . . . *something* spoke to me . . .

Understand me, I did not say that *someone* spoke, I did not say that anything *audible* spoke. But I know that, unlocking those velvet arms which clung to me, I stood up slowly—and, still slowly, turned and looked back at the frowning black rocks.

Merciful God! My heart beats wildly now when I recall that moment.

Motionless as a statue, but in a crouching attitude, as if about to leap down, he who had warned me so truly stood upon the highest point of the rocks watching us!

How long did I remain thus?

I cannot pretend to say; but when I turned to Sakîna—she lay trembling on the ground, with her face hidden in her hands.

Then, down over the piled-up rocks, this mysterious and ominous being came leaping. Old man though he was, he descended with the agility of a mountain goat—and sometimes, in the difficult places, *he went on all fours.*

Crossing the intervening strip of sand, he stood before me. You have seen the reproach in the eyes of a faithful dog whose master has struck him unjustly? Such a reproach shone out from the yellow eyes of this desert wanderer. I cannot account for it; I can say no more. . . .

It was impossible for me to speak; I trembled violently; such a fear and such a madness of sorrow possessed me that I would have welcomed any death —to have freed me from that intolerable reproach.

He suddenly pointed towards the horizon where against the curtain of the dawn black figures appeared.

I fell upon my knees beside Sakîna. I was a poor, pitiable thing; the madness of my passion had left me, and already I was within the great Shadow; I could not even weep; I knew that I had brought Sakîna out into that desolate place—to die.

And now the man whose ways were unlike human ways began to babble insanely, gesticulating and plucking at me. I cannot hope to make you feel one little part of the emotion with which those instants were laden. Sakîna clung to me trembling in a way I can never forget—never, never forget. And the look in her eyes! even now I cannot bear to think of it, I cannot bear——

Those almost colorless lizards which dart about in the desert places with incredible swiftness were now coming forth from their nests; and all the while the black figures, unheard as yet, were approaching along the path of the sun.

My mad folly grew more apparent to me every moment. I realized that this which so rapidly was overtaking me had been inevitable from the first. The strange wild man stood watching me with that intolerable glare, so that my trembling companion shrank from him in horror.

But evidently he was seeking to convey some idea to me. He gesticulated constantly, pointing to the approaching Arabs and then over his shoulder to the frowning rock behind. Since it was too late for flight—for I knew that the white mare with a double burden could never outpace our pursuers—it occurred to me at the moment when the muffled beat of hoofs first became audible, that this hermit of the rocks was endeavoring to induce me to seek some hiding-place with which no doubt he was acquainted.

How I cursed the delay which had enabled the Arabs to come up with us! I know, now, of course, that even had I not delayed, our ultimate capture was certain. But at the moment, in my despair, I thought otherwise.

And now I cursed the stupidity which had prevented me from following this weird guide; I even thought wrathfully of the poor frightened child, whose weakness had necessitated the delay and whose fears had contributed considerably to this later misunderstanding.

The pursuing party, numbering four, and led by

Saïd Mohammed, was no more than five hundred yards away when I came to my senses. The hermit now was tugging at my arm with frightful insistence; his eyes were glaring insanely, and he chattered in an almost pitiable manner.

"Quick!" I cried, throwing my arm about Sakîna, "up to the rocks. This man can hide us!"

"No, no!" she whispered, "I dare not——"

But I lifted her, and signing to the singular being to lead the way, staggered forward despairingly.

The distance was greater than it appeared, the climb incredibly difficult. My guide held out his hand to me to assist me to mount the slippery rocks; but I had much ado to proceed and also to support Sakîna.

Her terror of the man and of the place to which he was leading us momentarily increased. Indeed, it seemed that she was becoming mad with fear. When the man paused before an opening in the rocks not more than fifteen or sixteen inches in height, and wildly waving his arms in the air, his elfin locks flying about his shoulder, his eyes glassy, intimated that we were to crawl in—Sakîna writhed free of my grasp and bounded back some three or four paces down the slope.

"Not in there!" she cried, holding out her little hands to me pitifully. "I dare not! He would devour us!"

At the foot of the slope, Saïd Mohammed, who had dismounted from his horse, and who, far ahead of the others, was advancing towards us, at that moment raised his gun and fired. . . .

Can I go on?

It is more years ago than I care to count, but it is fresher in my mind than the things of yesterday. A lonely old age is before me, my friends—for I have been a solitary man since that shot was fired. For me it changed the face of the world, for me it ended youth, revealing me to myself for what I was.

Something more nearly resembling human speech than any sound he had yet uttered burst from the lips of the wild man as the report of Saïd Mohammed's shot whispered in echoes through the mysterious labyrinths beneath us.

Fate had stood at the Sheikh's elbow as he pulled the trigger.

With a little soft cry—I hear it now, gentle, but having in it a world of agony—Sakîna sank at my feet . . . and her blood began to trickle over the black rocks on which she lay.

*   *   *   *   *   *

The man who professes to describe to you his emotions at such a frightful moment is an impostor. The world grew black before my eyes; every emotion of which my being was capable became paralysed.

I heard nothing, I saw nothing but the little huddled figure, that red stream upon the black rock, and the agonized love in the blazing eyes of Sakîna. Groaning, I threw myself down beside her, and as she sighed out her life upon my breast, I knew— God help me—that what had been but a youthful

amour, was now a life's tragedy; that for me the
light of the world had gone out, that I should never
again know the warmth of the sun and the gladness
of the morning. . . .

The cave man, with a dog-like fidelity, sought
now to drag me from my dead love, to drag me into
that gloomy lair which she had shrunk from entering. His incoherent mutterings broke in upon my
semi-coma; but I shook him off, I shrieked curses
at him. . . .

Now the Bedouins were mounting the slope, not
less than a hundred yards below me. In the growing light I could see the face of Saïd Mohammed. . . .

The man beside me exerted all his strength to
drag me back into the gallery or cave—I know not
what it was; but with my arms locked about Sakîna
I lay watching the pursuers coming closer and closer.

Then, those persistent efforts suddenly ceased, and
dully I told myself that this weird being, having
done his best to save me, had fled in order to save
himself.

I was wrong.

You have asked me for a story of the magic of
Egypt, and although, as you see, it has cost me tears
—oh! I am not ashamed of those tears, my friends!
—I have recounted this story to you. You say,
where is the magic? and I might reply: the magic
was in the changing of my false love to a true. But
there was another magic as well, and it grew up
around me now at this moment when I lay inert,
waiting for death.

From behind me, from above me, arose a cry—
a cry. You may have heard of the Bedouin song,
the 'Mizmûne':

> "Ya men melek ana dêri waat sa jebb,
> Id el' ish hoos' a beb hatsa azât ta lebb."

You may have heard how when it is sung in a
certain fashion, flowers drop from their stalks?
Also, you may have doubted this, never having
heard a magical cry.

I do not doubt it, my friends! For I *have* heard
a magical cry—this cry which arose from behind
me! It started some chord in my dulled consciousness which had never spoken before. I turned my
head—and there upon the highest point of the rocks
stood the cave man. He suddenly stretched forth
his hands.

Again he uttered that uncanny, that indescribable
cry. It was not human. It was not animal. Yet
it was nearer to the cry of an animal than to any
sound made by the human species. His eyes gleamed
with an awful light, his spare body had assumed a
strange significance; he was transfigured.

A third time he uttered the cry, and out from one
of those openings in the rock which I have mentioned, crept a jackal. You know how a jackal avoids
the day, how furtive, how nocturnal a creature
it is? but there in the golden glory which proclaimed the coming of the sun, black silhouettes
moved.

A great wonder possessed me, as the first jackal
was followed by a second, by a third, by a fourth,

by a fifth. Did I say a fifth? . . . By five hundred
—by five thousand!

From every visible hole in the rocks, jackals
poured forth in packs. Wonder left me, fear left
me; I forgot my sorrow, I became a numbed intelligence amid a desert of jackals. Over a sea of moving
furry backs, I saw that upstanding crag and the
weird crouching figure upon it. Right and left,
above and below, jackals moved . . . and all turned
their heads towards the approaching Bedouins!

Again—again I heard that dreadful cry. The
jackals, in a pack, thousands strong, began to advance upon the Bedouins! . . .

Not east or west, north or south, could you
hope to find a braver man than was the Sheikh Saïd
Mohammed; but—he fled!

I saw the four horsemen riding like furies into
the morning sun. The white mare, riderless, gal-
loped with them—and the desert behind was yellow
with jackals! For the last time I heard the cry.

The jackals began to return!

Forgive me, dear friends, if I seem an emotional
fool. But when I recovered from the swoon which
blotted out that unnatural spectacle, the wizard—
for now I knew him for nothing less—had dug a
deep trench—and had left me, alone.

Not a jackal was in sight; the sun blazed cruelly
upon the desert. With my own hands I laid my
love to rest in the sands. No cross, no crescent
marks her resting-place; but I left my youth upon
her grave, as a last offering.

You may say that, since I had sinned so grievously, since I had betrayed the noble confidence of Saïd Mohammed, my host, I escaped lightly.

Ah! you do not know!

And what of the strange being whose gratitude I had done so little to merit but yet which knew no bounds? It is of him that I will tell you.

Years later—how many it does not matter, but I was a man with no illusions—my restless wanderings (I being still a desert bird-of-passage) brought me one night to a certain well but rarely visited. It lay in a depression, like another well that I am fated often to see in my dreams, and, as one approached, the crowns of the palm trees which grew there appeared above the mounds of sand.

I was alone and tired out; the next possible camping-place—for I had no water—was many miles away. Yet it was written that I should press on to that other distant well, weary though I was.

First, then, as I came up, I perceived numbers of vultures in the air; and I began to fear that someone near to his end lay at the well. But when, from the top of a mound, I obtained a closer view, I saw a sight that, after one quick glance, caused me to spur up my tired horse and to fly—fly, with panic in my heart.

The brilliant moon bathed the hollow in light and cast dense shadows of the palm stems upon the slope beyond. By the spring, his fallen face ghastly in the moonlight, in a clear space twenty feet across, lay a dead man.

Even from where I sat I knew him; but, had I doubted, other evidence was there of his identity. As I mounted the slope, thousands of fiery eyes were turned upon me.

God! that arena all about was alive with jackals —jackals, my friends, eaters of carrion—which, silent, watchful, guarded the wizard dead, who, living, had been their lord!

II

LURE OF SOULS

I

THIS is the story which Bernard Fane told me one afternoon as we sat sipping China tea in the Heliopolis Palace Hotel, following a round upon the neighboring links.

The life of a master at the training college (said Fane) is beastly uneventful, taken all around; not even *your* keen sense of the romantic could long survive it. The duties are not very exacting, certainly, and in our own way I suppose we are Empire builders of a sort; but when you ask me for a true story of Egyptian life, I find myself floored at once.

We all come out with the idea of the mystic East strong upon us, but it is an idea that rarely survives one summer in Cairo. Personally, I made a more promising start than the average; an adventure came my way on the very day I landed in Port Said, in fact it began on the way out. But alas! it was not only the first, but the last adventure which Egypt has offered me.

I have not related the story more than five hundred times, so that you will excuse me if I foozle it in places. I will leave you to do the polishing.

On my first trip out, then, I joined the ship at Marseilles, and saw my cabin trunk placed in a nice deck berth, with the liveliest satisfaction. Walking along the white promenade deck, I felt no end of a man of the world. Every Anglo-Indian that I met seemed a figure from the pages of Kipling, and when I accidentally blundered into the *ayahs'* quarters, I could almost hear the jangle of the temple bells, so primed was I with traditions of the Orient—the traditions one gathers from books of the lighter sort, I mean.

You will see that in those days I was not a bit *blasé;* the glamour of the East was very real to me. For that matter, it is more real than ever, now; Near or Far, the East has a call which, once heard, can never be forgotten, and never be unheeded. But the call it makes to those who have never been there is out of tune, I have learned; or rather, it is not in the right key.

Well, I had a most glorious bath—I am sybarite enough to love the luxuriance of your modern liner —got into blue serge, and felt no end of an adventurer. There was a notice on the gangway that the steamer would not leave Marseilles until ten o'clock at night, but I was far too young a traveller to risk missing the boat by going ashore again. You know the feeling? Consequently I took my place in the saloon for dinner, and vaguely wondered why nobody else had dressed for the function. I was a proper Johnny Raw, no end of a Johnny Raw, but I enjoyed it all immensely, nevertheless. I personally superintended the departure of the ship, and believed that every deck-hand took me for a hardened globetrotter; and when at last I sought my cosy cabin, all spotlessly white, with my trunk tucked under the bunk, and, drawing the little red curtain, I sat down to sum up the sensations of the day, I was thoroughly satisfied with it all.

Gad! novelty is the keynote of life, don't you think? When one is young, one envies older and more experienced men, but what has the world left of novelty to offer them? The simple matter of joining a steamboat, and taking possession of my berth, had afforded me thrills which some of my fellow-passengers—those whom I envied the most for the stories of life written upon their tanned features—could only hope to taste by means of big-game hunting, now, or other far-fetched methods of thrill-giving.

It wore off a bit the next day, of course, and I found that once one has settled down to it, ocean traveling is merely floating hotel life. But many of my fellow-passengers (the boat was fairly full) still appealed to me as books of romance which I longed to open. And before the end of that second day, I became possessed of the idea that there was some deep mystery aboard. Since this was my first voyage, something of that sort was to be expected of me; but it happened that I stood by no means alone in this belief.

In the smoking-room, after dinner, I got into conversation with a chap of about my own age who was bound for Colombo—tea-planting. We chatted on different topics for half an hour, and discovered that we had mutual friends, or rather, the other fellow discovered it.

"Have you noticed," he said, "a distinguished-looking Indian personage, who, with three native friends, sits at the small corner table on our left?"

Hamilton—that was my acquaintance's name—was my right-hand neighbor at the chief officer's table, and I recollected the group to which he referred immediately.

"Yes," I replied; "who are they?"

"I don't know," answered Hamilton, "but I have a suspicion that they are mysterious."

"Mysterious?"

"Well, they joined at Marseilles, just before yourself. They were received by the skipper in person, and two of them were closeted in his cabin for twenty minutes or more."

"What do you make of that?"

"Can't make anything of it, but their whole behavior strikes me as peculiar, somehow. I cannot quite explain myself, but you say that you have noticed something of the sort, yourself?"

"They certainly keep very much to themselves," I said. Hamilton glanced at me quickly.

"Naturally," he replied.

Not desiring to appear stupid, I did not ask him to elucidate this remark, although at the time it meant nothing to me. Of course I have learned since, as everyone learns whose lines are cast among Orientals, that iron barriers divide the races. But at the time I knew nothing of this—as will shortly appear.

During breakfast on the following morning, I glanced several times at the mysterious quartette. They had been placed at a separate table and were served with different courses from the rest of the passengers. I was not the only member of the company who found them interesting, but the Anglo-Indians on board, to a man, left the native party severely alone. You know the icy aloofness of the Anglo-Indians?

My second day at sea wore on, uneventfully enough; the bugle had already announced the hour for dressing, and the boat-deck outside my berth, where I had had my chair placed, was practically deserted, when something occurred to turn my thoughts from the four Indians. It was a glorious evening, with the sun setting out across the Mediterranean in such a red blaze of glory that I sat watching it fascinatedly, my book lying unheeded on the deck beside me. Right and left of me men occupying the other deck cabins had lighted up, and were busily dressing. Right aft was a corner cabin, larger than the others, and suddenly I observed the door of this to open.

A slim figure glided out on to the deck, and began to advance toward me. It proved to be that of a woman or girl dressed in clinging black silk, and wearing a *yashmak!* She had a richly embroidered shawl thrown over her head and shoulders, and in that coy half-light she presented a dazzlingly beautiful picture.

It was my first sight of a *yashmak,* and, because

it was worn by a marvelously pretty woman, the thousands seen since have never entirely lost their charm for me. I could detect the lines of an exquisitely chiseled nose, and the long dark eyes of the apparition were entirely unforgettable. The hand with which she held her shawl about her was of ivory smoothness, and, like a little red lamp, a great ruby blazed upon the index finger.

With her high-heeled shoes tapping daintily upon the deck she advanced; then, suddenly perceiving that the promenade was not entirely deserted, she turned, but not hastily or rudely, and glided back to her cabin.

I have endeavored to outline for your benefit the state of my mind at this period, hinting how keenly alive I was to romance of any sort, provided it wore the guise of the Orient; so that it will be unnecessary for me to explain how strong an impression this episode made upon me. The Indian party was forgotten, and as I hastily dressed and descended to dinner, I scarcely listened to Hamilton when he bent toward me and whispered something about the "Strong Room."

My gaze was roaming about the spacious saloon. Even in those days I might have known better; I might have known that no Mohammedan woman would take her meals in a public saloon. But I was too dazzled by my memories to summon to my aid such fragments of knowledge respecting Eastern customs as were mine.

*　　　*　　　*　　　*　　　*　　　*

Well, some little time elapsed before I saw or heard anything further of the houri. I began to settle down to the routine of the trip, and (you know how news circulates through a ship?) it was not very long before I knew as much as any of the other passengers knew.

Hamilton was a sort of filter through which it all came to me, and of course it was not undiluted, but colored with his own views. The lady of the *yashmak*, he informed me, was a member of the household of a wealthy Moslem in the neighborhood of Damascus. She was travelling via Port Said, and taking a Khedivial boat from there to Beyrût. He was a perfect mine of information, but his real interest was centered all the time on the party of four Indians.

"They are emissaries of the Rajah of Bhotana," he informed me confidentially. "The mystery begins to clear up. You must have read about a month ago that Lola de l'Iris was selling some of her jewelery and devoting the proceeds to the founding of an orphanage or something of the kind; quite a unique advertisement. Well, the famous Indian dia mond presented to her by one of the crowned heads of Europe was amongst the bunch which she sold; and after staying in the West for over fifty years, it is again on its way back to the East where it came from."

I began to recollect the circumstances, now; the historic Indian diamond—I do not know Hindustanî, but its name translated means "Lure of Souls"—

had been in the possession of the dancer for many years, and its sale for such a purpose had turned the limelight upon her most enviably. It was a new idea in advertising, and had proved an admirable success.

So the four reticent gentlemen were the guardians of the diamond. Under normal circumstances this might have been interesting, but, as I have tried to make clear, another matter engrossed my attention. In fact, I was living in a dream-world.

Of course, my opportunity came, in due course. One evening, as I mooned on the shadowy deck—which was quite deserted, because an extempore dance was taking place on the deck below—*she* came gliding along towards me. I could see her eyes sparkling in the moonlight.

At first I feared that she was going to turn back. She hesitated, in a wildly alluring manner, when first she saw me sitting there watching her. Then, turning her head aside, she came on, and passed me. I never took my eyes off that graceful figure for a moment.

Coming to the rail, she leaned and looked out toward the coast of Crete, where silver tracings in the blue marked the mountain peaks; then, shivering slightly, and wrapping her embroidered shawl more closely about her shoulders, she retraced her steps.

Not a yard from where I sat, she dropped a little silk handkerchief on the deck!

How my heart leapt at that! the rest was a magical whirl; and ten seconds later I was chatting with her.

She spoke fluent French, but little English.

She appealed to me in a way that was new and almost irresistible; it was an appeal quite Oriental, sensuous—indescribable. I just wanted to take her in my arms and kiss those tantalizing lips; talking seemed a waste of time. Of course, I cannot hope to make you understand; but it was extraordinary. I felt that I was losing my head; the glances of those long dark eyes were setting me on fire.

Suddenly, she terminated this, our first *tête-à-tête*. She raised her finger to her veiled lips and glided away into the shadows like a phantom A sentence died, unfinished, on my tongue. I turned, and looked over my shoulder.

Gad! I got a fright! A most hideous Oriental of some kind, having only one eye but that afire with malignancy, was watching me from where he stood half concealed by a boat.

My lily of Damascus was guarded!

Humming, with an assumption of unconcern, I strolled away and joined the dancers below.

II

That was the beginning, then. I cursed to think how short a time was at my disposal; but since, the very next morning, I found myself enjoying a second delicious little stolen interview, I perceived that my company was not unacceptable.

What? oh, I had lost my head entirely; I admit it. It was an effort to speak of matters ordinary, topics of the ship; my impulse was to whisper delicious nonsense into those tiny ears. However, I forced myself to talk about things in general, and told her that the famous diamond, Lure of Souls, was aboard.

This was news to her, and she seemed to be tremendously interested. Her interest was of such a childish sort, so naïve, that the project grew up in my mind at that very moment—the project that was to terminate so disastrously. It was hardly a matter of so many words; there was nothing definite about the thing at all, and this, our second interview, was cut short in much the same manner as the first.

"*Ssh! Mustapha!*"

With those whispered words, and a dazzling smile, this jewel of Damascus who interested me so much more deeply than the Rajah's diamond, departed hurriedly—and I turned to meet again the malignant gaze of the wall-eyed guardian.

The sort of romance in which I was steeped at that time flourishes and grows fat upon incidents of this kind. I have searched my memory many a time since then, for some word or hint to prove that the conversation about the diamond was opened and guided in a desired direction by the lady of the *yashmak;* but excluding transmission of thought, I could never find any evidence of the kind—have never been able to do so.

Certainly my memories of that period are hazy except in regard to Nahèmah. If I were an artist, I could paint her portrait from memory without

the slightest error, I think. She occupied my
thoughts to the exclusion of all else. But the project
was formed and carried out. Hamilton was one of
those popular men who seem born to occupy the
chair at any kind of meeting at which they may be
present; he organized almost every entertainment
that took place on board. At first he was not at all
keen on the idea.

"There are all sorts of difficulties," he said; "and
one doesn't care to ask a favor of a native. At any
rate one doesn't care to be refused."

But I had set my heart upon gratifying Nahèmah's curiosity, and, with the aid of Hamilton, it
was all arranged satisfactorily. The native guardians of the diamond were rather flattered than
otherwise, and a select little party of the "best"
people on board met in the chief officer's cabin to
view Lure of Souls.

The difficulty in regard to Nahèmah was readily
overcome by Hamilton the energetic, and Dr. Patterson's wife "took her up" for the occasion in a delightfully patronizing manner. The four swarthy,
polite Orientals were there, of course; several other
ladies in addition to Mrs. Patterson and Nahèmah,
the chief officer, myself, Hamilton, and a sepulchral
Scotch curate, the Rev. Mr. Rawlingson, whom I
had scarcely noticed hitherto, and whose presence at
this "select" gathering rather surprised me.

The sea was like a sheet of glass, and this was
the hottest day which I had yet experienced. It
was about an hour before lunch-time when we

gathered to view the diamond; and Mr. Brodie, the
chief officer, exercised his pawky humor in a series
of elaborate pantomimic precautions, locking the
door with labored care, and treating the ladies of
the company to Bluebeard glances of frightful
intensity.

Phew! if we had only known! . . .

Finally one of the Indians took out the diamond
from its case—which had been brought from the
strong-room a few minutes before. It was a wonderful thing, I suppose, of quite unusual size, and it
sparkled and gleamed in the sunlight streaming
through the open porthole in an absolutely dazzling
fashion. I had ranged myself close beside Nahèmah.
Each of us was permitted to handle the stone. It
was I who passed it to her, Mr. Rawlingson having
passed it to me. She held it in the palm of her
little hand, and her eyes sparkled with childish delight as she bent to examine the gem. Then a very
strange thing happened.

From somewhere behind me—I was sitting with
my back to the porthole—a dull gray object came
leaping and twirling; and a scorpion—I have never
seen a larger specimen—fell upon Nahèmah's wrist!

She uttered a piercing cry, dropped the diamond
and brushed the horrid insect from her wrist; then
fell swooning into my arms. . . .

A scene of incredible confusion followed. The
four Indians, ignoring the presence of the scorpion,
dropped like cats upon the floor, seeking for Lure
of Souls. Mrs. Patterson and I carried Nahèmah

to the sofa hard by and laid her upon it. Just as we did so the scorpion darted from between the end of the sofa and the wardrobe, and the chief officer put his foot upon it.

Ensuing events were indescribable. Since the diamond had not yet been picked up, obviously the cabin door could not be unlocked; so in the stuffy atmosphere of the place it was a matter of some difficulty to revive Nahèmah. Meanwhile, four wild-eyed Indians were creeping about amongst our feet—like cats, as I have said before.

In the end, just as the girl began to revive somewhat, it became evident that Lure of Souls was missing. A pearl shirt button, the ownership of which we were unable to establish, was picked up, but no diamond.

The chief officer showed himself a man of priceless tact. He rang for the stewardess, and the ladies were shepherded to a neighboring, vacant cabin. Then the door was relocked, and Mr. Brodie proceeded to strip, placing his garments one by one upon the little folding table for examination. He was not satisfied until every man present had overhauled them. We all followed his example, the Rev. Mr. Rawlingson last of all . . . and Lure of Souls was still on the missing list!

Then we gave the chief officer's cabin such a turnout as it had never had before, I should assume. Our quest was unrewarded. Meanwhile, the ladies had been submitted to a similar search in the adjoining cabin; same result.

With great difficulty we succeeded in hushing up the matter to a certain extent; but the captain's language to the chief officer was appalling, and the chief officer's remarks to Hamilton were equally unparliamentary; whilst Hamilton seemed to consider that he was justified in placing the whole blame upon me, which he did in terms little short of insulting. The four Indians apparently regarded all of us with equal suspicion and animosity.

I could not foresee the end. The thing was so sudden, so serious, that at the time it banished even thoughts of Nahèmah from my mind. I anticipated that we should all find ourselves arrested when we reached Port Said.

Later in the day Hamilton walked into my cabin and placed a little cardboard box upon the dressing-table. It contained the crushed body of the scorpion.

"Where did that scorpion come from?" he demanded abruptly.

It was a question which already had been asked fully a thousand times, yet no one had discovered an intelligent reply.

I shook my head.

"It came from the open porthole," he replied, "and as it's a thousand to one against a scorpion being aboard, somebody was *carrying* it for this very purpose—somebody who was on the deck outside the chief officer's cabin *and who threw the scorpion* into the cabin."

"But such a deadly thing. . . ."

"Have a good look," said Hamilton, turning the

insect over with a lead pencil; "this one isn't deadly at all. See!—his tail has been cut off!"

I looked and stifled an exclamation. It was as Hamilton had said. The scorpion was harmless.

*   *   *   *   *   *

I never once set eyes upon Nahèmah again until we arrived at Port Said. Then I saw her preparing to go ashore in one of the boats. I managed to join her, ignoring the scowls of her one-eyed attendant, and we arrived at the quay together. Right there by the water's edge a most curious scene was being enacted. Surrounded by two or three passengers and a perfect ring of uniformed officials, Hamilton, very excited, watched his baggage being turned out upon the ground. He saw me approaching.

"Hang it all, Fane," he cried, "this is disgraceful!—I don't know upon whose orders they are acting, but the beastly police are searching my baggage for the diamond. . . ."

I thought it very extraordinary and said as much to the Rev. Mr. Rawlingson, who was one of the onlookers.

"It is very strange indeed," he said mildly, turning his gold-rimmed spectacles in my direction.

A moment later, to my horror and indignation, Nahèmah was submitted to the same indignity! The crowd had been roped off from the part of the quay upon which we stood, and I could see that the whole thing had been arranged beforehand in some way, probably by wireless from the ship. Curiously, as I thought at the time, my own baggage was not examined in this way, but I was detained long enough to lose sight of Nahèmah and her one-eyed guardian. When I got to the hotel I indulged in some reflection. It occurred to me that Hamilton was bound for Colombo, which made it rather singular that he should have had his baggage put ashore at Port Said.

I should have liked to have searched the town for my lady of the *yashmak*, but having no clue to her present whereabouts, realized the futility of such a proceeding. My last thought before I fell asleep that night was that some day in the near future I should visit Damascus.

III

I saw very little of Port Said, for we had arrived in the early morning and I was departing for Cairo by a train leaving shortly before midday. I wandered about the quaint streets a bit, however, and wondered if, from one of the latticed windows overhanging me, the dark eyes of Nahèmah were peering out.

Although I looked up and down the train fairly carefully, I failed to find among the passengers anyone whom I knew, and I settled down into my corner to study the novel scenery uninterruptedly. The shipping in the canal fascinated me for a long time as did the figures which moved upon its shores. The ditches and embankments, aimlessly wandering footpaths, and moving figures which seemed to belong to a thousand years ago, seized upon my imagination as they seize upon the imagination of every traveller when first he beholds them.

But, properly speaking, my story jumps now to Zagazig. The train stopped at Zagazig; and, walking out into the corridor and lowering a window, I was soon absorbed in contemplation of that unique town. Its narrow, dirty, swarming streets; the millions of flies that boarded the train; the noisy vendors of sugar cane, tangerine oranges and other commodities; the throng beyond the barriers gazing open-mouthed at me as I gazed open-mouthed at them—it was a first impression, but an indelible one.

I was not to know it was written that I should spend the night in Zagazig; but such was the case. Generally speaking, I have found the service on the Egyptian State Railway very good, but a hitch of some kind occurred on this occasion, and after an hour or so of delay, it was definitely announced to the passengers that owing to an accident to the permanent way, the journey to Cairo could not be continued until the following morning.

Then commenced a rush which I did not understand at first, and in which, feeling no desire to exert myself unduly, I did not participate. Half an hour later I ascertained that the only two hotels which the place boasted were full to overflowing, and realized what the rush had meant. It was all part of the great scheme of things, no doubt; but when, thanks to the kindly, if mercenary, offices of the International Sleeping Car attendant, I found myself in possession of a room at a sort of native *khân* in the lower end of the town, I experienced no very special gratitude towards Providence.

I have enjoyed the hospitality of less pleasing caravanserai since, but this was my first experience of the kind, and I thought very little of it.

My room boasted a sort of bed, certainly, but without entering into details, I may say that there were earlier occupants who disputed its possession. The plaster of the walls—the place apparently was built of a mixture of straw and dried mud—provided residence not only for mosquitoes, but also for ants, and the entire building was redolent of an odor suggestive of dried bones. That smell of dried bones is characteristic, I have learned, of the sites of ancient Egyptian cities (Zagazig is close to the ruins of ancient Bubastis, of course); one gets it in the temples and the pyramids, also. But it was novel to me, then, and not pleasing.

I killed time somehow or other until the dinner hour; and the train, which now reposed in a siding, became a rendezvous for those who desired to patronize the dining-car. Evidently no sleeping-cars were available (or perhaps that idea was beyond the imagination of the native officials), and having left a trail of tobacco smoke along the principal native street, I turned into my apartment which I shared with the ants, mosquitoes—and the other things.

An examination of my rooms by candle-light revealed the presence of a cupboard, or what I thought to be a cupboard, but opening the double doors I saw that it was a window, latticed and overlooking a lower apartment; so much I perceived by the light of an oil lamp which stood upon the table. Then, stifling a gasp of amazement, I hastily snuffed my candle and peered down eagerly at that incredible scene. . . .

Nahèmah, longer veiled, was sitting at the table, and opposite to her was seated the hideous wall-eyed attendant!

They were conversing in low tones, so that, strive as I would, I could not overhear a word. You ask me why I spied upon the lady's privacy in this manner? For a very good reason.

Midway between the two, upon the rough boards of the table, lay Lure of Souls, twinkling and glittering like a thing of incarnate light.

I observed that there was a door to the room below, almost immediately opposite the window through which I was peering . . . and this door was opening very slowly and noiselessly. At least, *I* could hear no noise, but the one-eyed man detected something, for suddenly he started up and did a remarkable thing. Snatching up the diamond from the table, he clapped it into the eyeless cavity of his skull and turned in a twinkling to face the intruder.

Then the door was thrown open, and Hamilton leapt into the room.

I could scarcely credit my senses. Honestly, I thought I was dreaming. Hamilton's whole face was changed: a hard, cunning look had come over it, and he held a revolver in his hand. Nahèmah sprang to her feet as he entered, but he covered the pair of them with his revolver, and pointing to the one-eyed man muttered something in a low voice. Rage, fear, rebellion chased in turn across the evil features of One-eye; but there was something about Hamilton's manner that cowed.

Manipulating the sunken eyelids as though they had been of rubber, the guardian of the veiled lady slipped the diamond into the palm of his hand and tossed it, glittering, on to the table.

Hamilton's expression of triumph I shall never forget. One step forward he took and was about to snatch up the gem when—out of the dark cavity of the doorway behind him stepped a second intruder.

It was the Rev. Mr. Rawlingson!

The reverend gentleman's behavior was most unclerical. He leapt upon the unsuspecting Hamilton like a panther and screwed the muzzle of a revolver into that gentleman's right ear with quite unnecessary vigor.

"You have been wasting your time, Farland!" he snapped in a voice that was quite new to me. "That is, unless you have turned amateur detective."

He made no attempt to reach for the diamond, but just held out his hand, and with his eyes fixed upon Hamilton, silently commanded the latter to hand over the gem. This Hamilton did with palpable reluctance. Mr. Rawlingson, who, though still clerically garbed, had discarded his spectacles, slipped the stone into his pocket, snatched the revolver from Hamilton's hand and jerked his thumb in the direction of the open door. Hamilton shrugged his shoulders and walked out of the room. For scarce a moment did Rawlingson's eyes turn to follow the retreating figure, but the chance was good enough for the wall-eyed man.

He launched himself through space like nothing so much as a kangaroo, bearing Rawlingson irresistibly to the floor! With his lean hands at the other's throat he turned his solitary eye upon Nahèmah, muttering something gutturally. After a moment's hesitation she ran from the room.

* * * * * *

Twenty seconds later I was downstairs, and ten seconds after that was helping Rawlingson to his feet. He was considerably shaken and boasted a very elegant design in bruises which was just beginning to reveal itself upon his throat; but otherwise he was unhurt.

"I have lost her, Mr. Fane!" were his first words. "She knows this part of the world inside out. I have no case against Farland, but I am sorry to have lost the woman."

Was my mind in a whirl? Did I think that madness had seized me? Replies both in the affirmative; I was simply staggered.

I always go to pieces with this part of the yarn, being an unpractised narrator, as I have already explained; but I may relieve your mind upon one point. I never saw Nahèmah and the one-eyed man again, nor have I since set eyes upon Hamilton. Mr. Rawlingson, the last time I heard from him, was in similar case.

The explanation of the whole thing was something of a blow to me, of course. The lily of Damascus who had fascinated me so hopelessly was no Eastern at all; you will have guessed as much. She was a Frenchwoman, I believe; at any rate they had a long record up against her in Paris. She had gone out after Lure of Souls, and very ingeniously had made me her instrument. As Mr. Rawlingson explained to me, what had probably taken place was this:

The harmless scorpion, specially brought along for some such purpose, had been thrown into the chief officer's cabin from the open porthole by the one-eyed villain. That had been the cue for Nahèmah to drop the shirt button, and, whilst the occupants of the cabin were in confusion, to toss the diamond out on to the deck where her accomplice was waiting. The search of their effects had been futile, of course; no one had thoughts of searching the eye-cavity of her Eastern companion.

Where did Hamilton come in? Hamilton was one James Farland, an American crook of the highest accomplishments, known to the police of the entire civilized world. He, too, had gone out for Lure of Souls, but the woman, his professional competitor, had proved too clever for him.

The Rev. Mr. Rawlingson? He was Detective-Inspector Wexford of New Scotland Yard. Yes, it's a rotten story, from a romantic point of view.

DOORS OF SOULS

III

THE SECRET OF ISMAIL

I

MUSTAPHA MIRZA knew it—Mustapha Mirza, the blind Persian who makes shoes hard by the Bâb ez-Zuwêla and in the very shadow of the minarets of Muayyâd; Hassan es-Sîwa of the Street of the Carpet-sellers in the Mûski, Hassan, who, where another man has hands, has but hideous stumps, knew it, and because of him it was that Abdûl Moharli sought it—Abdûl the mendicant who crouches on the steps of the Blue Mosque muttering, guttural, inarticulate, and pointing to the tongueless cavity of his mouth. Now I know it; but not from Abdûl Moharli: may Allah, the Great, the Compassionate, defend me!

I say "May Allah defend me," yet I am no Moslem; I have no spot of Egyptian blood in my veins. No, I am a pure Greek of Cos, of Cos the home of the loveliest women in the world; and my mother was one of these, whilst my father was a Cretan, and a true descendent of Minos. My story perhaps will not be believed, for always it has been my fate to be maligned. You will ask, perhaps, what I was doing in the Mâzi Desert between Beni Suêf and the Red Sea, but I reply that my cotton interests—for I have cotton interests in the Delta—often lead me far afield. You do not understand the cotton industry or this explanation would be unnecessary. It is only those who do not understand the cotton industry that speak of *hashish*. *Hashish!* I leave it to the Egyptians and the Jews to deal in *hashish;* I am neither a Jew nor an Egyptian, but a Greek of Cos, who would not soil his hands with such a trade —no.

Upon my business, then, my legitimate business, I found myself with a small company of servants encamped by the Wâdi Araba. At the Wâdi Araba I had a commercial acquaintance, a sheikh of the Mâzi Arabs. Those villains who say that he was a "go-between," that my business was not with him, but through him with a port of the Red Sea, dare not say as much to my face; for there is a law in the land—even in the land of Egypt, now that the British hold power here.

I had reached the point, then, whereat it was my custom to meet my business acquaintance and to discuss certain affairs in which we were interested. My servants had erected the tent in which I was to sleep, and the camels lay in a little limestone valley to the west, their eyes mild because they knew that the day's work was ended; for it is a foolish mistake to suppose that the eye of a camel is mild at any other time. The camel knows the secret name of Allah—and that name is Rest.

The violet after-glow, which is the most wonderful thing in Nature, crowned the desert with glory right away to the porphyry mountains. I stood at

my tent door looking westward to the Nile. I stood
looking out upon the waste of the sands, the eternal
sands which are a belt about Egypt; and my thoughts
running fleetly before me, crossed the desert, crossed
the Nile, and came to rest in the verdant, fertile
Fàyûm, its greenness sweet to look upon in the heat
of such an evening, its palms fashioned in ebony
black against the wondrous sky. Yes, I, who am a
Greek, love the Fàyûm more than any spot on earth;
the modern clamor and dust of Cairo are hateful to
me, although my business often takes me there, and
also to Alexandria, the most European city in the
East, and to me the most detestable. But my business is in the Delta and it is a good business, so why
should I complain?

I stood at my tent door, and I thought of many
things, though little of the matters which had brought
me there; a faint cool breeze fanned my brow, and
about me was that great peace which comes to Egypt
with the touch of night. My servants were silent in
their encampment, and the shrieking of the camels
had ceased. About me, then, all was sleeping; only
I was awake, only I was there to receive Abdûl
Moharli and his secret—the secret of Ismail.

By the pattering of his bare feet upon the sand,
I first learned of his coming, but for a long time I
could not see him, for his way led him through the
valley where the camels slept, and a mound obscured
my view. But presently I heard his panting breaths
and his little delirious cries of fear, which were like
sobs, and presently, again, I saw him staggering

over the slope. At the sight of me he uttered one last gasping cry and fell forward on his face unconscious—like a dead man.

I hurried to him, stooped and raised him. His face was dreadful to look upon. His eyes were sunken in his skull, and his flesh shrivelled as by long fasting. His beard was filthy, knotted and unkempt, and his hair a black mat streaked with dirty gray. He was thin as a mummy and the bones protruded through his skin. He was as one who is dying from excess of *hashish*.

Ah! I know how they look, those poor fools who poison themselves with the Indian hemp. I wonder Allah does not strike down the villain who places that poison within their reach. I use the term "Allah" because my business brings me much in contact with the natives, but I am no Moslem, as I have related. Father Pierre of Alexandria can tell you how devoted a Christian I am.

Drink and food revived him somewhat; and as I sat beside him in my tent that night he babbled to me, half deliriously; he raved, and to another it might have seemed the fancies of a poor madman which he poured into my ears. For he spoke of a secret oasis and of a sheikh who had lived since the days of Sultan Kalaûn; of a treasure vast as that of Suleyman—and of magic, black magic; of the transmuting of gold and the making of diamonds.

But I, who am a Greek, and one who has lived all his life between Alexandria and the Red Sea; I who know the Garden of Egypt as another knows the

palm of his hand—I detected in this delirium the
shadow of a truth. To me it became evident that
this wretched being who had fled, a hunted thing,
over the trackless desert for many days and nights
—it became evident to me, I say, that he spoke of
the far-famed secret of Ismail.

You would ask: What is the secret of Ismail?
I would tell you, ask it of Hassan the Handless, of
Mustapha, the blind Persian of the Bâb ez-Zuwêla;
better still, ask it of any son of the Fàyûm, of any
man of the Mâzi. None of them will answer you,
for none save Hassan and Mustapha knows the
strange truth—Hassan and Mustapha, and Abdûl
Moharli . . . and no one of these three knows all,
nor will reveal what he knows.

Ah! how my heart leapt and how my eyes must
have gleamed in the darkness of the tent, yet how
cold a fear clutched at the life within me. The night
seemed suddenly to become a thin curtain veiling
eyes that watched, the empty desert a hiding-place
for unseen multitudes that listened; the faint breeze
raising the flap of the tent, ever so gently, ever so
softly, assumed the shape of a malignant hand that
reached for my throat, that sought to stifle me ere
the secret, the deathly secret of Ismail should be
mine.

Abdûl Moharli was the name of this wanderer;
and as he spoke to me, gulping down great draughts
of water between the words, ever he glanced to right
and left, over his shoulder and all about him.

"It is four days from here," he whispered hoarsely; "due south in the direction of the porphyry quarries and the Mountain of Smoke. There is a tiny village and all the inhabitants are of the race of Saïd Ebn al As, being descendants of the companion of the prophet. I had long supposed that this race of heretics was extinct; but it is not so, O my benefactor; with these eyes, have I seen the houses wherein they dwell. By the strategy of which I have spoken did I penetrate to their secret dwelling-place and win their unsuspecting love."

And then, clutching me to him with his bony hands, he spoke in hushed and fearful tones of the house of the Sheikh Ismail Ebn al As. It was the fabled treasure of this holy man which had been the lodestone drawing Abdûl Moharli out into the desert. Something of his fear, of his constant apprehension seized upon me too; and as he glanced tremblingly first over this shoulder and then over that, so likewise did *I* glance, until I seemed to crouch in a world of spies listening to a secret greater than that of the Universe.

I pronounced the *Takbîr*, "Great is the Lord!" —a superstitious custom which I have acquired from my business acquaintances. I made the sign of the Cross and called upon the name of the Holy Virgin. Almost I feared to listen further, yet I lacked the courage to abstain.

"Not with mine eyes have I beheld the treasure of Ismail," he whispered to me, this shadow of a man, this living mummy, those same eyes rolling in their sunken sockets; "nor with mine ears have I heard it named. These hands have never touched it; yet the secret of Ismail is *my* secret."

So far he had proceeded and no further, when a slight noise, that was not of my imagination, came from immediately outside the tent. On the instant I sprang forth . . . but no one was there and nothing now disturbed the solitude of the desert about me. A moment I stood, peering to left and right, into the void of the velvet dusk; no more than a moment, I can swear, yet long enough for that dreadful thing to happen—that thing which sometimes haunts my dreams.

Shrill and awful upon the silence it burst; the scream of a stricken man. It stabbed me like a knife; and as a creature of clay I stood, unable to stir or think. It died away, in a long wail of pain, that gave place to a guttural, inarticulate babbling —a choking, sobbing sound indescribable, but that may not be forgotten once it has been heard.

No living thing, as I can tesitfy, entered or left the tent; so far the evidence of my senses bears me. But that one had entered and left it, unseen, I learned, when, throwing off this palsy of horror, I staggered back to the side of the one who knew the secret of Ismail.

He lay writhing upon the ground; blood issued from his mouth. The tongue of Abdûl Moharli had been torn out!

II

Three weeks later I had my first sight of the secret oasis. The fate from which Abdûl had fled had overtaken him as I have related, in my tent, and from that moment until we parted company—for this poor wretch survived his mutilation—not another hint could I glean from him respecting the discovery for which he had paid so terrible a price.

In the first place, he lacked the accomplishment of writing and in the second place his fear of the vengeance of Ismail had become a veritable madness. I left him at Beni Suêf, filled with a determination to probe this mystery for myself. Suitably prepared for such an undertaking I set out alone from Dér Byâd, and undertook the four days' journey which I had planned.

In a little gorge, arid, shadeless, in which only a few stunted tamarisks grew, but affording a sort of hiding-place for myself and my camel, I made my base of operations. Provisions of a sort I had plenty, but for water I must depend on the secret oasis, which I estimated to be not more than four miles distant. In the dead of night I set out, naking for a series of mounds or hillocks rising up from the rocky face of the plateau. Cautiously I ascended their slopes, ever watchful and with eagerly beating heart; and it was lying prone upon the crest of the greatest of these that I first saw the village and the oasis.

There was nothing extraordinary in the appearance of the village; it presented to the eye the usual group of small, squat houses clinging to the trunks of the palm trees and surrounding a shrine or mosque boasting a wooden minaret. There were tilled fields and palm groves to the left of the village and a large house surrounded by white walls embracing extensive gardens. My spirits rose high. Within that house lay the secret of Ismail.

I determined to approach from the left, where I should be able to take advantage of the far-cast shadows of the palm groves and of the direction of the faint breeze; for most of all I feared the dogs, without which no Arab village is complete. Sure enough, although I had elected to approach the left of the village and although I crawled laboriously upon hands and knees, the accursed brutes apparently scented me or heard me and made night hideous with their clamor.

Flat upon the ground I lay, awaiting the dogs who bore down upon me snarling, their fangs bared. I had come prepared for this; but, mysteriously, at a point by the end of the palm grove and some twenty yards away from me, the pack halted, and after a time became silent. This was unaccountable but fortunate; and after waiting a while longer to learn if anyone had been aroused by the outcry, I advanced towards the wall of the garden, passing stealthily from palm to palm.

I observed that the mosque was a more important building than I had supposed, with a tomb on the right of the entrance surmounted by a white dome.

A passage leading to the courtyard, which presented a charming picture in the moonlight, its fountain overshadowed by acacias, reminded me very much of that in the Mosque of Muayyâd in Cairo. As in the latter, a double arcade surrounded it on three sides and the columns were of some kind of marble and sculptured with inscriptions in Arabic. I had a glimpse of a blue-tiled sanctuary, through a fine *mushrabîyeh* screen beneath the pointed arches. Arabesques in colored glass rendered the windows very beautiful to look upon. Nothing stirred within the village, as I crept along the narrow lane separating the mosque from the wall of the garden. Beyond prospecting the ground, I had no definite plans for to-night; but Fate had willed it that I was to become more deeply involved in the affair than I had designed or intended.

A side door opened from the garden at a spot nearly opposite the little wooden platform which served as the minaret of the mosque; and the mud bricks of the porch were so broken and decayed by time that I perceived here an opportunity of mounting to the top of the wall, an opportunity of which I instantly availed myself.

Yes, in spite of my peaceful calling (I have explained that I have cotton interests in the Delta) my life has not been unadventurous nor have I ever hesitated to incur risk where profit might be gained. Therefore, having climbed to the top of the wall, unmolested, and perceiving at a spot some little distance to the right a sort of trellis overgrown with purple blossom, I did not hesitate to make for it and to descend into the garden. I had just completed the descent, and stood looking cautiously about me, when a sound disturbed the silence—a sound so entirely unexpected, in that place, at such an hour, that it turned my blood cold, bringing to my mind all those stories of the black magic for which the people of this oasis were famed.

It was the sound of a woman singing; and although the song she sang was a familiar Arab love song and the voice of the singer was sweet, if very mournful, the effect, as I have said, was weird to a degree.

> *Ashik yekul l'il hammám hát le genáhak yom*
> (A lover said to a dove, "Lend me your wings for
> a day," etc.)

Overcoming the fear and astonishment which momentarily had deprived me of action, I advanced with the utmost caution in the direction from whence this mysterious singing seemed to proceed. Passing an angle of the house, where the stucco wall ran sheerly up to a *mushrabîyeh* window, I perceived before me a smaller, detached building in the form of a sort of pavilion. Some fine acacias overhung its white and glistening dome, in which were little windows of colored glass. Concealed in the shadow of the house, I stood looking towards this smaller building, observing with astonishment that it possessed a massive, bronze-mounted door.

Indeed, in many respects, and in spite of the charming picture which its jeweled appearance presented, it might well have been the tomb of some holy

Sheikh. But seated on an old-fashioned *mastabah* before the entrance were two huge negroes of most ferocious aspect, armed with scimitars which glittered evilly in the light of the moon!

I drew back sharply into the shelter of the projecting wall. One of the negroes seemed to slumber, but the wicked black eyes of his companion were widely open and he revealed his ivory teeth in a frightful leer. The beating of my heart almost suffocated me, for I ascribed that ghastly grimace to the fact that the negro had detected my presence and was already gloating over the pleasing prospect of my swift and bloody despatch. For many agonized moments I lurked there, one hand clutching the stucco wall and the other resting upon the butt of a new Colt magazine pistol which I had taken the precaution to purchase in Alexandria a week earlier.

When again I ventured to protrude my head, I learned how groundless my fears had been; I realized that the loathsome contortion of the negro's countenance represented a smile of appreciation. He was listening to the unseen singer whose voice now stole again upon the silence of the night! His blubber lips drooped open cavernously and his fierce little eyes blinked in stupid rapture.

It appeared to me, now, that the sweet voice proceeded from some subterranean place: I thought that I was listening to the song of a *ginneyeh*. I remembered how the Sheikh Ismail was reputed to be the son of an *Efreet* and an Arabian princess, and to have lived in that oasis for generations, since the reign of the Sultan Mohammed Nâsir ibn-Kalaûn, who had expelled him from Cairo as a magician. He was said to possess the secrets of Geber and of Avicenna—the great Ibn Sina of Bokhara; to possess the Philosophers' Stone and the *Elixir Vitæ*. In this pavilion with the bronze door I beheld the magician's treasure-house, guarded, within, by a *ginneyeh* and, without, by ghouls or black *Efreets!*

You will understand that these childish superstitions sometimes overcome me, because I have lived so long among those who believe them; but to me, a Greek, possessing the consolation of the true religion, it was only momentary, this cold fear which belongs to ignorance and is bred in the blood of the Moslem but finds no place in the heart of a true Christian.

And now the Fates again took a hand in the game. The pack of curs in the distant palm grove set up a sudden tempest of sound, so that they seemed to have become possessed of a million devils. It was a disturbance infinitely louder and more prolonged than that with which the dogs had greeted my appearance, and I had barely time to throw myself flat in the depths of a black and friendly shadow ere the two negroes, monstrous in the moonlight, passed me silently and trotted off in the direction from whence the uproar proceeded. You will say, no doubt, that a madness as great as that of the dogs possessed me; but because what I tell you is true, you must not be surprised to find it strange.

Allowing the negroes time to reach the gate for

which I divined them to be making, I ran across the moon-bathed garden to the door of the pavilion.

You must understand that my madness was not entirely without method; for I had a vague plan in my mind: it was to ascertain the character of the lock upon the bronze door (for you must know that I am skilled in the craft of the locksmith), and then, passing beyond the pavilion, which I was assured was the treasure-house of Ismail, to make my escape over the garden wall at some point to the west and return to my base in the desert ravine armed with a knowledge of the enemy's dispositions.

But, as I have said, the Fates took a hand. The sweet-voiced singer ceased her song as I approached the pavilion; and, at the moment that I set foot upon the lower step, her voice—by Allah! whose Name be exalted, it was sweet as honey!—addressed to me these words:

"O my master, at last thou art come! Here is the key! enter ere they return."

Whilst I stared blankly upward to the open lattice from whence the invisible speaker thus addressed me, an antique key wrapped in a piece of perfumed silk, fell almost upon my head!

III

Dazed though I was by the complete unexpectedness of this happening I doubt if I should have had the temerity to pursue the matter further that night but for the sound of fleetly running footsteps of which at this moment I became aware.

My escape was cut off! If I endeavored to pass around the pavilion in accordance with my original plan I should undoubtedly be perceived. My only hope lay in accepting the invitation so singularly given. With trembling hands I fitted the key to the cumbersome lock, opened the door, and entered the pavilion. My presence of mind had not completely deserted me and before closing the door I withdrew the key.

I found myself in a saloon of extraordinary magnificence, furnished with mattresses covered with silk and lighted by hanging lamps and by candles, and having at its upper end a couch of alabaster decorated with pearls and canopied by curtains of satin peacock-blue. From a carved wooden archway draped with cloth of gold there leaped forth a girl of such surpassing loveliness that her image must forever reside in my heart together with those of the saints.

Conceive all the dark-eyed beauties of Oriental poetry, of Hafiz, of Omar, of Attâr, and from each distil the very essence of female loveliness; though you combine them all in one rapturous vision of delight you will have conceived but a feeble shadow of shadows of this wondrous reality who now stood panting before me, her red lips parted and her bosom tumultuous.

I think if the light in her eyes had been for me I could gladly have died for her and found death sweet; but as her gaze met mine a pitiful change took place in that lovely countenance. Her color fled and she swayed and almost fell.

"Oh," she whispered, "thou art not my beloved! O Allah! this is some snare that Ismail hath set for my feet! Who art thou? who art thou?"

But because of the excess of the loveliness of the speaker, from whom I could not remove my eyes, and because as I stood in that perfumed apartment it seemed to me that I was no longer a real man, but a figment of some *Efreet's* dream, I found myself incapable of both speech and action.

Yet I was speedily to know that the Fates, which had thrust me into that saloon—nay, which had brought me across the desert to that secret oasis— were not yet wearied of their sport.

A soft call, a lover's signal (for no true Believer will whistle at night, since to do so is to summon the evil *ginn*) sounded from immediately outside the bronze door, followed by a muffled rapping upon the door itself!

"Saîd, my beloved!" cried the girl wildly, and ran towards the door.

At that very moment, and whilst I stood there like a man of clay, I heard the negro guardians returning to their posts; I heard the clatter of their sandals and I heard their guttural cries of rage! Uttering a long tremulous sigh, the beautiful occupant of the pavilion fell swooning upon the floor.

A loud imperious voice now rose above the sounds of conflict which had commenced outside the pavilion;

I heard the sound of many running feet, and—my blood turned to ice—that of a key being inserted in the lock of the bronze door! Power of action returned to me, though I confess that I now grew sick with dread. Only one hiding-place was possible: the first I could reach.

I leaped across the lovely form extended upon the floor and dropped, almost choking with emotion, behind the alabaster couch. I had barely gained this cover when the door was hurled open and a tall, excessively gaunt, and hawk-faced old man entered, his eyes blazing, his thin nostrils quivering, and his lean hands opening and closing at his sides in a sort of clutching movement horribly suggestive and terrifying.

He was followed by the two negroes, who were dragging between them a young Egyptian of prepossessing appearance down whose pale face blood was pouring from a wound in the brow.

Several other persons, principally servants of the *harêm*, brought up the rear.

Towering over the recumbent body of the girl, the terrible old man—in whom I could not fail to recognize the Sheikh Ismail—glared down at her for some moments in passionate silence; then he made as if to spurn her with his foot; then he clutched his long white beard with both hands and plucked at it frenziedly, whilst tears began to course down his furrowed cheeks, which had the frightful appearance of those of a mummy.

"O light of mine eyes!" he exclaimed; "O shame

of my house! O reproach of my white hairs!"

He recovered himself by dint of a stupendous effort and turning a fiery glance upon the captive:

"Cast him down upon the floor," he cried, "that I may spit upon him, who is a scorn among swine and the son of a disease!"

To my unspeakable horror, the Sheikh then strode across the saloon and seated himself upon the alabaster couch! I almost choked with fear; I felt my teeth beginning to chatter and the beating of my heart sounded in my ears like the throb of a *darâbukeh*. The Sheikh, fortunately ignorant of my proximity, thus addressed the unfortunate young man who lay at his feet:

"Know, O disgrace of thy mother, that thy death hath been decided upon, and it shall visit thee in a most painful and unfortunate manner. O thou spawn of offal, learn that I have been aware of thy malevolent intentions since first thou didst seek to penetrate into my secret. What! am I heir to all the wisdom of the ages, that I should remain ignorant of the presence of such as thee, O thou gnat's egg, in my house? When the partner in thine infamy didst steal the key of the door from me, thinkest thou that mine eyes were blind to the theft, O thou foredoomed carrion? It was in order that thy culpability should be made manifest that I permitted thee to enter. Thy double stratagem for quelling and then exciting the dogs, in order that the guards might be drawn from their posts, was known to me, and the negroes had received my orders to run to the gate in seeming accordance with thine accursed desires, O filthy insect!''

Throughout the time that this dreadful old man thus addressed his victim, the latter crouched upon the floor, apparently paying no heed to his words but keeping an agonized glance fixed upon the lovely form of the girl. I was now in a condition of such profound and dejected fear as I had never known before and trust I may never know again. The Sheikh continued:

"Learn of the fate of some of those who sought the secret of Ismail before thee. One there was, Mustapha Mirza, a Persian, who came hither to despoil me. With his eyes did he behold my treasure. To-day *he hath no eyes!* And there was one Hassan of the Khân Khalîl. He dared to lay violent hands upon the treasure of my house—the 'treasure' not of gold nor jewels but of fairest flesh and blood. To-day *he hath no hands!* Wouldst like to know of Abdûl Moharli, who learned much of this "secret" of mine, and would have spoken of it? His tongue I threw to the carrion crows! *Thou,* O sink of iniquity, hast not only seen with thine eyes, heard with thine ears and laid thy filthy hands upon the treasure of Ismail; thou hast approached thy foul lips to this peach of Allah's garden! thou hast . . .''

He choked in his utterance and seemed upon the point of hurling himself upon the young man before him: but again he recovered his composure after a great effort and proceeded:

"The unpleasant punishments visited upon those

others shall likewise fall to thy portion, since thou hast committed like crimes; but this shall only be in order to prepare thee for a most protracted and painful death. Bear him forth into the courtyard."

As one who dreams an evil dream, I saw the company stream out of the saloon, the wretched prisoner in their midst. When at last the bronze door was reclosed and I found myself alone with the swooning girl, I could scarce believe that even this respite was mine.

I offered a prayer to St. Antony of the Thebaïd—my patron saint—as I listened to the sound of their receding footsteps; when I was aroused from the lethargy of fear into which I had fallen by a distant scream—a long wailing cry. . . .

* * * * * *

I have often asked myself: How did I make my escape from that dreadful village? You will remember that I had the purloined key of the bronze door in my possession? Then it was to this in the first place that I owed my preservation. To regain the garden was a simple matter, for the Sheikh and his bloodthirsty following were engaged in the courtyard of the house, but to St. Antony be all praise for the circumstance that the little door opposite the mosque had been left open—possibly by the unhappy Saïd,—and to St. Antony be all praise that a second time I avoided the dogs. . . .

Dawn found me staggering down into that friendly ravine which sheltered my camel. I was utterly exhausted, for I bore a burden, but triumphant, deliri-

ous with joy and rapture, because my burden was so
sweet. You may question me of these matters, and I
shall reply: As well as my cotton interests I have
now another interest in the Delta—the lovely
"Secret" of the Sheikh Ismail Ebn al As!*

* Readers of *Tales of Abû Tabâh* will recognize Mizmûna, "The
Lady of the Lattice," the story of whose recovery by the bereaved
Sheikh has already been related.

IV

HARÛN PASHA

I

I WILL tell you this story (said Ferrier of the Egyptian Civil) with one reservation; comments are to be reserved for some future time. I can only tell you what I saw with my own eyes and heard with my own ears; I offer no explanation; I pass on the story; you can take it or leave it.

Some of you will remember Dunlap—I don't mean Robert Dunlap, who is chief officer of the *Pekin,* but Jack Dunlap his cousin, the irrigation man who used to be stationed at Assuan.

You remember the build of the beggar?—the impression of scaffolding his figure conveyed? I always used to think of him as an iron framework, and he had the most hard-bitten head-piece I have ever struck; steel blue eyes and a mouth that was born shut. The dash of ginger in his hair, complexion, and constitution made up a Scotch brew that was very strongly flavored.

He came down to Cairo one spring, and a lot of us got together in the club—on a Sunday night, I remember, it was. The conversation got along that silly line; what we were all doing, and why we were doing it, what we had really intended to do, and how Fate had butted in and made sailors of those that had meant to be parsons, engineers of the poets, and tramps of the chaps who had proposed to become financiers.

Well, we had traveled up and down this blind alley for hours, I should think, when Dunlap mounted on his hind legs and took the rug with the proposition that nothing—*nothing*—was impossible of achievement to the man of single purpose. Some-one put up an extreme case; asking Dunlap how he should handle the business of the son of a respectable greengrocer who, with singleness of purpose, proposed to become king of England.

He said it was not a fair case, but he accepted the challenge; and the way this junior greengrocer, under Dunlap's guidance, plunged into politics, got elected M.P., wormed himself into the confidence of the entire Empire by a series of brilliant campaigns conducted from John o' Groats to Van Diemen's Land; induced the reigning monarch, publicly, to advocate his own abdication; established a sort of commonwealth with his ex-Majesty on the board and Dunlap occupying a post between that of a protector and a Roman Cæsar—well, it was wonderful.

Of course, you can judge of the lateness of the hour from the fact that a group of moderately intelligent men tolerated, and contributed to, a chat of this nature. But what brings me down to the story is the few words which I exchanged with Dunlap at the break-up of the party, when he was leaving.

His cousin Robert, as you know, is well on the rippity side; but Jack, with all his fine capacity for

heather-dew, had always struck me as something of
a psalmster. I've heard that Bacchus holds the keys
of truth, and it may be right; for out on the steps
of the club, I said to Jack Dunlap:

"It seems you don't practise what you preach?"

"Don't I?" he snapped hardly. "What do you
suppose I am doing here?"

"Engineering, I take it. Do you aspire to a pede-
stal beside De Lesseps?"

"De Lesseps be damned!" he retorted sourly.
"Look at these."

He held out his hands, hardened with manual toil
—the hands of a grinder.

"Clearly you are a glutton for work," I said.

"I am aiming at never doing another hand's stroke
in my life," he replied, with an odd glint in his blue
eyes. "My idea of life—*life*, mind you, not mere
existence—is to be a pasha—one of the old school,
with gate porters, orange trees, fountains, slaves,
mosaic pavements, a marble bath."

He mixed his ambitions oddly.

"Someone to do all the shifting for me, and even
the thinking; to hold a book in front of me if I wanted
to read, to poke my pipe in my mouth, and to take
it out when I wanted to blow smoke rings—and to
know when I wanted it taken out without being told."

"On your showing, you are traveling by the
wrong road."

"Am I?" he snapped viciously. "Just wait
awhile."

That was all the indication I had of Dunlap's

ideas, and remembering the time of night and other circumstances, I did not count upon it worth a brass farthing; putting it down to the heather-dew rather than to any innate viciousness of the man. But listen to the sequel, which shifts us up just about twelve months, to the spring of the following year, in fact.

II

I had seen no more of Dunlap, and concluded that he was back in Assuan, or somewhere on the river, foozling with his irrigation again. I never had the clearest conception of the work of his department, by the way. An irrigation man once started to explain to me about his section, mixing up surveying paraphernalia in his talk, telling me something about an allowance of half an inch variation in half a mile of bank, or chat to that effect; but I couldn't quite make it out. My impression of Dunlap at business was very hazy; I pictured him measuring the bank of the Nile with a six-foot rule, and periodically kneeling down in the smelly mud to footle with a spirit-level. But he was a Senior Wrangler, as you remember, and a man, too, of more substantial accomplishments, and he drew five hundred a year from the Egyptian Government; so that probably I underestimated his usefulness.

At any rate, I had forgotten his iron framework and mahogany countenance, together with his response (under the afflatus of heather-dew) at the time of which I am now speaking.

A little matter had cropped up which touched me on a weak spot; and with a mob of jabbering Egyptians and one very placid Bedouin flooding my room, I found myself thinking again of Dunlap and envying him his intimate acquaintance with Arabic.

Although I had been in the country quite twice as long as Dunlap, my Arabic was far from perfect, for I have always been a rotten linguist. Dunlap, as I now remembered, might have passed for a native (excepting his Scottish headpiece), and I ascribed his proficiency to an inherent trick of mimicry. There was something of the big ape about him; and after one function at which we both were present, I remember how he convulsed the entire club with an imitation of a certain highly placed Egyptian dignitary, voice and gesture being equal in comic effect to Cyril Maude at his best. In fact, if you notice, you will find that the best linguists, as a rule, have a marked apish streak in their composition.

Well, here was I at my wits' ends to grasp twenty points of view at one and the same time; no two expressed in quite the same dialect, and each orator more excited than another. You know the brutes?

That got me thinking of Dunlap, and even after the incident was closed, I found myself thinking of him. Some friends from home were staying at Shepheard's, and of course they had claimed me as dragoman; not that I objected in the least, for one of the party—when it was possible to dodge her mother—was, well, a very agreeable companion, you understand.

On this particular morning we were doing the bazaars. I have found by comparison that the average tourist knows far more of the Mûski than the average resident; in the same way, I suppose that for information regarding the Tower of London or the British Museum, one must go, not to a Cockney, but to an American visitor. At any rate, my party told me more than I could tell them, and my job degenerated into that of a mere interpreter. In the matter of purchases, I possibly saved them money, but their knowledge of the wares was miles ahead of my own. These up-to-date guide books must be very useful reading, I think.

Although I had tried hard to rush them past that dangerous quarter, the *Gôhargîya,* the ladies of the party had discovered a shop where little trays of loose gems, turquoises, rubies, bits of lapis-lazuli, and so forth, were displayed snarefully.

After that I knew where I could find them up to any time before lunch; I knew they were safe enough for the rest of the morning; and accepting my defeat at the hands of the jewel merchant who turned his slow eyes upon me and shrugged apologetically, I drifted off, after a decent interval (leaving young Forrest, who, mysteriously, had turned up, to do the cavalierly), intending to visit my acquaintance, Hassan, in the *Sûk el-Attârin* (Street of the Perfumers), not twenty yards away.

You know Hassan? A large, mysterious figure in the shadows of his little shop, smoking amber-scented cigarettes as though he liked them, and turn-

ing his sleepy eyes slowly upon each passer-by. Well,
I drifted around in his direction.

Right at the corner of the street, a big limousine
was standing; an up-to-date car, fawn cushions, sil-
ver-plated fittings, and simply stuffed with fresh-cut
flowers. A useful-looking Nubian was chauffeur, and
on the step squatted a fat and resplendent being in
all the glory of much gold braid.

These *harêm* guards are rarely seen in Cairo
nowadays—they belong to the other picturesque
Oriental institutions which have begun to fade with
the cresent of Islâm. There was something start-
lingly incongruous about this full-grown specimen,
that bloated representative of Eastern despotism
squatting on the step of an up-to-date French car.

It was a kind of all-round shock; I cannot describe
how it struck me. It was something like running
into Martin Luther at the Grand National or Nero,
say, at an aviation meeting.

This was a frightfully hot morning, and the
adipose object on the car step was slumbering bliss-
fully. A moment later I spotted the charge which
he was guarding with such sedulous care. She was
seated in Hassan's shop—well back in the shadows—
a gauzy white vision, all eyes and *yashmak*. A confidential female servant accompanied her. They
made a pleasing picture enough, and a more suitable
setting could not well be found. It was an illustrated
page of the *Arabian Nights,* and it appealed strongly
even to my jaded perceptions.

Of course, I was not going to interrupt the

tête-à-tête; but from where I stood I could observe
the group very well whilst remaining myself un-
observed. It presently became evident that the lady
of the *yashmak,* under the pretence of purchasing
perfumes, was merely killing time, and my interest
increased as the hour of noon grew near and the
artistic group remained unbroken. You know the
Mosque of El-Ashraf by Hassan's shop? Its minaret
almost overhung the place. Well, in due course,
out popped the *mueddin.*

"*La il aha illa Allah. . . .*"

There he was a very sweet-voiced singer, as I
noted at the time, telling them there was no God
but God, and all the rest of it; and presently he
worked round to the side of the gallery overlooking
Hassan's shop.

Then I could see which way the wind blew. He
seemed to be deliberately singing *at* the picturesque
trio—and the dark eyes of the lady of the *yashmak*
were lifted upward—in reverence, perhaps; but I
hardly thought so.

There was no doubt about the *mueddin's* final
glance, as he turned and retired from the gallery.
I remained where I was until the *yashmak* left the
shop; and as she had to pass quite close to me in
order to rejoin the waiting car, I had a good look
at her.

It was just an impression, of course, an impression of red lips under the white gauze, an oval
Oriental outline, with very fine eyes—notably fine,
where fine eyes are common—and a little exquisitely

chiseled nose; a bewitching face. Just that one
glimpse I had and a vague impression of rustling
silk with the tap of high heels. A faint breath of
musk still proclaimed itself above the less pleasing
odors of the street; then, the female attendant having cuffed the slumbering Silenus into wakefulness,
the car moved off and this *harêm* lily vanished
from the bazaar.

I knew that my party was safe for another half
an hour, at any rate, so I nipped along to Hassan's
shop. Of course, he began brazenly by declaring
that no ladies had been there that morning. I
had expected it, and the attitude confirmed my
suspicions.

Presently, when his boy had made fresh coffee,
and Hassan, from the black cabinet, had produced
some real cigarettes, we got more intimate. There
was a scarcity of European visitors that morning;
and excepting one interruption by a party of four
American ladies, I had Hassan to myself for half
an hour.

He raised his fat finger to his lips when I pressed
my question, and rolled his eyes fearfully.

"She is from the palace of Harûn Pasha," he
whispered with more sidelong glances. "Ah!
effendim, I fear. . . .

We smoked awhile; then—

"The Pasha's wife?" I inquired.

"It is the Lady Zohara," he said.

This did not add greatly to my information; but
I continued: "And the *mueddin?*"

"Ah!—do not whisper it. . . . That is my brother, Saïd!"

"He raises his eyes very high?"

"Not so, *effendim;* it is she who raises her eyes. I fear—I fear for Saïd. The Pasha . . . you have heard of him?"

"I may have heard his name," I replied; "but I am quite unfamiliar with his reputation."

Hassan shook his head gloomily.

"He is the last of his race," he explained; "the race of the Khalîfs. He inhabits the ancient palace —but much has been rebuilt, and much added—in Old Cairo, close behind the Coptic Church. . . ."

"I did not know that such a palace even existed."

Again Hassan raised his finger to his lips.

"He is not like the other pashas," he said; "in the house of Harûn Pasha are observed to-day all the old customs as in the day of his great ancestor Harûn al-Raschîd."

"But a motor-car!"

"Ah, *effendim,* he does not scorn to employ modern comforts, nor do I mean that he is a strict Moslem. But you saw the one who sat upon the step? The *harêm* of the Pasha is well guarded; not only by such as he, but by the Nubians and by the other mutes."

"Mutes!"

"He has many slaves. His agent in Mecca procures for him the pick of the market."

"But there is no such thing as slavery in Egypt!"

"Do the slaves know that, *effendim?*" he asked simply. "Those who have tongues are never seen outside the walls—unless they are guarded by those who have no tongue!"

It was a curious sidelight upon a more curious possibility and I was much impressed.

"Your brother——"

"Alas! I have warned him! I fear, most sincerely I fear, that one dark night the same will befall him that befell the son of my cousin, Ali."

"And what was that?"

"He climbed the wall of the Pasha's garden. There is a fig tree growing close beside it at one place. Someone assisted him to descend on the other. But he had been betrayed; the Nubian mutes took him—and they——"

He bent and whispered in my ear.

"Impossible!" I cried—"impossible! *báss! báss!*"

"Not so, *effendim*—nor was that all. After that they——"

"Enough, Hassan, enough!" I cried. "*Usbûr!*"

Hassan sighed, raising fearful eyes to the minaret.

III

There has been nothing you are likely to disbelieve so far; but now—well, I specified at the beginning—no comments. Let me tell the story in my own way, and you have permission to *think* what you please.

There was a dance at Shepheard's that night, and

young Forrest rather interfered with my plans again as to one of the members of the English party; I think I have referred to her before? That sent me home in a bad humor—at least not home; for as I was standing over by the Ezbekîyeh Gardens, wondering whether to go along to "Jimmy's" or not, I formed a sudden determination to go and have a look at the abode of Harûn Pasha instead!

Mind you, I was not surprised to have lived in Cairo all these years without having heard of the place; I had learned things about the Mûski in the morning, from my tourist friends, which had revealed to me something of my pitiable ignorance But I was determined to mend my ways, so to speak, and I thought I would turn my restless mood to good purpose, by improving my knowledge of my neighbors.

I induced the torpid driver of an *arabîyeh* to drive me out to Old Cairo. He obviously considered me to be even more demented than the rest of my countrymen, but since the fare would be a substantial one, he tackled the job. Mad expedition? Quite so; but you appreciate the mood?

After we had passed a certain quarter—a quarter which never sleeps—there was nothing livelier than decayed tombs *en route*. In the chill of the evening I began to weigh up my own foolishness appreciatively, but having got so far as the Coptic Church —you know the church I mean?—I was not going back unsatisfied; so I told my man to wait, and started off to look for the famous palace.

I must say the scene was impressive; a sky full
of diamonds and a moon just bursting with light.
The liquid night—sounds of the Nile alone disturbed
the silence, and the buildings might have been made
of mother-o'-pearl, so flawless and pure did they
seem, gleaming there under the moon.

Well, I wandered up some narrow streets—past
ruins of former important houses, and all that—
until I found myself in the shadow of a high wall
which obviously was kept in good repair. I followed
this for some distance, and I could see trees on the
other side; at one place a perfect mat of those purple
flowers hung over the top; gorgeous things; the
name begins with a B, but I can never remember it.
This seemed promising, and as there was not a soul
in sight, nor, on the visible evidences, a habitable
building near me, I began to fossick for a likely
place to climb up.

Presently I found the spot, and at the same time
confirmation of my belief that these were the pre-
cincts of the Pasha. A fig tree grew beside the wall,
affording an admirable means of reaching the top
—a natural ladder. In a jiffy I was up . . . and
overlooking one of the most glorious gardens I had
ever seen or dreamt of!

It must have been planned by an artist simply
soaked in the lore of the Orient. It set me thinking
of Edmond Dulac's illustrations to the *Arabian
Nights*. Apart from those pages, you never saw
anything like it, I swear. The position of each tree
was a study; the arrangement of the flowerbeds was

poetic—that is the only word for it; there was a
pond with marble seats around and a flight of steps
with big copper urns filled with growing flowers,
mosaic paths, and lesser pools with fountains playing. I peered down into the water, and the moon
rays glittered magically upon the scales of the golden
carp which darted there. And all this fairy prospect
was no more than an introduction, as it were, a sort
of lead-up, to the Aladdin's Palace beyond.

I saw now that what with palms and the natural
rise of the land back from the Nile, the wonderful
palace, with its terraces and gleaming domes, must
actually be invisible from all points; a more secret
locality one could not well imagine.

As to this magician's abode, which lay before me,
I shall not attempt to describe it. But turn to the
illustrations which I have menioned, or to those of
Burton's big edition; I will leave it to the artist's
and your imagination to fill up the canvas.

Lights shone out from a hundred windows. Out
of the ghostly, tomb-like silence of Old Cairo, I
had clambered into a sort of fairyland; I stood
there with the spray from a fountain wetting me,
and rubbed my eyes. Honestly, I should not have
been surprised to find myself dreaming. Well, you
may be sure I was not going back yet; there was
not a living soul to be seen in the gardens, and I
meant to have a peep into the palace, whatever the
chances.

The likeliest point, as I soon determined, was to
the west—where a long, low wing of the building

extended, and was lost, if I may use the term, in a great bank of verdure and purple blooms. I took full advantage of the ample shadow cast by the trees, and came right up under the white wall without mishap.

To my right, the wall was obviously modern, but to my left, although in the distance and under the moon it had seemed uniform, it was built of sandstone blocks and was evidently of great age. The palace proper, you understand, was fully forty yards east; the place before me was a sort of low extension and evidently had no real connection with the residential part.

Just above my head was a square window, ironbarred, but this did not look promising, and cautiously, for I was hampered by the creepers which grew under the wall, I felt my way further west. Presently I encountered a pointed door of black, time-seared wood, and heavily iron-studded. Then, with alarming suddenness, the quietude of my adventure was broken; things began to move with breathless rapidity.

A most dreadful screaming and howling split the stillness and made me jump like a startled frog!

The sound of a lash on bare flesh reached me from some place behind the pointed door. Screams for mercy in thick, guttural Arabic, mingled and punctuated with horrifying shrieks of pain, informed my ignorance unmistakably that mediæval methods yet ruled in the civilized Near East.

Screams and supplications merged into a dull

moaning; but the whistle of the lash continued uninterruptedly. Then that too ceased, and dimly came the sounds of a muffled colloquy; a sort of gurgling talk that got me wondering.

I had just time to creep away and conceal myself behind a thick clump of bushes, when the door was thrown open, and the most gigantic negro I have ever set eyes upon appeared in the opening, outlined against the smoky glare from within. He had one gleaming bare arm about the neck of an insensible man, and he dragged him out into the garden as one might drag a heavy sack; dropping him all in a quivering heap upon the very spot which I had just vacated!

The negro, who was stripped to the waist and whose glistening body reminded me of a bronze statue of Hercules, stood looking down at the insensible victim, with a hideous leer. I ventured to raise myself ever so slightly; and in the ghastly, sweat-bedaubed face of the tortured man—whose bare shoulders were bloody from the lash—I recognized the Silenus of the limousine!

In response to a guttural inarticulate muttering by the black giant, a second Nubian, of scarcely lesser dimensions, emerged from the dungeon with a jar of water. He drenched the swooning man, evidently in order to revive him; and, when the wretched being ultimately fought his way back to agonized consciousness—to my horror he was seized, dragged in through the doorway again, and once more I heard the whistle of the lash being applied to

his lacerated back, the skin of which was already
in ribbons.

I suppose there are times when the most discreet
man is snatched outside himself by circumstances?
The door of this beastly torture-room had not been
reclosed, and before I could realize what I was about,
I found myself inside!

The wretched victim had been hauled up to a beam
by his bound wrists, and the huge Nubian was putting all his strength into the wielding of the cat-o'-
nine-tails, drawing blood with every stroke; whilst
his assistant hung on to the rope running through a
pulley-block in the low ceiling.

All in a sort of whirl (I was raving mad with
indignation) I got amongst the trio, and landed a
clip on the jaw of the son of Erebus which made his
teeth rattle like castanets.

Down came the fat sufferer all in a heap in his
own blood. Down went my man, and began to cough
out broken molars. Then it was my turn; and down
I went with the second mute on top of me, and the
pair of us were playing hell all about the blood-
spattered floor—up, down, under, over—straining,
punching, kicking . . . then my antagonist introduced
gouging, and I had to beat the mat.

It had been a stiff bout, and the stinking shambles
were whirling about me like a bloody maelstrom.
When things settled down a bit, I found myself lying
in a small cell skewered up like a pullet, and with a
prospect of iron grating and stone-flagged passage
before me. I was more than a trifle damaged, and

my head was singing like a kettle. If I had thought that I dreamed before, it was a struggle now to convince myself that this was not a nightmare.

Amid the rattling of chains and dropping of bars, a fantastic procession was filing down the passage. First came a hideous, crook-backed apparition, hook-nosed, and bearing a lantern. Behind him appeared two guards with glittering scimitars. Behind the guards walked a fourth personage, black-robed and white-turbaned—a sort of dignified dragoman, carrying an enormous bunch of keys.

The iron grating of my dungeon was unlocked and raised, and I was requested, in Arabic, to rise and follow. Realizing that this was no time for funny business, I staggered to my feet, and between the two Scimitars marched unsteadily through a maze of passages with doors unlocked and locked behind us, stairs ascended and stairs descended.

From empty passages, our journey led us to passages richly carpeted and softly lighted. By a heavy door opening on to the first of the latter, we left the squinting man; and, with the two Scimitars and Black Robe, I found myself crossing a lofty pavilion.

The floor was of rich mosaic, and priceless carpets were spread about in artistic confusion. Above my head loomed a great dome, lighted by stained glass windows in which the blue of lapis-lazuli predominated. By golden chains from above swung golden lamps burning perfumed oil and flooding the pavilion with a mellow blue light. There were inlaid tables and cabinets; great blue vases of exquisite Chinese

porcelain stood in niches of the wall. The walls
were of that faintly amber-tinted alabaster which
is quarried in the Mokattam Hills; and there were
fragile columns of some delicately azure-veined
marble, rising, graceful and slender, ethereal as
pencils of smoke, to a balcony high above my head;
then, from this, a second series of fairy columns
crept in blue streaks up into the luminous shadows
of the dome.

We crossed this place, my heel taps echoing hollowly and before a curtained door took pause. An
impressive interval of perfumed silence; then in
response to the muffled clapping of hands, the curtain
was raised and I was thrust into a smaller apartment
beyond.

I found myself standing before a long *diwan*,
amid an opulence of Oriental appointment which surpassed anything which I could have imagined. The
atmosphere was heavy with the odor of burning
perfumes, and, whereas the lofty pavilion afforded
a delicate study in blue, this chamber was voluptu-
ously amber—amber-shaded lamps, amber cushions,
amber carpets; everywhere the glitter of amber and
gold.

Amid the amber sea, half immersed in the golden
silks of the daïs, reclined a large and portly Sheikh;
full and patriarchal his beard, wherein played amber
tints, lofty and serene his brow, sweeping up to the
snowy turban. From a mouthpiece of amber and
gold he inhaled the scented smoke of a *narghli*. Behind him, upon a cushioned stool, knelt a female

whose beauty of face and form was unmistakable, since it was undisguised by the filmy artistry of her attire. With a gigantic fan of peacock's feathers, she cooled the Sheikh, and dispersed the flies which threatened to disturb his serenity. A second houri received in her hands the amber mouthpiece as it fell from her lord's lips; a third, who evidently had been playing upon a lute, rose and glided from the apartment like an opium vision, as I entered between the guardian Scimitars.

I found myself thinking of Saint Saen's music to *Samson and Delilah;* the barbaric strains of the exquisite *bacchanale* were beating on my brain.

Black Robe advanced and knelt upon the floor of the *dîwan.*

"We have brought the wretched malefactor into your glorious presence," he said.

The Pasha (for I knew, beyond doubt, that I stood before Harûn Pasha) raised his eyes and fixed a stern gaze upon me. He gazed long and fixedly, and an odd change took place in his expression. He seemed about to address me, then, apparently changing his mind, he addressed the recumbent figure at his feet.

"Have the slaves returned with the female miscreant and her partner in Satan?" he demanded sternly.

"Lord of the age," replied the other, rising upon his knees, "they are expected."

"Let them be brought before me," directed the Pasha, "upon the instant of their arrival. Has

Misrûn confessed his complicity?"

"He fainted beneath the lash, excellency, but confessed that he slept—that pig who prayed without washing and whose birth was a calamity—on several occasions when accompanying the lady Zohara."

"Leave us!" cried the Pasha. "But, first, unbind the prisoner."

He swept his arm around comprehensively, and everyone withdrew from the apartment, including the Scimitars (one of whom cut my lashings) and the lady of the fan. I found myself alone with Harûn Pasha.

IV

"Sit here beside me!" directed the Pasha.

Being yet too dazed for wonder or protest, I obeyed mechanically. My exact situation was not clear to me at the moment and I was a long way off knowing how to act.

"I am much disturbed in mind, and my bosom is contracted," continued the Pasha, with a certain benignity, "by reason of a conspiracy in my *harêm*, which came to a head this night, and which led to the loss of the pearl of my household, a damsel who cost me her weight in gold, who entangled me in the snare of her love and pierced me with anguish. Know, O young Inglîsi, that love is difficult. Alas! she who had captivated my reason by her loveliness fled with a shame of the Moslems who defamed the sacred office of *mueddin!* In truth he is naught but the son of a disease and a consort of camels. My soul cries out to Allah and my mind is a nest of wasps. Relate to me your case, that it may turn me from the contemplation of my sorrows. At another time, it had gone hard with you, and penalties of a most unfortunate description had been visited upon your head, O disturber of my peace; but since this child of filth and progeny of mules has shattered it forever, your lesser crime comes but as a diversion. Relate to me the matters which have brought you to this miserable pass.''

There was some still little voice in my mind which was trying to speak to me, if you understand what I mean. But what with the suffocating perfume of ambergris (or it may have been frankincense), my incredible surroundings, and the buzzing of my maltreated skull, I simply could *not* think connectedly.

A memory was struggling for identification in my addled brain; but whether it was due to something I had seen, heard, or smelled, I could not for the life of me make out. I heard myself spinning my own improbable yarn as one listens to a dreary and boresome recitation; *I* didn't seem to be the raconteur; my mind was busy about that amber room, furiously chasing that hare-like memory, which leaped and doubled, dived under the silken cushions, popped up behind the Pasha, and flicked its ears at me from amid the feathers of the peacock fan.

I driveled right on to the end of my story, mechanically, without having got my mind in proper working order; and when the Pasha spoke again— there was that wretched memory still dodging me, sometimes almost within my grasp, but always just eluding it.

"Your amusing narrative has diverted me," said the Pasha; and he clapped his hands three times.

It never occurred to me, you will note, to assert myself in any way; I accepted the lordly condescensions of this singular personage without protest. You will be wondering why I didn't kick up a devil of a hullabaloo—declare that I had come in response to screams for assistance—wave the dreaded name of the British Agent under the Pasha's nose, and all that. I can only say that I didn't; I was subdued; in fact I was down, utterly down and out.

Black Robe entered with eyes averted.

"Well, wretched vermin!" roared the Pasha in sudden wrath; "do you tell me they are not here?"

The man, with his head bumping on the carpet, visibly trembled.

"Most noble," he replied hoarsely, "your lowly slave has exerted himself to the utmost——"

"Out! son of a calamity!" shouted the Pasha— and before my astonished eyes he raised the heavy *narghli* and hurled it at the bowed head of the man before him.

It struck the white turban with a resounding crack, and then was shattered to bits upon the floor. It was a blow to have staggered a mule. But Black Robe, without apparent loss of dignity, rose and departed, bowing.

The Pasha sat rocking about, and plucking madly at his beard.

"O Allah!" he cried, "how I suffer" He turned to me. "Never since the day that another of your race (but, this one, a true son of Satan) came to my palace, have I tasted so much suffering. You shall judge of my clemency, O imprudent stranger, and pacify your heart with the spectacle of another's punishment."

He clapped his hands twice. This time there was a short delay, which the Pasha suffered impatiently; then there entered the squint-eyed man, together with the two Scimitars.

"I would visit the dungeon of the false Pasha," said my singular host; and, rising to his feet, he placed his hand upon my shoulder and indicated that we were to proceed from the apartment.

Led by Crook Back, in whose hand the gigantic bunch of keys rattled unmelodiously, and followed by the Scimitars, we proceeded upon our way; and it was beyond the powers of my disordered brain to dismiss the idea that I was taking part in a Christmas pantomime. Many steps were descended; many heavy doors unbolted and unbarred, bolted and barred behind us; many stone-paved passages, reminding me of operatic scenery, were traversed ere we came to one tunnel more gloomy than the rest.

Upon the right was a blank stone wall, upon the left, a series of doors, black with age and heavily iron-studded. The only illumination was that furnished by the lantern which Crook Back carried.

Before one of the doors the Pasha paused.

"In which is Misrûn?" he demanded.

"In the next, excellency," replied the jailer—for such I took to be the office of the hunchback.

As he spoke, he held the lantern to the grating.

I found myself peering into a filthy dungeon, the reek of which made me ill; and there, upon the stone floor, lay poor Silenus! He raised his eyes to the light.

"Lord of the age," he moaned, lifting his manacled wrists, "glory of the universe, sun of suns! I have confessed my frightful sin, and most dire misfortunes. Of your sublime mercy, take pity upon the meanest thing that creeps upon the earth——"

"Proceed!" said the Pasha.

And with the moaning cries of Misrûn growing fainter behind us, we moved along the passage. Before a second door, we halted again, and the jailer raised the lantern.

"Look upon this!" cried the Pasha to me—"look well, and look long!"

Shudderingly I peered in between the bars. It had come home to me how I was utterly at the mercy of this man's moods. If he had chosen to have me hurled into one of his dungeons, what prospect of release would have been mine? Who would ever know of my plight? No one! And beyond doubt I was in the realm of an absolute monarch. I silently thanked my lucky stars that my lot was not the lot of him who occupied this second dungeon.

As the dim light, casting shadow bars across the filthy floor, picked out the features of the prisoner, I gave a great start. Save that the beard was more

gray, longer, filthy and unkempt, and that, in place
of the nearly shaven skull, this unhappy being displayed dishevelled locks, the captive might easily
have passed for the Pasha.

I met the eye of this terrible despot.

"Look upon the false Pasha," he said; "look upon
the one who thought to dispossess me! For years,
by his own miserable confession, he studied me in
secret. When I journeyed to my estates in Assuan"
(I started again) "he was watching—watching—
always watching. His scheme, which was whispered
into his ear by the Evil One, was no plant of sudden
growth, but a tree, that, from a seed of Satan planted
in fertile soil, had flourished exceedingly, tended by
the hand of villainous ambition."

I clutched at the bars for support. The stench
of the place was simply indescribable; but it was
neither the stench nor the bizarre incidents of the
night which accounted for my dizziness: it was the
sudden tangibility of that hitherto elusive memory.

In build, in complexion, in certain mannerisms
underlying the dignified assumption, Harûn Pasha
might well have been the twin brother of Jack
Dunlap!

A frightful possibility burst upon me like a bomb;
clutching the bars with quivering hands, I stared
and stared at the wretched impostor in the cell.
Could it be? Had he been mad enough to make some
attempt upon the Pasha? And was this his end?

I looked around again. I searched the bearded
features of the Pasha with eager gaze. Good God!

either I was going mad, or incredible things had been done, were being done, in Cairo.

I had not seen Dunlap for a year, remember, and in the ordinary way I did not see him more than half a dozen times in twelve months, so that, all things considered, it was not so remarkable that I had overlooked the resemblance. A full beard and mustache, artificially darkened eyelashes, a shaven head and a white turban, are effectual disguises; but if you can imagine Dunlap—the Dunlap you remember—so arrayed, then you have Harûn Pasha. Imagine Harûn Pasha, dirty, bedraggled, a hopeless captive . . . and you have the prisoner who crouched upon the straw in that noisome dungeon!

For the second time that night I was lifted out of myself. I turned on the man beside me in a blazing fury.

"You villain!" I shouted at him, and clenched my fists— "do you *dare* to confine a Britisher in your stinking cellars. By God! sir . . ."

Harûn Pasha clapped his hand over my mouth; the two guards had me by the arms from behind. But my cries had aroused the man in the dungeon, and, as I was dragged down the passage, these moaning words reached me, spoken in Arabic:

"Help! help! Englishman! A crime has been committed! I appeal to Lord——."

A door was slammed fast with a resounding bang, and the rest of the captive's appeal was lost to me. One of my guards had substituted his hand for that of the Pasha, but now it was removed; and, speechless with rage, I found myself being thrust up stone stairs—and I realized that by a moment's indiscretion, I had ruined everything.

Back in the amber apartment once more, with the two Scimitars at the door and Harûn Pasha reclining upon the cushions, I found speech.

"What are you going to do with me?" I demanded.

"My son," replied the Pasha with benignity, "I pardon all! Your great courage and address, together with the modesty of your deportment, and the spirit of adventure which has brought you to your present unfortunate case, plead for you in a manner which my clemency cannot resist. It is my unhappy lot often to be called upon to punish. Tonight, those gloomy dungeons which you have seen will echo, alas, with the howls of miserable wretches who are responsible for the loss of the pearl of my soul; for I am persuaded that she has fled with the son of offal who profaned the words of Allah from the minaret. This being so, I would temper my proper severity with a merciful deed. You shall never speak of what you have seen within these walls, save in terms suitably disguised. You shall never seek to return, nor, by speech with any man, to confirm whatsoever you may suspect. Upon this warranty, you shall depart in peace."

He clapped his hands twice, and a houri of most bewitching aspect glided into the *dîwan*.

"Bring sherbet!" ordered the Pasha.

The maiden departed; and whilst I was yet trying

to come to a decision (the Pasha had mentioned no alternative, but my imagination was equal to the task of supplying one!) she returned with a tray upon which were porcelain cups and two vessels of beautifully chased gold.

Harûn Pasha decocted a sparkling beverage, and, with his own hands, passed the brimming cup to me.

*   *   *   *   *   *

I knew you would not believe it; but I warned you, and I made a stipulation. Your idea is that I must be a poor sort of animal to accept so dishonorable a compromise? I agree. But the situation was even more peculiarly difficult than is apparent to you at the moment. Without *seeking* the information, I learned from Hassan of the Scent Bazaar that his brother had indeed fled with the beauteous Lady Zohara, no one knew whither; and this confirmation of the Pasha's sorrows touched a very tender spot in my heart!

Then there is another little point.

When the Pasha removed the elaborate stopper from the first of the golden vessels to which I have just referred, *my* eye alone perceived that a bottle, bearing a familiar black and white label, was contained in this golden casing. The flavor of the decoction with which we sealed our infamous bargain clinched the matter.

I was absolutely thrust out of the presence chamber before I had time for another word; but, looking back from the door and meeting the eye of the Pasha,

I encountered a most portentous wink. Therefore I have stuck to my bargain.

Oh! I have not given much away. The Pasha is not called Harûn, and the palace is nowhere near the Coptic Church in Old Cairo. Because, you see, I only knew one man who winked in quite that elaborate fashion—and his name was Jack Dunlap!

V

IN THE VALLEY OF THE SORCERESS

I

CONDOR wrote to me three times before the end (said Neville, Assistant-Inspector of Antiquities, staring vaguely from his open window at a squad drilling before the Kasr-en-Nîl Barracks). He dated his letters from the camp at Deir-el-Bahari. Judging from these, success appeared to be almost within his grasp. He shared my theories, of course, respecting Queen Hatasu, and was devoting the whole of his energies to the task of clearing up the great mystery of Ancient Egypt which centres around that queen.

For him, as for me, there was a strange fascination about those defaced walls and roughly obliterated inscriptions. That the queen under whom Egyptian art came to the apogee of perfection should thus have been treated by her successors; that no perfect figure of the wise, famous, and beautiful Hatasu should have been spared to posterity; that her very cartouche should have been ruthlessly removed from every inscription upon which it appeared, presented to Condor's mind a problem only second in interest to the immortal riddle of Gîzeh.

You know my own views upon the matter? My monograph, "Hatasu, the Sorceress," embodies my opinion. In short, upon certain evidences, some adduced by Theodore Davis, some by poor Condor, and some resulting from my own inquiries, I have come to the conclusion that the source—real or imaginary—of this queen's power was an intimate acquaintance with what nowadays we term, vaguely, magic. Pursuing her studies beyond the limit which is lawful, she met with a certain end, not uncommon, if the old writings are to be believed, in the case of those who penetrate too far into the realms of the Borderland.

For this reason—the practice of black magic—her statues were dishonored, and her name erased from the monuments. Now, I do not propose to enter into any discussion respecting the reality of such practices; in my monograph I have merely endeavored to show that, according to contemporary belief, the queen was a sorceress. Condor was seeking to prove the same thing; and when I took up the inquiry, it was in the hope of completing his interrupted work.

He wrote to me early in the winter of 1908, from his camp by the Rock Temple. Davis's tomb, at Bibân el-Mulûk, with its long, narrow passage, apparently had little interest for him; he was at work on the high ground behind the temple, at a point one hundred yards or so due west of the upper platform. He had an idea that he should find there the mummies of Hatasu—and another; the latter, a certain Sen-Mût, who appears in the inscriptions of the reign as an architect high in the queen's favor. The archæological points of the letter do not concern us in the least, but there was one odd little paragraph which I had cause to remember afterwards.

"A girl belonging to some Arab tribe," wrote Condor, "came racing to the camp two nights ago to claim my protection. What crime she had committed, and what punishment she feared, were far from clear; but she clung to me, trembling like a leaf, and positively refused to depart. It was a difficult situation, for a camp of fifty native excavators, and one highly respectable European enthusiast, affords no suitable quarters for an Arab girl—and a very personable Arab girl. At any rate, she is still here; I have had a sort of lean-to rigged up in a little valley east of my own tent, but it is very embarrassing."

Nearly a month passed before I heard from Condor again; then came a second letter, with the news that on the eve of a great discovery—as he believed —his entire native staff—the whole fifty—had deserted one night in a body! "Two days' work," he wrote, "would have seen the tomb opened—for I am more than ever certain that my plans are accurate. Then I woke up one morning to find every man Jack of my fellows missing! I went down into the village where a lot of them live, in a towering rage, but not one of the brutes was to be found, and their relations professed entire ignorance respecting their whereabouts. What caused me almost as much anxiety as the check in my work was the fact that Mahâra—the Arab girl—had vanished also. I am wondering if the thing has any sinister significance.''

Condor finished with the statement that he was making tremendous efforts to secure a new gang. "But," said he, "I shall finish the excavation, if I have to do it with my own hands."

His third and last letter contained even stranger matters than the two preceding it. He had succeeded in borrowing a few men from the British Archæological camp in the Fáyûm. Then, just as the work was restarting, the Arab girl, Mahâra, turned up again, and entreated him to bring her down the Nile, "at least as far as Dendera. For the vengeance of her tribesmen," stated Condor, "otherwise would result not only in her own death, but in mine! At the moment of writing I am in two minds what to do. If Mahâra is to go upon this journey, I do not feel justified in sending her alone, and there is no one here who could perform the duty," etc.

I began to wonder, of course; and I had it in mind to take the train to Luxor merely in order to see this Arab maiden, who seemed to occupy so prominent a place in Condor's mind. However, Fate would have it otherwise; and the next thing I heard was that Condor had been brought into Cairo, and was at the English hospital.

He had been bitten by a cat—presumably from the neighboring village; and although the doctor at Luxor dealt with the bite at once, traveled down with him, and placed him in the hand of the Pasteur man at the hospital, he died, as you remember, in the night of his arrival, raving mad; the Pasteur treatment failed entirely.

I never saw him before the end, but they told me that his howls were horribly like those of a cat. His eyes changed in some way, too, I understand; and, with his fingers all contracted, he tried to *scratch* everyone and everything within reach.

They had to strap the poor beggar down, and even then he tore the sheets into ribbons.

Well, as soon as possible, I made the necessary arrangements to finish Condor's inquiry. I had access to his papers, plans, etc., and in the spring of the same year I took up my quarters near Deir-el-Bahari, roped off the approaches to the camp, stuck up the usual notices, and prepared to finish the excavation, which, I gathered, was in a fairly advanced state.

My first surprise came very soon after my arrival, for when, with the plan before me, I started out to find the shaft, I found it, certainly, but only with great difficulty.

It had been filled in again with sand and loose rock right to the very top!

II

All my inquiries availed me nothing. With what object the excavation had been thus closed I was unable to conjecture. That Condor had not reclosed it I was quite certain, for at the time of his mishap he had actually been at work at the bottom of the shaft, as inquiries from a native of Suefee, in the

Fáyûm, who was his only companion at the time, had revealed.

In his eagerness to complete the inquiry, Condor, by lantern light, had been engaged upon a solitary night-shift below, and the rabid cat had apparently fallen into the pit; probably in a frenzy of fear, it had attacked Condor, after which it had escaped.

Only this one man was with him, and he, for some reason that I could not make out, had apparently been sleeping in the temple—quite a considerable distance from Condor's camp. The poor fellow's cries had aroused him, and he had met Condor running down the path and away from the shaft.

This, however, was good evidence of the existence of the shaft at the time, and as I stood contemplating the tightly packed rubble which alone marked its site, I grew more and more mystified, for this task of reclosing the cutting represented much hard labor.

Beyond perfecting my plans in one or two particulars, I did little on the day of my arrival. I had only a handful of men with me, all of whom I knew, having worked with them before, and beyond clearing Condor's shaft I did not intend to excavate further.

Hatasu's Temple presents a lively enough scene in the daytime during the winter and early spring months, with the streams of tourists constantly passing from the white causeway to Cook's Rest House on the edge of the desert. There had been a goodly number of visitors that day to the temple below, and one or two of the more curious and venturesome had scrambled up the steep path to the little plateau which was the scene of my operations. None had penetrated beyond the notice boards, however, and now, with the evening sky passing through those innumerable shades which defy palette and brush, which can only be distinguished by the trained eye, but which, from palest blue melt into exquisite pink, and by some magical combination form that deep violet which does not exist to perfection elsewhere than in the skies of Egypt, I found myself in the silence and the solitude of "the Holy Valley."

I stood at the edge of the plateau, looking out at the rosy belt which marked the course of the distant Nile, with the Arabian hills vaguely sketched beyond. The rocks stood up against that prospect as great black smudges, and what I could see of the causeway looked like a gray smear upon a drab canvas. Beneath me were the chambers of the Rock Temple, with those wall paintings depicting events in the reign of Hatasu which rank among the wonders of Egypt.

Not a sound disturbed my reverie, save a faint clatter of cooking utensils from the camp behind me—a desecration of that sacred solitude. Then a dog began to howl in the neighboring village. The dog ceased, and faintly to my ears came the note of a reed pipe. The breeze died away, and with it the piping.

I turned back to the camp, and, having partaken of a frugal supper, turned in upon my campaigner's bed, thoroughly enjoying my freedom from the routine of official life in Cairo, and looking forward to the morrow's work pleasurably.

Under such circumstances a man sleeps well; and when, in an uncanny gray half-light, which probably heralded the dawn, I awoke with a start, I knew that something of an unusual nature alone could have disturbed my slumbers.

Firstly, then, I identified this with a concerted howling of the village dogs. They seemed to have conspired to make night hideous; I have never heard such an eerie din in my life. Then it gradually began to die away, and I realized, secondly, that the howling of the dogs and my own awakening might be due to some common cause. This idea grew upon me, and as the howling subsided, a sort of disquiet possessed me, and, despite my efforts to shake it off, grew more urgent with the passing of every moment.

In short, I fancied that the thing which had alarmed or enraged the dogs was passing from the village through the Holy Valley, upward to the Temple, upward to the plateau, and was approaching *me*.

I have never experienced an identical sensation since, but I seemed to be audient of a sort of psychic patrol, which, from a remote *pianissimo*, swelled *fortissimo*, to an intimate but silent clamor, which beat in some way upon my brain, but not through the faculty of hearing, for now the night was deathly still.

Yet I was persuaded of some *approach*—of the coming of something sinister, and the suspense of waiting had become almost insupportable, so that I began to accuse my Spartan supper of having given me nightmare, when the tent-flap was suddenly raised, and, outlined against the paling blue of the sky, with a sort of reflected elfin light playing upon her face, I saw an Arab girl looking in at me!

By dint of exerting all my self-control I managed to restrain the cry and upward start which this apparition prompted. Quite still, with my fists tightly clenched, I lay and looked into the eyes which were looking into mine.

The style of literary work which it has been my lot to cultivate fails me in describing that beautiful and evil face. The features were severly classical and small, something of the Bisharîn type, with a cruel little mouth and a rounded chin, firm to hardness. In the eyes alone lay the languor of the Orient; they were exceedingly—indeed, excessively—long and narrow. The ordinary ragged, picturesque finery of a desert girl bedecked this midnight visitant, who, motionless, stood there watching me.

I once read a work by Pierre de l'Ancre, dealing with the Black Sabbaths of the Middle Ages, and now the evil beauty of this Arab face threw my memory back to those singular pages, for, perhaps owing to the reflected light which I have mentioned, although the explanation scarcely seemed adequate, those long, narrow eyes shone catlike in the gloom.

Suddenly I made up my mind. Throwing the

blanket from me, I leapt to the ground, and in a flash had gripped the girl by the wrists. Confuting some lingering doubts, she proved to be substantial enough. My electric torch lay upon a box at the foot of the bed, and, stooping, I caught it up and turned its searching rays upon the face of my captive.

She fell back from me, panting like a wild creature trapped, then dropped upon her knees and began to plead—began to plead in a voice and with a manner which touched some chord of consciousness that I could swear had never spoken before, and has never spoken since.

She spoke in Arabic, of course, but the words fell from her lips as liquid music in which lay all the beauty and all the deviltry of the "Siren's Song." Fully opening her astonishing eyes, she looked up at me, and, with her free hand pressed to her bosom, told me how she had fled from an unwelcome marriage; how, an outcast and a pariah, she had hidden in the desert places for three days and three nights, sustaining life only by means of a few dates which she had brought with her, and quenching her thirst with stolen water-melons.

"I can bear it no longer, *effendim*. Another night out in the desert, with the cruel moon beating, beating, beating upon my brain, with creeping things coming out from the rocks, wriggling, wriggling, their many feet making whisperings in the sand— ah, it will kill me! And I am for ever outcast from my tribe, from my people. No tent of all the Arabs though I fly to the gates of Damascus, is open to me, save I enter in shame, as a slave, as a plaything, as a toy. My heart"—furiously she beat upon her breast—"is empty and desolate, *effendim*. I am meaner than the lowliest thing that creeps upon the sand; yet the God that made that creeping thing made me also—and you, you, who are merciful and strong, would not crush any creature because it was weak and helpless."

I had released her wrist now, and was looking down at her in a sort of stupor. The evil which at first I had seemed to perceive in her was effaced, wiped out as an artist wipes out an error in his drawing. Her dark beauty was speaking to me in a language of its own; a strange language, yet one so intelligible that I struggled in vain to disregard it. And her voice, her gestures, and the witch-fire of her eyes were whipping up my blood to a fever heat of passionate sorrow—of despair. Yes, incredible as it sounds, despair!

In short, as I see it now, this siren of the wilderness was playing upon me as an accomplished musician might play upon a harp, striking this string and that at will, and sounding each with such full notes as they had rarely, if ever, emitted before.

Most damnable anomaly of all, I—Edward Neville, archæologist, most prosy and matter-of-fact man in Cairo, perhaps—*knew* that this nomad who had burst into my tent, upon whom I had set eyes for the first time scarce three minutes before, held me enthralled; and yet, with her wondrous eyes upon me, I could summon up no resentment, and could offer but poor resistance.

"In the Little Oasis, *effendim*, I have a sister who will admit me into her household, if only as a servant. There I can be safe, there I can rest. O *Inglisi*, at home in England you have a sister of your own! Would you see her pursued, a hunted thing from rock to rock, crouching for shelter in the lair of some jackal, stealing that she might live—and flying always, never resting, her heart leaping for fear, flying, flying, with nothing but dishonor before her?"

She shuddered and clasped my left hand in both her own convulsively, pulling it down to her bosom.

"There can be only one thing, *effendim*," she whispered. "Do you not see the white bones bleaching in the sun?"

Throwing all my resolution into the act, I released my hand from her clasp, and, turning aside, sat down upon the box which served me as chair and table, too.

A thought had come to my assistance, had strengthened me in the moment of my greatest weakness; it was the thought of that Arab girl mentioned in Condor's letters. And a scheme of things, an incredible scheme, that embraced and explained some, if not all, of the horrible circumstances attendant upon his death, began to form in my brain.

Bizarre it was, stretching out beyond the realm of things natural and proper, yet I clung to it, for there, in the solitude, with this wildly beautiful creature kneeling at my feet, and with her uncanny powers of fascination yet enveloping me like a cloak,

I found it not so improbable as inevitably it must have seemed at another time.

I turned my head, and through the gloom sought to look into the long eyes. As I did so they closed and appeared as two darkly luminous slits in the perfect oval of the face.

"You are an impostor!" I said in Arabic, speaking firmly and deliberately. "To Mr. Condor"—I could have sworn that she started slightly at sound of the name—"you called yourself Mahâra. I know you, and I will have nothing to do with you."

But in saying it I had to turn my head aside, for the strangest, maddest impulses were bubbling up in my brain in response to the glances of those half-shut eyes.

I reached for my coat, which lay upon the foot of the bed, and, taking out some loose money, I placed fifty piastres in the nerveless brown hand.

"That will enable you to reach the Little Oasis, if such is your desire," I said. "It is all I can do for you, and now—you must go."

The light of the dawn was growing stronger momentarily, so that I could see my visitor quite clearly. She rose to her feet, and stood before me, a straight, slim figure, sweeping me from head to foot with such a glance of passionate contempt as I had never known or suffered.

She threw back her head magnificently, dashed the money on the ground at my feet, and, turning, leaped out of the tent.

For a moment I hesitated, doubting, questioning

my humanity, testing my fears; then I took a step forward, and peered out across the plateau. Not a soul was in sight. The rocks stood up gray and eerie, and beneath lay the carpet of the desert stretching unbroken to the shadows of the Nile Valley.

III

We commenced the work of clearing the shaft at an early hour that morning. The strangest ideas were now playing in my mind, and in some way I felt myself to be in opposition to definite enmity. My excavators labored with a will, and, once we had penetrated below the first three feet or so of tightly packed stone, it became a mere matter of shoveling, for apparently the lower part of the shaft had been filled up principally with sand.

I calculated that four days' work at the outside would see the shaft clear to the base of Condor's excavation. There remained, according to his own notes, only another six feet or so; but it was solid limestone—the roof of the passage, if his plans were correct, communicating with the tomb of Hatasu.

With the approach of night, tired as I was, I felt little incliniation for sleep. I lay down on my bed with a small Browning pistol under the pillow, but after an hour or so of nervous listening drifted off into slumber. As on the night before, I awoke shortly before the coming of dawn.

Again the village dogs were raising a hideous outcry, and again I was keenly conscious of some ever-nearing menace. This consciousness grew stronger as the howling of the dogs grew fainter, and the sense of *approach* assailed me as on the previous occasion.

I sat up immediately with the pistol in my hand, and, gently raising the tent flap, looked out over the darksome plateau. For a long time I could perceive nothing; then, vaguely outlined against the sky, I detected something that moved above the rocky edge.

It was so indefinite in form that for a time I was unable to identify it, but as it slowly rose higher and higher, two luminous eyes—obviously feline eyes, since they glittered greenly in the darkness— came into view. In character and in shape they were the eyes of a cat, but in point of size they were larger than the eyes of any cat I had ever seen. Nor were they jackal eyes. It occurred to me that some predatory beast from the Sûdan might conceivably have strayed thus far north.

The presence of such a creature would account for the nightly disturbance amongst the village dogs; and, dismissing the superstitious notions which had led me to associate the mysterious Arab girl with the phenomenon of the howling dogs, I seized upon this new idea with a sort of gladness.

Stepping boldly out of the tent, I strode in the direction of the gleaming eyes. Although my only weapon was the Browning pistol, it was a weapon of considerable power, and, moreover, I counted upon the well-known cowardice of nocturnal animals. I was not disappointed in the result.

The eyes dropped out of sight, and as I leaped to the edge of rock overhanging the temple a lithe shape went streaking off in the greyness beneath me. Its coloring appeared to be black, but this appearance may have been due to the bad light. Certainly it was no cat, was no jackal; and once, twice, thrice my Browning spat into the darkness.

Apparently I had not scored a hit, but the loud reports of the weapon aroused the men sleeping in the camp, and soon I was surrounded by a ring of inquiring faces.

But there I stood on the rock-edge, looking out across the desert in silence. Something in the long, luminous eyes, something in the sinuous, flying shape had spoken to me intimately, horribly.

Hassan es-Sugra, the headman, touched my arm, and I knew that I must offer some explanation.

"Jackals," I said shortly. And with no other word I walked back to my tent.

The night passed without further event, and in the morning we addressed ourselves to the work with such a will that I saw, to my satisfaction, that by noon of the following day the labor of clearing the loose sand would be completed.

During the preparation of the evening meal I became aware of a certain disquiet in the camp, and I noted a disinclination on the part of the native laborers to stray far from the tents. They hung together in a group, and whilst individually they seemed to avoid meeting my eye, collectively they watched me in a furtive fashion.

A gang of Moslem workmen calls for delicate handling, and I wondered if, inadvertently, I had transgressed in some way their iron-bound code of conduct. I called Hassan es-Sugra aside.

"What ails the men?" I asked him. "Have they some grievance?"

Hassan spread his palms eloquently.

"If they have," he replied, "they are secret about it, and I am not in their confidence. Shall I thrash three or four of them in order to learn the nature of this grievance?"

"No thanks all the same," I said, laughing at this characteristic proposal. "If they refuse to work to-morrow, there will be time enough for you to adopt those measures."

On this, the third night of my sojourn in the Holy Valley by the Temple of Hatasu, I slept soundly and uninterruptedly. I had been looking forward with the keenest zest to the morrow's work, which promised to bring me within sight of my goal, and when Hassan came to awaken me, I leaped out of bed immediately.

Hassan es-Sugra, having performed his duty, did not, as was his custom, retire; he stood there, a tall, angular figure, looking at me strangely.

"Well?" I said.

"There is trouble," was his simple reply. "Follow me, Neville Effendi."

Wondering greatly, I followed him across the plateau and down the slope to the excavation. There I pulled up short with a cry of amazement.

Condor's shaft was filled in to the very top, and presented, to my astonished gaze, much the same aspect that had greeted me upon my first arrival!

"The men——" I began.

Hassan es-Sugra spread wide his palms.

"Gone!" he replied. "Those Coptic dogs, those eaters of carrion, have fled in the night."

"And this"—I pointed to the little mound of broken granite and sand—"is their work?"

"So it would seem," was the reply; and Hassan sniffed his sublime contempt.

I stood looking bitterly at this destruction of my toils. The strangeness of the thing at the moment did not strike me, in my anger; I was only con cerned with the outrageous impudence of the missing workmen, and if I could have laid hands upon one of them it had surely gone hard with him.

As for Hassan es-Sugra, I believe he would cheerfully have broken the necks of the entire gang. But he was a man of resource.

"It is so newly filled in," he said, "that you and I, in three days, or in four, can restore it to the state it had reached when those nameless dogs, who regularly prayed with their shoes on, those devourers of pork, began their dirty work."

His example was stimulating. *I* was not going to be beaten, either.

After a hasty breakfast, the pair of us set to work with pick and shovel and basket. We worked as those slaves must have worked whose toil was directed by the lash of the Pharaoh's overseer. My back acquired an almost permanent crook, and every muscle in my body seemed to be on fire. Not even in the midday heat did we slacken or stay our toils; and when dusk fell that night a great mound had arisen beside Condor's shaft, and we had excavated to a depth it had taken our gang double the time to reach.

When at last we threw down our tools in utter exhaustion, I held out my hand to Hassan, and wrung his brown fist enthusiastically. His eyes sparkled as he met my glance.

"Neville Effendi," he said, "you are a true Moslem!"

And only the initiated can know how high was the compliment conveyed.

That night I slept the sleep of utter weariness, yet it was not a dreamless sleep, or perhaps it was not so deep as I supposed, for blazing cat-eyes encircled me in my dreams, and a constant feline howling seemed to fill the night.

When I awoke the sun was blazing down upon the rock outside my tent, and, springing out of bed, I perceived, with amazement, that the morning was far advanced. Indeed, I could hear the distant voices of the donkey-boys and other harbingers of the coming tourists.

Why had Hassan es-Sugra not awakened me?

I stepped out of the tent and called him in a loud voice. There was no reply. I ran across the plateau to the edge of the hollow.

Condor's shaft had been reclosed to the top!

Language fails me to convey the wave of anger, amazement, incredulity, which swept over me. I looked across to the deserted camp and back to my own tent; I looked down at the mound, where but a few hours before had been a pit, and seriously I began to question whether I was mad or whether madness had seized upon all who had been with me. Then, pegged down upon the heap of broken stones, I perceived, fluttering, a small piece of paper.

Dully I walked across and picked it up. Hassan, a man of some education, clearly was the writer. It was a pencil scrawl in doubtful Arabic, and, not without difficulty, I deciphered it as follows:

"Fly, Neville Effendi! This is a haunted place!"

Standing there by the mound, I tore the scrap of paper into minute fragments, bitterly casting them from me upon the ground. It was incredible; it was insane.

The man who had written that absurd message, the man who had undone his own work, had the reputation of being fearless and honorable. He had been with me before a score of times, and had quelled petty mutinies in the camp in a manner which marked him a born overseer. I could not understand; I could scarcely believe the evidence of my own senses.

What did I do?

I suppose there are some who would have abandoned the thing at once and for always, but I take it that the national traits are strong within me. I went over to the camp and prepared my own breakfast; then, shouldering pick and shovel, I went down into the valley and set to work. What ten men could not do, what two men had failed to do, one man was determined to do.

It was about half an hour after commencing my toils, and when, I suppose, the surprise and rage occasioned by the discovery had begun to wear off, that I found myself making comparisons between my own case and that of Condor. It became more and more evident to me that events—mysterious events—were repeating themselves.

The frightful happenings attendant upon Condor's death were marshaling in my mind. The sun was blazing down upon me, and distant voices could be heard in the desert stillness. I knew that the plain below was dotted with pleasure-seeking tourists, yet nervous tremors shook me. Frankly, I dreaded the coming of the night.

Well, tenacity or pugnacity conquered, and I worked on until dusk. My supper despatched, I sat down on my bed and toyed with the Browning.

I realized already that sleep, under existing conditions, was impossible. I perceived that on the morrow I must abandon my one-man enterprise, pocket my pride, in a sense, and seek new assistants, new companions.

The fact was coming home to me conclusively that a menace, real and not mythical, hung over that valley. Although, in the morning sunlight and filled with indignation, I had thought contemptuously of Hassan es-Sugra, now, in the mysterious violet dusk so conducive to calm consideration, I

was forced to admit that he was at least as brave
a man as I. And he had fled! What did that night
hold in keeping for me?

      *   *   *   *   *   *

I will tell you what occurred, and it is the only
explanation I have to give of why Condor's shaft,
said to communicate with the real tomb of Hatasu,
to this day remains unopened.

There, on the edge of my bed, I sat far into the
night, not daring to close my eyes. But physical
weariness conquered in the end, and, although I have
no recollection of its coming, I must have succumbed
to sleep, since I remember—can never forget—a
repetition of the dream, or what I had assumed to be
a dream, of the night before.

A ring of blazing green eyes surrounded me. At
one point this ring was broken, and in a kind of
nightmare panic I leaped at that promise of safety,
and found myself outside the tent.

Lithe, slinking shapes hemmed me in—cat shapes,
ghoul shapes, veritable figures of the pit. And the
eyes, the shapes, although they were the eyes and
shapes of cats, sometimes changed elusively, and
became the wicked eyes and the sinuous, writhing
shapes of women. Always the ring was incomplete,
and always I retreated in the only direction by
which retreat was possible. I retreated from those
cat-things.

In this fashion I came at last to the shaft, and
there I saw the tools which I had left at the end of my
day's toil.

Looking around me, I saw also, with such a pang of horror as I cannot hope to convey to you, that the ring of green eyes was now unbroken about me.

And it was closing in.

Nameless feline creatures were crowding silently to the edge of the pit, some preparing to spring down upon me where I stood. A voice seemed to speak in my brain; it spoke of capitulation, telling me to accept defeat, lest, resisting, my fate be the fate of Condor.

Peals of shrill laughter rose upon the silence. The laughter was mine.

Filling the night with this hideous, hysterical merriment, I was working feverishly with pick and with shovel filling in the shaft.

The end? The end is that I awoke, in the morning, lying, not on my bed, but outside on the plateau, my hands torn and bleeding and every muscle in my body throbbing agonisingly. Remembering my dream—for even in that moment of awakening I thought I had dreamed—I staggered across to the valley of the excavation.

Condor's shaft was reclosed to the top.

VI

POMEGRANATE FLOWER

I

THERE are not so many *Antereeyeh* (story-tellers) in Cairo now (said my acquaintance, Hassan of the Scent Bazaar, staring, reflectively, at two American ladies paying fabulous prices for the goods of his mendacious neighbor on the left). They have adopted other, and more lucrative, professions; but in my father's time, it was an excellent business.

For one thing, the stories which you call the *Arabian Nights* are no longer recited, because they are said to be unlucky. This has considerably reduced the story-teller's stock-in-trade; for unless a man is blessed with much originality, he cannot well refrain from using in his narratives some part of the thousand and one tales.

To this day, however, there is in the city of Cairo a tale-teller of much repute. With his tale-telling he combines the profession of a barber; and like the famous barber of the *Arabian Nights* bears the nickname Es-Samit (the Silent). An old man is this Es-Samit, who no more will know his ninetieth year, of dark countenance, and white beard and eyebrows, with small ears like the ears of a gazelle, and a long nose like that of a camel, and a haughty aspect.

This barber enjoys every comfort in his declining years by reason of his amusing manner, and because his ridiculous stories and disclosures respecting his six brothers (for in all things he resembles, or claims to resemble, his famous namesake) divert all who hear them, causing him whose bosom is contracted with woe to swoon with excessive laughter, and filling the saddest heart with joy; such is the absurd loquacity and impertinence of the barber called Es-Samit, the Silent.

It chanced one day that I found myself at the wedding festivities of a prosperous merchant distantly related to me; and for the entertainment of his guests, this wealthy man, in addition to the usual dances and songs, had engaged Es-Samit to divert us with one of his untruthful stories. In order to refresh the *Anteree's* mendacity, the host thus addressed the barber—

"O Es-Samit, thou silent one! it hath come to my ears that in thine exceeding paucity of speech thou hast omitted, hitherto, to relate the story of thy seventh brother. Since thou hast a seventh brother, let not thy love of silence (in thee even greater than in thy famous ancestor) deprive us of a knowledge of his depravity, but acquaint us with his case."

"O Merchant Prince!" replied the barber, "to none other than thyself—so handsome, so liberal, and of such excellent morality—would I break my vow, to speak of that wretched villain, that malevolent mule, that vilest of the vile, my twin brother Ahzab."

My cousin, feigning astonishment at the manner of his speech, said—

"Thy twin brother, O Es-Samit, was not, like thee, a man of rectitude, of exalted mind, and of enlightened intelligence?"

"Alas!" replied the barber, "he was a dog of the most mongrel kind. My bosom is pierced when I utter his accursed name! At the hands of Ahzab, my twin brother, I met with every indignity, and with penalties of a most unfortunate description."

When the host heard this, he laughed exceedingly, saying—

"Acquaint us, O Es-Samit, with his shameless misdeeds."

The barber, sighing as though his soul sought rest from all earthly afflictions, proceeded as follows:

Know, O light of my eyes! that my other brother, Ahzab, was born in the city of Cairo, and his birth was unattended by a darkening of the sun and other unpleasant calamities only by reason of the fact that *I* was born in the same hour!

My twin brother, Ahzab, was blessed with handsome stature, an elegant shape, a perfect figure, with cheeks like roses, with eyebrows meeting above an aquiline nose brightly shining. In short, this shame of my mother was endowed with all those perfections which Allah (whose name be exalted) had also bestowed upon me; but his heart was the heart of a serpent, and he lacked the nobility of mind which thou hast observed in thy servant, O Paragon of wisdom!

When we were yet in the bloom and blossom of handsome youth, a dispute arose between us, and for many moons I saw not Ahzab, but pursued my occupation as a barber and teller of wonderful stories in a distant part of the city. In this way it befell that I knew of his state only by report, until one day as I sat before my shop observing if the ascendent of the hour were favorable to one who waited to be shaved, there came to me a negro most handsomely dressed, who said:

"My Master, Ahzab the Merchant, desires that you repair as soon as possible to his magazine. He hath urgent need of thee."

Upon hearing these words, and observing the richness of the negro's apparel, I perceived that those reports which had come to me, respecting Ahzab's wealth, were no more than true; and I spoke thus to myself:

"Within the vilest heart may bloom the flower of brotherly affection. Ahzab desires to share with me, the most enlightened of his family, this good fortune which hath befallen him."

Accordingly, I shut up my shop, dismissing the one who waited to be shaved, and followed the black to the Khân Khalîl, where were the shops of the wealthy silk merchants. My brother received me affectionately, embracing me and saying:

"O Es-Samit, ever have I loved thee. Lo! Thou growest more like myself each year. Save that thou art more dignified and noble. Enter into this private apartment with me, for it is important that no one shall see thee."

Much surprised at his words, I followed him to an elegant apartment above the shop, and there he ordered the servants to roast a lamb and to bring to us fruit and wine; and while we thus pleasantly employed ourselves, he unfolded to me his case.

"Know, O my brother, that I have accumulated great wealth; and this I have done by observing those wise precepts of conduct laid down by thee. By the charm of my speech, which I have fashioned upon thine, and the elegance of my manner, in which I have, though poorly, imitated thine own, and by the dignity and the modesty of my conduct, I have endeared all hearts and am esteemed above all the other merchants in Cairo.

"It is necessary that I repair to Damascus, and during my absence I wish nothing better than that thou shouldst take my place here. This will be favorable to both of us; for I will reward thy services with five hundred piastres and an interest in my affairs, and thou wilt pass for me; for all will say, 'Lo! Ahzab the Merchant waxes more handsome each day; such is the benign influence of righteous prosperity and conscious rectitude!' My affairs stand thus and thus, and my steward, who will be in our confidences, will acquaint thee with all matters necessary. Thou wilt wear my costly garments, and sit in my shop. Each evening thou wilt secretly repair to thine own abode."

Upon hearing those words, my bosom swelled with joy; for I observed that Ahzab had not failed to perceive my exalted qualities. We sat far into the night in conversation respecting our plans; and on the following day, Ahzab having departed secretly for Damascus, I repaired to his shop, as arranged, and took my seat there.

But the number of the persons who saluted me, and by the manner of their speech, I perceived, more and more, the great prosperity of my brother; and being of a thoughtful mind, I passed the days very pleasantly in contemplation of my good fortune.

Upon the fourth day after the departure of my brother, as I sat in his shop, there came past a damsel accompanied by female attendants. This damsel was riding upon a mule with a richly embroidered saddle, with stirrups of gold, and she was covered with an *izar* of exquisite fabric; and about her slender waist was a girdle of gold-embroidered silk. I was stricken speechless with the beauty and elegance of her form; and when she alighted and came into the shop, the odors of sweet perfumes were diffused from her, and she captivated my reason by her loveliness.

Seating herself beside me, she raised her *izar*, and I beheld her black eyes. And they surpassed in beauty the eyes of all human beings, and were like the eyes of the gazelle. She had a mouth like the Seal of Suleyman, and hair blacker than the night of affliction; a forehead like the new moon of Ramadan, and cheeks like anemones, with lips fresher than rose petals, teeth like pearls from the sea of distraction, and a neck surpassing in whiteness molten silver, above a form that put to shame the willow branch.

She spoke to me, saying:

"O Ahzab! I have returned as I promised thee!"

At the sound of her voice, by Allah (whose name be exalted!) I was entangled in the snare of her love; fire was burning up my heart on her account; a consuming flame increased within my bosom, and my reason was drowned in the sea of my desire.

Perceiving my state, she quickly lowered her veil in pretended displeasure, and desired to look at some pieces of silk. While she thus employed herself, she surpassed the branches in the beauty of her bending motions, and my eyes could not remove themselves from her. I thus communed with myself:

"O Es-Samit, thou didst contract with thy brother to do this and that, and to render unto him a proper account of thy dealings. But though he hath made thee no mention of his affair with this damsel—it is important that thou conductest this matter as he would have done, so that he cannot reproach thee with negligence!" For I was ever a just as well as a discreet and silent man.

Accordingly I spoke as follows:

"O my mistress, who art the most lovely person God has created, rend not my heart with thy displeasure, but take pity upon me. Know that love is difficult, and the concealment of it melteth iron

and occasioneth disease and infirmity. Thou hast
returned as thou didst promise; therefore I conjure
thee, conceal not thy face from thy slave!"

The damsel thereupon raised her head and put
aside her veil, casting a glance upon me and looked
sideways at the attendants, and placed one finger
upon her lips; so that I knew her to be as discreet
as she was lovely. She laughed in my face, and said:

"I will take this piece of embroidered silk that
I have chosen. What is the price?"

And I answered:

"One hundred piasters; but I pray thee let it
be thine, and a gift from Ahzab!"

Upon this, she looked into my eyes and the sight
of her face drew from me a thousand sighs, and took
the silk, saying:

"O my master, leave me not desolate!"

So she departed, while I continued sitting in the
market-street until past the hour of afternoon
prayer, with disturbed mind enslaved by her beauty
and loveliness. I returned to my house and supper
was placed before me, but reflecting upon the damsel,
I could eat nothing. I laid myself down to rest,
but passed the whole night sleepless, communing
with myself how I could best carry out this affair
and obtain possession of the damsel . . . for my
brother, Ahzab!

II

Scarcely had daybreak appeared when I arose
and repaired to the market-place and put on a suit

of my brother's clothing, richer and more magnificent than that I had worn the day before; and having drunk a cup of wine, I sat in the shop. But all that day she came not, nor the next, but upon the third day she came again, attended only by one attendant, and she saluted me and said in a speech never surpassed in softness and sweetness:

"O my master, reproach me not that I thus reveal the interest I have in thee, but I could not speak to thee when my women were in hearing; and this one is in my confidence. I have told thee that my father will never give me to thee because of my rank, but thou hast wounded my heart, and more and more do I love thee each day—for each day thou growest more beautiful and elegant. Forever I must be desolate. Alas! I have placed thy letter in the box thou didst give me, and no day passes that it is not wet with my tears. Farewell! O my beloved!"

On hearing this, my love and passion grew so violent that I almost became insensible. The damsel rose to leave the shop, and the one who was with her spoke softly in her ear; but she shook her head, expressing displeasure, and went away.

When I perceived that indeed she was gone, verily the tears descended upon my cheek like rain, and my soul had all but departed. My heart clung to her—I followed in the direction of her steps through the market-place, and lo! the attendant came running back to me, and said:

"Here is the message of my mistress: 'Know that my love is greater than thine, and on Friday next my servant will come to thee and tell thee how thou mayest see me for a short interview before my father comes back from prayers.' "

When I heard these words of the girl, the anguish of my heart ceased, and I was intoxicated with love and rapture, and in my joy and longing, I omitted to ask the girl the abode of her mistress—neither did I know the name of my beloved; but reflecting upon these matters, I returned to my brother's shop, and sat there until late, and then I repaired secretly to my abode.

I paused in a quiet street, and seated myself upon a *mastabah* to scent the coolness of the air, and to abandon myself to exquisite reflections.

But no sooner had I thus seated myself than a negro of gigantic stature, and most hideous aspect, suddenly appeared from the shadow of a door, and threw himself upon me, exclaiming:

"This is thine end, as it was written, O Ahzab the Merchant!"

By Allah! (whose name be exalted) I thought it was even as he said; and none but myself had fallen into sudden dissolution, but that everything slippery is not a pancake, and the jar that is struck may yet escape unbroken.

So it befell that by great good fortune and by the exercise of my agility and intelligence, I tripped the negro and his head came in contact with the *mastabah,* and before he could recover himself, I held to his ebony throat the blade of a razor which, by the mercy of God, and because it was a custom of my profession, I carried in my *kamar*.

"O thou dog!" I exclaimed, "prepare to depart to that utter darkness and perdition that awaits assassins! For assuredly I am about to slay thee!"

But he humbled himself to the ground before me, and embraced my feet, crying:

"Have mercy, O my master! I but obeyed the commands!"

"Of whom, thou vile and unnamable vermin?" I asked of him.

"Of whom else but Abu-el-Hassan, the son of the Kadî! For hath he not revealed to thee that for what has passed with Jullanar (Pomegranate Flower), the daughter of the Walî, he will slay thee?"

"He hath revealed this to me?" I asked of him, astonished at his words.

And he replied: "Thou knowest, master, it was by my hand that the message was borne."

Whereupon I praised Allah (whose name be exalted) and spurned the slave with my foot, saying:

"Depart, O thou black son of filth, and report that I am dead. I give thee thy wretched life; depart!"

But when he had gone, I again lifted up my voice in thanksgiving. And having come to my abode, I performed the preparatory ablution, and recited the prayer of night-fall; after which I recited the chapters "Ya-Sîn" (The Cow) and "Two Preventatives." For I perceived that this was the true purport of my brother's absence, and that in his love and affection he had resigned to me this affair, well knowing that I should perish!

It was by the mercy of Allah, the Compassionate, the Merciful, that my case was not as he had foreseen. The damsel called Jullanar, daughter of the Walî, was famed from Cairo to the uttermost islands of China for her elegance and loveliness, and I knew that my beloved could be none other than she, and that Abu-el-Hassan, son of the Kadî, could be none other than the betrothed chosen of her father the Walî.

I slept not that night, but passed the hours until sunrise reflecting upon this matter, and upon the dangers which awaited my father's handsome son on Friday. And I went not to the market on the next day, but sent a message to my brother's steward saying that I was smitten with sickness and enjoining him to acquaint the girl, who presently would come, where I was to be found.

Thus it befell that at noon on Friday the same girl that had been with Jullanar came to me, sent thither from the shop of Ahzab by the steward, saying:

"O my master, answer the sumons of my mistress. This is the plan that I have proposed to her: Conceal thyself within one of the large chests that are in thy shop, and hire a porter to carry thee to the house of the Walî. I will cause the *bowwab* to admit the chest to the apartment of the Lady Jullanar. She doth trust her honor to thy discretion, by reason of her love for thee, and because she will die if she see thee not to bid thee farewell. I will **arrange** for thee to be secretly conveyed from the house, **ere** the Walî returns.''

And at her words I was like to have swooned with ecstasy; and I forgot, in the transport of love and delight, the black assassin and the threatened vengeance of Abu-el-Hassan. I set at naught my fears at trusting my father's favorite son within the walls of the Walî's house. I thought only of Jullanar of the slender waist and heavy hips, of the dewy lips, more intoxicating than wine, and the eyes of my beloved like wells of temptation to swallow up the souls of men.

I shaved and went to the bath, and repaired to the shop of Ahzab. My brother's steward was not there, whereat I rejoiced, and arrayed myself in the most splendid suit that I could find, and having perfumed myself with essences and sweet scents, I summoned a boy and said:

"Go thou and bring here a porter. Order him to carry yon large chest to the house of the Walî, near the Mosque of Ibn-Mizheh, and ask for the lady Jullanar who hath purchased this box and a number of things which are in it. See that he be a strong man, for the box is very heavy."

The boy replied. "On the head," and departed on his errand.

Thereupon I commended my soul to Allah, and entered the box, closing the lid upon me. Scarcely had I concealed myself, when the porter entered and lifted the chest. The boy assisted him to take it upon his back, and he bore it out into the market-street.

"Now by the beard of the Prophet(on whom be peace)," I exclaimed to myself, "it is well that I am named Es-Samit, the Silent; for had it been otherwise, I must have lifted up my voice against this son of perdition who carries me with my soles raised to heaven!"

The porter conveyed me for some distance, panting beneath the weight of the box, and, presently, coming to a *mastabah*, dropped one end of the box upon it, whilst he rested himself.

"Now as Allah is great, and Mohammed his only prophet," I said in my beard, "I am fortunate in that I have acquired a paucity of diction. There is no other in Cairo, but the joy of my mother, that could refrain from speech when dropped upon his skull on a stone bench!"

After a while, the porter raised the chest again, and resumed his journey, presently coming to the house of the Walî, and dropping the box into the courtyard.

"Allah be praised!" I said. "For if this porter, whose name be accursed, did but carry me a quinary further, my silence would become even more surprising than it is; for my affair would finish, and I should speak no more to any man!"

The *bowwab* now cried out:

"What is in this chest?"

"Purchases of the lady Jullanar," said the girl, whom I recognized by her voice. "Permit the porter to carry it to her apartments."

"I must obey the orders of the Walî my master," replied the door-keeper. "The box must be opened."

I was bereft of the power to control myself, and seized with a colic from excess of fear; I almost died from the violent spasms of my limbs.

"O Es-Samit!" I said, "this is the reward of him whom love leads to the house of the Walî!"

I felt certain that my destruction approached. The intoxication of love now ceased in me, and reflection came in its place. I repented of what I had done, and prayed a happy solution of my dangerous case.

Whether as a result of my prayers, I know not, but some arrangement was come to, and the porter once more raised the chest, and, striking my head upon the end of it at each step, bore me up to the apartments of Jullanar, which I thus entered feet first.

He deposited the box, lid downward, upon the soft mattress of a *dîwan,* so that I found myself upon all fours, like a mule with my face between my hands! Ere I could break my habitual silence, he lifted some heavy piece of furniture—I know not what—and placed it on top of the box!

A voice sweeter than the songs of the Daood spoke:

"Slave! what art thou doing?"

"I *am* thy slave!" spoke another voice, at the accursed sound whereof I almost died of spleen. "Knowest thou me not, my beloved? I have devised a new stratagem and come to thee in the guise of a porter! But lo! beneath my uncomely garments, I am Ahzab, thy lover!"

III

As a man who sleeps ill after a protracted feast, I heard her answer, saying:

"Is it true thou hast come to me, or is this a dream?"

"Verily, it is true!" answered the accursed, the vile, the unspeakable Ahzab, my brother—for it was he. "From the time when I first saw thee, neither sleep hath been sweet to me, nor hath wine possessed the slightest flavor! I have come to thee thus, fragrant bloom of the pomegranate, because I would not have thee see me in a posture so undignified as that of one crouched in a box! So that thy people might be compelled to give me access to thine apartments, I have put a mendicant in my place, rendering the chest heavy!"

And she said, "Thou art welcome!" and embraced him.

By Allah (whose name be exalted), I gnawed my beard until I choked!

"Thou art changed, beloved!" she said to him; "thou art always beautiful, but to-day thou seemest less rosy-cheeked to mine eyes!"

The accursed Ahzab, like an enraged mule, kicked the box wherein I dissolved in flames of wrath.

"I am burnt up with love and longing for thee!" he replied. "O my love! how beautiful thou art!"

Whereat my command of silence forsook me! As Allah is the one god, and Mohammed his only Prophet, I became as one possessed of a devil!

"Robber!" I cried; and my words lost themselves within the box. "Cheat! accursed disgrace of my father! infamy of my race! O dog! O unutterable dirt!"

Jullanar cried out in fear, but my accursed brother took her in his bosom, soothing her with soft words.

"Fear not, O my beloved!" he said. "I gave the mendicant wine that his heart might warm to his lowly task, but I fear he has become intoxicated!"

"O thou liar!" I cried. "O malevolent scoundrel! O son of a disease!" And with all my strength I sought to raise the weight that bore me down; but to no purpose.

"Know, my beloved," continued my thrice-accursed brother, "what I have suffered on thy account. But three days since I was attacked by four gigantic negro assassins despatched by Abu-el-Hassan to slay me! But I vanquished them, killing one and maiming a second, whilst the others escaped and ran back to their wretched master."

"O unutterable liar!" I groaned. For I was near to hastening my predestined end both from suffocation and consuming rage. "Thou didst fly, thou jackal! from that peril, and reapest the fruits of my courage and dexerity! O, mud! O, stench!"

"Lest he should despatch a number too great for me to combat, I have lurked in hiding, delight of souls! in a most filthy hovel belonging to a barber!"

"May thy tongue turn into a scorpion and bite thee!" I cried. "My abode is as clean as the palace of the Khedive! Thou hast never entered it, O thou gnat's egg! Thou hast hidden in I know not what hole, like the unclean insect thou art, until thy steward (may his beard grow backward and smother him!) informed thee of this! O Allah! (to whom be ascribed all might and glory) give me strength to move this accursed box that I may crush him!"

Scarce had I uttered the last word, when a girl came running into the apartment, crying: "Fly, my master! O my mistress! The Walî! the Walî!"

Upon hearing these words, my rage departed from me and in its place came excessive fear. My breath left my body, and my heart ceased to beat.

"He that falleth in the dirt be trodden on by camels," I reflected. "It is not enough, O Es-Samit, that thou hast suffered the attack of the assassin; that thou hast all but died of fear at the door of the Walî's house; that thou hast been torn from the arms of the loveliest creature God hath created; thou are destined, now, O most unfortunate of men, to be detected by the Walî in his daughter's apartments, concealed in a box!"

And I pronounced the *Takbîr*, crying, "O Allah! thy ways are inscrutable!"

"Fly, my beloved!" cried Jullanar to Ahzab. "My women will conceal thee!" Wherewith she swooned and fell upon the floor senseless.

"Quick! follow me closely, O my master!" cried the girl, and I heard my perfidious brother depart from the room by one door, as the Walî entered by another.

"Ah!" cried the Walî, clapping his hands. "Slaves! what is this?

And people came running to his command; some carrying out the lady Jullanar to her sleeping apartment, and sprinkling rose-water upon her, and some remaining.

"What is in this box upon the *dîwan!*" demanded the Walî. "Bring it hither and open it!"

At that I knew that I was lost, and my soul as good as departed, and I bade farewell to life and invoked Mohammed (whom may God preserve) to intercede for me that I might die an easy death.

The chest was dragged into the middle of the floor and thrown open.

"Name of my mother!" exclaimed the Walî. "It is Ahzab the Merchant! It is the villain who hath presumed to make love to my daughter! O Allah! my daughter hath disgraced me! By the beard of the Prophet, I can no more hold up my head among honest men!"

And he slapped his face and plucked his beard, and fell insensible upon the floor. As he did so, I leaped from the box and would have escaped, but two blacks seized me; and the noise, or the refreshing quality of the rose-water with which the women were sprinkling him, revived the Walî, who recovered, fixing upon me a terrible gaze.

"O thou dog!" he said; "thou who hast wrought my disgrace! As thou didst enter my house in

yonder box, in yonder box shalt thou quit the world!
Cast him back again, fasten the box with ropes, and
throw it into the Nile at nightfall!"

IV

Now were my powers of silence most surprisingly
displayed. For I spoke no word, but dumb as a
tongueless man, I allowed myself to be knocked backward into the box. The lid closed upon me, ropes
bound about the box, and the seal of the Walî affixed
to it. Negroes carried it out, and threw it into some
cellar to await nightfall.

"O Es-Samit!" I said, "this is the end that was
appointed to thy father's wisest son! To this pass
thy silence and wisdom have brought thee! O Allah
(to whom be all glory), grant that one of the fishes
that eat me in the Nile shall be served up to Ahzab,
my twin brother, and choke him!"

And then my thoughts turned to Jullanar, and I
sighed and groaned; and the torments I suffered
through lying drawn up in the box were delights to
the agonies that my reflections respecting her case
occasioned in me; so that, with the excess of my woe
and misery, I became insensible. How long I remained so I know not, but I was awakened by a
knocking at the lid of the box, and the voice of the
Walî spoke, saying:

"Prepare to die, O wretch! for my servants are
about to convey thee to the river and cast thee in!

Thou dog! who didst presume to raise thine eyes to my daughter!—know that this is the reward of such malefactors; for assuredly if thou escapest alive, thou shalt wed Jullanar!"

Whereat he laughed until he almost swooned and kicked the box until I thought he had burst it. Blacks raised me, and I was borne down a long flight of steps and onward in I know not what direction.

"From here?" said one of them, and through a crack in the lid, I saw the light of a torch, and the whispering of the river came to my ears.

"Yes!" replied another.

And I commended my soul to Allah as the box was swung to and fro and hurled through the air. With a sound in my ears as of the shrieking of ten thousand *efreets*, I was plunged into the water!

Far under the surface I went and knew all the agonies of dissolution; but the box was strongly and cunningly made and rose again; then it began to fill and sink once more, and again I tasted of the final pangs. Throughout all this time, a strong current was bearing the box along, and presently, as, for the fiftieth occasion, I was seeking to die and to end my misery, I heard voices.

The most miserable life is sweet to him who feels it slipping from his grasp, and I summoned sufficient strength to raise a feeble cry.

"O Allah!" I cried, "if it be thy will, grant that these persons whose voices I hear take pity upon my unfortunate condition, and draw me forth."

Even as I spoke, something stayed the onward

progress of the box. It was a fisherman's net!
And the fishermen began to draw me into the boat,
I praising Allah the while.

But when they had the box upon the edge of the
boat, and heard my voice proceeding from within,
and saw the Walî's seal upon the lid—"By the beard
of the Prophet!" cried one, "this is some evil *ginn*
or magician whom the Walî hath imprisoned in this
chest! Allah avert the omen! Cast him back,
comrades!"

Alas! I could find no words wherewith to entreat
them to take pity; never had paucity of speech
served me so ill! A great groan issued from my
bossom as I was consigned again to the Nile!

Allah is great, and it was not written that I should
perish in that manner. For another current now
seized upon the box, and just as I was on the point
of dissolution, cast it upon a projecting bank, where
it was perceived by a band of four robbers, who
derived a livelihood from plundering such vessels
as lay unprotected in the river.

These waded out and dragged the box ashore. I
was too near my end to have spoken had I desired
to speak, but from my unfortunate adventure with
the fishermen, I had learned that silence was wisdom,
now as always. Thus I lay in the box like a dog that
has been all but drowned, and listened to the words
of my rescuers.

These were arguing respecting the contents and
value of the box, one holding this opinion and another
that. One, who seemed to be their leader, was about

to unfasten the ropes, but another claimed that this was his due. So, from angry words, they came to blows, and by the grace of God (whose name be exalted) they drew their knives, and three of the four were slain. The fourth removed the ropes and opened the box, thinking to enjoy, alone, the treasures which he supposed it to contain.

Whereupon I uprose and looked up to where Canopus shone, and said:

"There is no God but God! Praise be to Allah who has preserved me from an unfortunate and unseemly end!"

At that, the robber, with wild cries of fear, turned and ran, and I saw him no more. Such, O bountiful patron, is the disgraceful story of the dog Ahzab, my seventh and twin broteher. But all that which I endured happened by Fate and Destiny, and from that which is written there is no escape nor flight.

*   *   *   *   *   *

Our worthy host (concluded Hassan) laughed heartily at this story, saying:

"O Es-Samit, it is evident to me that thy paucity of speech alone preserved thee from drowning! But acquaint us, I beg, with the fate of thy dog of a brother, and of thy beautiful Pomegranate Flower."

"O glory of beholders!" replied the barber, "by the mouth of the girl who was in Jullanar's confidence—Ahzab, that shame of mules, learned, whilst in hiding, how the Walî had said in the presence of many witnesses: 'Assuredly if thou escapest alive, thou shalt wed Jullanar.'"

"Tellest thou me that he had the effrontery to demand the fulfilment of a pledge so spoken, O Es-Samit?"

"Alas!" replied the barber, with tears pouring like rain down the wrinkles of his aged cheek, "he lived with her the most joyous, and most agreeable, and most comfortable, and most pleasant life, until they were visited by the terminator of delights, and the separator of companions!"

THE END.

www.ingramcontent.com/pod-product-compliance
Lightning Source LLC
Chambersburg PA
CBHW011520240626
47154CB00009B/2896